DEAD PEOPLE SLEEP

A MURDER SQUAD THRILLER #BOOK 2

LIAM HANSON

BLOODHOUND
— BOOKS —

Print ISBN 978-1-913942-16-8

ALSO BY LIAM HANSON

Lies People Tell - Murder Squad Thriller #1

For my parents, who made me what I am today.

When you breathe in, you inspire. When you don't breathe, you…
expire.
Jeffrey B. Gross

1

He'd murdered his own mother only a few days earlier. Closed his hands around her scrawny neck and throttled all signs of life out of her. It was sheer impulse on his part; the culmination of years of pent-up anger and frustration.

She'd seldom shown love. Had pushed him away at a young age, preferring instead the *comforts* provided by men who came and went when Father was busy at work.

As a boy, he saw it all.

Every sordid detail.

Mother and women like her cared for no one but themselves. Were nothing but common whores. And for that alone, he despised them.

When she'd upped sticks and left without so much as a cursory wave goodbye, it came as no surprise to him. But not so Father – who for reasons understood only by himself – chose Christmas Eve as a suitable day on which to end it all.

As a six-year-old, the boy had bounced out of bed, eager to get downstairs. '*He's been!*' he'd yelled, opening the glass door at the foot of the staircase. But there was no shiny new bicycle propped against the plump arm of the sofa. No bulging stocking, nor tubes of jelly sweets. Only a swollen-tongued corpse rotating on the end of an improvised noose.

They'd taken him away after that. Put him in care, saying *he* was to blame. Next were the beatings, and abuse of the most wicked kind. They were shaping him. Moulding a killer, though they couldn't have known.

He'd withdrawn inside himself just to survive day to day; like a snail seeking the protection of its hardened shell.

Then along came a woman unlike any other he'd previously met. She'd rescued him from the horrors of the children's home, bringing him up as her own, preventing him from walking the wrong path in life. He'd never have achieved anywhere near the level of success he now knew, were it not for Aunt Freda.

He was crying again; caught in the terrible memory of her death to cancer only a few months earlier. Her passing had left fewer honourable people in the world, the balance shifting in favour of women like Mother.

When Aunt Freda had lain on her deathbed, she'd taken his hand in hers, telling him to do what he knew was right. That was her message to him. His new purpose in life. One that involved redressing the skewed balance between good and evil.

And here he was.

Outside the home of a shameless whore.

About to get started...

2

Killing Mother had given him nowhere near the buzz he felt lying in wait for the unsuspecting woman. The anticipation alone sent a shot of adrenaline coursing through him – and had he not shaved his body from head-to-foot earlier, every hair on it would have stood proud.

He'd taken no chances.

Had planned each move with a military-type precision.

The automatic wiper blades swung in a wide arc, juddering across the dirty windscreen of the Volvo with a series of squeaks, the glass not wet enough for smooth operation. The sound interrupted the moment and irritated him. Switching them off, he checked the rear-view mirror for the umpteenth time and saw no sign of his victim as yet.

She wouldn't be long. He knew that already. Had previously sat and watched her arrive home on at least a half-dozen occasions.

The local newspapers and television channels didn't understand. He was no stalker, as they so authoritatively claimed. What he was doing had a greater purpose. There was a difference between the two things, even if *they* failed to comprehend that.

Another check of the empty mirror.

His first victim – the *prototype* – would arrive on foot, alone and on the same side of the road, before crossing almost twenty metres short of where he was waiting beneath the overhang of a leaning tree.

He'd have moved by then.

Knew just the place to hide.

He'd watch her open the low gate with an outstretched foot – an aversion to getting her soft fleece mittens wet, perhaps – the meandering garden path taking her round to the side entrance of the house.

To where the shadows are of the darkest kind, and nightmares lie in wait.

He turned the keys counterclockwise, shutting the engine down before removing the bunch from the ignition slot with a gloved hand. With his *bag-of-tricks* grasped tightly, Dr Richard Wellman stepped out of the silver Volvo estate and into the icy night air.

On the opposite side of the city, the hapless victim fell to his knees on a hard concrete floor, a muffled '*humpf*' escaping his bloodied lips when he landed. A bald man with a tattooed face – Billy Creed, to use his rightful name – limped circles around him.

Three other men watched silently. One carrying a machete and deep scowl.

'Were you part of it?' Creed asked, his thick neck straining against a button-down shirt collar. It was a question for which the gangster demanded an answer, not bullshit. 'Did they pay you to fuck up the repair on the security system?'

The CCTV engineer raised his head a few inches off the ground. Unnecessary, given that they'd earlier blinded him using his own broken thumbs as implements of torture. Mumbling an incoherent response through bubbles of red spit and broken teeth, he promptly lurched onto his front with little more than a dull thud.

The sound had a pigeon take flight overhead. A short hop to a safer perch on a rusted tractor at the far end of the draughty barn.

The place smelled of engine oil, neglect, and fear in bucketfuls.

'They couldn't have got into the club unseen if it wasn't for you not fixing the cameras.' Creed came to a halt with a sharp intake of breath and a foul mouth, and leaned on a polished cane. 'How much did that Gillighan bitch pay you to do it? Or was it that fat-fuck, Ken Ward?'

Just over two months had passed since the shooting at the Midnight Club, yet the shattered knee still plagued Creed both day and night. 'My best mate Denny died because of what you did there.' Creed prodded the engineer when he got no response. 'It's only right his little brother be the one to kill you.' Machete-man got his cue. 'For Denny,' Creed said over the sound of sharpened steel cleaving its way through human flesh and bone.

'*For Denny,*' the others repeated, as though ending a prayer.

Wellman had already dressed and positioned the prototype on the bed upstairs; the young woman's death needing to appear as though it had been from natural causes and not the foulest of play.

'You're dying,' he said, putting a hypodermic needle and empty syringe to one side of a nightstand that stood next to the bed. 'I've given you a neuromuscular blocking agent.' As a nurse, she'd understand the seriousness of the situation she found herself in. Would know she was helpless without him. Leaning on an elbow, he filled her lungs with a half-dozen of his own deep breaths, dry lips scratching against hers. 'You're temporarily paralysed. Dead within a matter of minutes if I were to get up and leave.'

The soft glow of an orange street lamp peeked through a chink in the curtains, illuminating what might have been a tear welling in the corner of the dying woman's eye.

There was nothing more than that. No struggle nor pleas for mercy.

'It's for the best in the long run,' Wellman said. 'I know you don't see it that way at the moment. And who would blame you?' His voice was educated. Reassuring under different circumstances.

But not these.

A dog barked somewhere to the east of them, no doubt disturbed by a rumble of thunder rolling in off the sea. Another answered in kind. This one larger.

Putting two fingers to the side of the woman's slim neck, he felt for a pulse. It was galloping. She was frightened and had every right to be. He lowered his head long enough to breathe life into her rapidly bluing face. 'We're almost done here,' he said, taking to his feet.

High-pitched laughter cut through the tension just then; rising from the pavement below. 'Sounds like they're having almost as much fun as we are,' he said, watching from the side of the bed. 'But I'm afraid *that's it* for the two of us.' He made an apologetic face. 'I'm needed back at the hospital. Lives to save and all that.'

Beneath the calm exterior, every survival mechanism in the woman's body would have been commanding her to move, fight, breathe. And scream.

Wellman pressed his fingers to the prototype's neck one last time. The heart was no longer tapping out its normal rate and rhythm. Had less volume too. 'Are you ready to die?'

She didn't answer.

Hadn't moved.

Was staring out into a deep and dark abyss.

3

A WEEK LATER

'It's Reece.' He clung to the exposed rafters of the old cottage roof in Brecon, an icy wind numbing him deep to the core. Behind him were snow-capped mountain peaks, and a low-level mist that made its daily pilgrimage into the Welsh valley below with the silence of a seasoned assassin. The detective had a mobile phone wedged between his good shoulder and bearded chin; a roofer's hammer gripped tightly between his knees. He hated heights and spoke without daring to look down. 'Yanto, shush that radio a minute, will you.' When his friend failed to respond to the request in time, Reece lobbed the hammer in the man's general direction. It broke a slate on contact and went sliding away out of sight.

Yanto straightened and glared at him. 'For fuck's sake, Brân, you could've killed me by there then.'

'The radio.' Reece jabbed a finger at it. 'Hang on,' he said for the caller's benefit. 'I can't hear a word you're saying.'

'Missed me by that much, you did.' Yanto measured the distance with a finger and thumb. 'Hell's wrong with you today?'

'Shut up, will you.' Reece shifted the phone to the other ear, gritting his teeth when the shoulder complained. 'No, not

8

you, ma'am.' He sat and listened for a good two minutes longer, all the while waving at the sulking Yanto, trying to get his attention so he could apologise. But he needn't have bothered. The man was legendary for his ability to keep something like this going for weeks on end if he decided to. 'I'm in Brecon, getting some outstanding jobs done on the cottage,' Reece said before finally tucking the handset away in a jacket pocket. 'Right, I'm off.' He couldn't be sure his voice had reached as far as the stone chimney stack, but from Yanto's sudden and angry reaction, he guessed it might have done.

'*Off*. Where to this time?'

Reece inched his way down the partially slated roof, on the seat of his jeans and soles of his boots. 'Oh shit,' he muttered, stretching a leg to slow himself down. He withdrew it, repositioned, and then felt for the ladder propped against the back of the building. 'You sure this thing's okay where it is?' Swearing loudly, he went over the side, not waiting for an answer.

'I'm warning you, Brân.' Yanto was on the move. Headed for the hammer that had since come to rest in a short stretch of sagging guttering. 'Get your arse back up here.'

'I can't,' Reece shouted down the throat of the wind. 'The chief super wants me back in Cardiff a week or two early. They're thin on the ground, what with Jenkins and me still being away on leave.'

'And who's gonna finish this lot?' Yanto pointed at the gaping hole in the roof, and palettes of Welsh slate stacked on the ground below. 'There's loads left to do yet.'

'It's not that bad.' Reece was walking on terra firma at last, his legs still wobbly after the ordeal of getting down the creaking ladder. Making his way across a wide expanse of gravel courtyard, he came to a halt on top of a frozen puddle, the thin ice splintering underfoot like a pane of glass. Smirking, he said, 'Won't take you much longer now we've broken the back of it.'

Yanto stabbed his leg at the air, just managing to stay upright on the roof's steep pitch. 'I haven't got time for this bollocks,' he said in a high-pitched whine. 'Got the farm and builders' yard to see to, I have.'

'Another day or two and you'll be done.' Reece opened the car door and got in.

'Don't you dare,' Yanto called over the noise of the engine starting up. He grabbed for the hammer, using an upright of steel scaffolding to support his weight, and flung it a good few metres short of the battered Peugeot when it pulled away. 'Bastard!'

The car's back end twitched violently as worn rubber sought purchase on a mix of ice and loose gravel, Reece laughing properly for the first time in well over a year. When Yanto and the cottage were out of sight, Reece leaned across the passenger seat and opened the glovebox. Rummaging amongst empty sweet packets and old music cassettes, he found the Stubby screwdriver, and poked its pointed end deep into one of several holes in the radio's front panel. He twisted it left and right until Led Zeppelin's 'Stairway to Heaven' had him toss the thing to one side.

Leaning forward in his seat, he dragged a fistful of dirty knuckles across the windscreen and watched the Storey Arms go by on his left. He leaned a bit further, ducking his head low until he saw her – Pen y Fan – the highest British peak south of Cadair Idris in Snowdonia, North Wales.

He'd scattered his father-in-law's ashes on the taller of the twins' summit only a few weeks previously. His wife, Anwen's, had rested there a full twelve months before that.

With Jimmy Page working his magic on a double-neck

Gibson guitar, Detective Chief Inspector Brân Reece floored the accelerator en route for the University Hospital in Cardiff.

The building was spreading like an aggressive cancer left to its own devices. Opened in 1971, they'd kept adding bits to it, rather than starting over with something fit for purpose. The mortuary was in the bowels of the hospital and well out of sight of most of the living.

Reece hadn't yet changed into something more appropriate for his visit, such was the urgency of Chief Superintendent Cable's call. He trudged the corridors in heavy boots and dirty jeans, attracting looks of disapproval from people who should have known better. 'Get over to the morgue,' was all she'd told him during their brief telephone conversation. 'We're moving quickly on this one. DC Morgan will fill you in when you get there.'

And so here he was. At the morgue, as directed.

Ffion Morgan stood behind a tall Perspex window, doing her level best to look beyond the whirring disk of a bone saw, and the mist of fine red spray that followed wherever it went. 'Boss,' she said on sight of him. 'The chief super mentioned you were on your way.'

'I've been on a roof,' Reece said in answer to her look of bewilderment.

'You?' She held on to the laugh, but not so the smirk. 'On a roof.'

'Take the piss if you want, but that's where I've been.' Reece came down the steps and took the space next to her. 'How are things with you?'

'Better before that,' Morgan said, swallowing when the skull cap came away from the top of the cadaver's head to reveal what looked like a big grey cauliflower. That's what she kept telling herself, anyway. 'It's just a cauli with flecks of dirt on it.'

Reece chuckled. 'I'd nearly forgotten how much you hate coming to these things.'

'Doesn't everybody?' Gagging, she lowered her gaze to the floor. 'How's the shoulder, by the way?'

'Lets me know it's still there,' he said, giving it a good rub. On the other side of the screen was a tall distinguished looking man dressed in black scrubs, green plastic apron, and white Wellington boots. 'What's the rush with this one, Twm? I normally get to see the body at the scene before you start taking it apart.'

The Home Office Forensic Pathologist stood with the deceased man's brain in both hands. Like it was a Pagan offering of some sort. On a shiny extraction table behind him was the rest of his patient, lying there like a hollowed-out canoe.

On an adjacent table was a naked old man, his skin as white as milk, except for red liver spots dotted over the surface of his body like a mild case of measles. Stood next to him was a female pathologist, busy rummaging through his insides as though picking the winning ticket from a weekend tombola. Resting on a metal tray near the old man was his entire alimentary canal: complete from tongue to rectum.

'Brân, good to see you back at work,' Pryce said. 'Looks like the Assistant Chief Constable has been getting it in the ear from someone further up the chain of command. What with this stalker all over the newspapers, and now a stabbing on the doorstep of the hospital – the politicians are having kittens.'

Reece moved his head side to side. It wasn't a nod. And it wasn't a shake. 'Even so, removing the body before the SIO gets a glimpse is a big no-no in my opinion.'

'Your pal authorised it,' Pryce said, resting the chilled brain in the bowl of a weighing scales.

'*Pal.*' Reece turned to Morgan for further explanation. 'Who's that?'

'DI Adams, boss.' The apologetic look she gave him did little to diffuse the awkward situation. 'I'll explain when we get over to the crime scene.'

'You do that.' The mere mention of Robert Adams's name went some way to ruining Reece's day. His attention was then drawn back to the nearest table and the body of the younger man. The mortuary team were in the early stages of reassembling him – albeit in clear plastic bags that were shoved into the gaping hole in his belly and chest. 'Who is he?' Reece asked.

Morgan shook her head. 'We've no idea as yet. No witnesses or anything else to help us out.'

'ID?'

'None we've found so far.'

Reece didn't think that unusual. If the motive had been theft, then there was little surprise in finding nothing on the victim's person. 'And where was he found?'

'Allensbank Road. Just outside the hospital boundary.'

'That's not your typical place for a gang-related stabbing.'

'I suppose he could have been assaulted elsewhere and then got dumped from the back of a car,' Morgan suggested. 'Maybe it was the closest they'd come to the emergency department without the risk of being seen.'

'What do you think, Twm?' Reece pressed his head against the glass. 'Could someone have dumped him?'

'It's possible. There *are* a few scuffs to the knees, hands and left cheek. Ffion might have something there. Difficult to say for sure, though.'

Reece nodded. 'Can you give us any more detail on the stabbing itself?'

'The blade penetrated the full thickness of the right

ventricle,' Pryce said with a serious look. 'That's the thinner side of the heart. Poor man didn't stand a chance once his attacker withdrew it.'

'And would he have died instantly?' Morgan asked.

'They seldom do.' Pryce stripped off his rubber gloves and deposited them in a bin marked *Clinical Waste Only*. 'The victim of the attack tends to bleed into the pericardium – the closed sac around the heart – and with nowhere else to go, the blood wells up and compresses the heart, causing full cardiovascular collapse and death within minutes if not treated.'

'The crime scene suggests the victim managed to walk only a few yards across the road before keeling over,' Morgan said.

Pryce used a foot to tap closed the stubborn bin lid. 'That sounds about right.'

'Anything else of interest?' Reece asked.

'No defence wounds,' the pathologist told him. 'The victim often grabs for the blade of the knife when it's thrust at them, sustaining terrible cuts in most instances. I've known some to lose fingers when it's pulled away again through their clenched hands.'

Reece looked beyond the pathologist; to where the anonymous man was being tucked into a black bag for his night in the fridge. 'But there's nothing like that in this case?'

Pryce shook his head. 'A solitary stab injury to the chest, and that's it.'

'That could mean he knew his attacker,' Morgan said. 'He'd have no reason to defend himself then. By the time he knew what was happening, it'd be over. Too late. Dead.'

Reece started up the steps, Morgan following closely. Holding the door open at the top, he waved her through ahead of him. 'You might well be right,' he said, overtaking to lead the way through the outer corridor. 'Come on then, show me the crime scene.'

4

There was a single white van – emblazoned with the South Wales Police emblem – and a patrol car blocking each of three routes off the T-junction with the hospital. There were blue lights, but no loud sirens. They'd reserved those for the early hours of the morning, in part, to piss off the locals.

People in hooded white coveralls, overshoes, and face masks, came and went with monotonous repetition. Carrying equipment. Labelling things for the record.

Uniformed officers walked shoulder-to-shoulder along the road and pavements, heads bowed like hungry crows in a freshly ploughed field. They were looking for the murder weapon. Hunting for the nugget that might help solve the case.

Their search had only just begun.

Enthusiasm for the job at hand not yet waning.

A squat yellow lorry from the council, together with its equally squat and rosy-cheeked driver, dealt with the drains. *Things of potential interest* laid out in muddy puddles on the broken tarmac for some unfortunate soul way down the pecking order to sift through.

Reece waved his warrant card at a confused-looking

constable in uniform, and ducked beneath a taut length of blue-and-white crime scene tape that was trying to break free of its mooring. 'I'm the senior investigating officer for this one,' he said, slapping at the tape. 'Shift yourself.'

'But I thought...' The constable left it there, not daring to take his half-hearted protest any further than that. He went back to what he was doing, which to the enquiring eye didn't seem to be anything of much use.

Reece left him to it, and without further discussion made his way towards a blue tent that billowed lopsidedly in the choppy wind. Had it not been for the heavy weights placed at each corner, it looked as though the thing might lift off at any moment and deposit itself on the busy road beneath the nearby flyover.

'What are *you* doing here?' The accent was unmistakably Brummie. The expression one of immediate irritation and disbelief. 'I'm the SIO for this case.'

'Not anymore, you're not.' Reece winked at Detective Inspector Robert Adams. 'Off you go then,' he said, shooing the man away as you would an annoying dog.

Adams stomped a short distance down the street, fumbling under his coveralls, presumably looking for a phone with which to call the station and Chief Superintendent Cable.

'Don't you think you should have taken handover from him first?' Morgan asked. 'I mean, he saw the body in situ, after all. Even came back to get a second look at the scene now it's gone.'

Reece disagreed. 'I'll get more sense from the photographs and a chat with Sioned Williams.'

'Okay,' she said. 'You're the boss.'

Reece leaned closer. 'What's he still doing here, anyway? The man's an out-and-out liability.'

'Hasn't improved any since you saw him last.' Morgan

watched the DI gesturing like a tic-tac man at the races. 'Rumour has it he's put in for a transfer back home.'

'Station canteen's his best bet.' Reece reached for a coverall. 'Hold on to me while I get my boot through the bottom of this thing, will you.'

Once suitably dressed and signed in with the scene guard, they went over to where the crime scene manager was talking with another woman. 'Morning, Sioned,' Reece said with his best effort at a smile.

The CSM double-took, and grinned widely. 'Brân, lovely to see you. I'd heard mutterings you were coming back sometime soon. How's the shoulder?'

'Better every day,' he lied. 'I thought I'd come get the details straight from the horse's mouth; save me having to spend any time with numpty over there.' Adams was still walking in circles further up the road, phone wedged against the side of his head. Reece gave him a wave just for the hell of it.

'Behave, will you.' Williams slapped his hand, making him lower it, and then put on her best look of disapproval. 'Horse's mouth, eh?'

'It was a compliment,' Reece said defensively. 'I meant, you're the go-to person on the team, not that you look like Shergar.'

'And you're full of shit.' She pushed him towards the gaping tent flap before he could cause any more trouble than he already had.

Inside were a couple more people dressed in white paper suits, and an area of pavement that was soaked with dark-coloured blood. Reece instantly felt his chest tighten, and pushed a finger beneath his collar to make more room. When that had little to no effect, he undid the top button of his shirt and loosened the tie. 'This is where the victim fell to the ground and died,' he thought he heard Sioned Williams say.

He shut his eyes. Opened them again and saw Anwen – his

dead wife – lying on that same stretch of road, bleeding to death. 'Brân,' someone said.

Was it Williams calling his name?

Or Anwen, perhaps?

He couldn't tell.

~

Reece was sat on the cemetery wall next to the tent when Morgan found him.

She perched herself on a section of damp stonework alongside. 'Another one of your flashbacks, boss?'

'I'm fine,' was Reece's only response to mention of the subject. Nodding at a line of yellow cones meandering towards them from the other side of the road he said, 'Stabbed over there, then came this way and died of his injuries.'

Morgan's gaze followed the trail. 'Looks like.'

Pressing his back against the railings, Reece snorted and shook his head.

She watched him. 'What?'

'It's a cemetery, isn't it? I just thought it ironic our victim would have been making his way towards it, like he knew he should try to get in.' Reece pushed off the wall. 'Come on, let's go see what else Sioned has to say.'

They found the CSM talking shop with the blood splatter analyst. There was lots of finger pointing going on as the couple followed the line of yellow cones.

'Better now?' Williams asked on sight of the DCI.

'Was he stabbed on the pavement over there?' Reece indicated a yellow cone with a black number 1 on it.

'Yep. He then staggered across the road, bleeding heavily, and succumbed to his injuries over...' Williams paused. 'I guess you've seen where he went down.'

'I don't suppose the attacker was kind enough to leave the knife hanging about for us to find?' Reece said hopefully. 'Twm Pryce reckons it's about four inches long, with a serrated edge.'

'No such luck, I'm afraid.'

Reece tutted. 'Inconsiderate bastard.'

'Killers usually are,' Williams said. 'There's no community spirit anymore.'

'You're telling me. This sort of thing rarely happened in my day.'

Morgan rolled her eyes at the other women, all three of them having previously heard what was coming next a dozen times or more.

Reece was oblivious to their mannerisms and began his well-versed account of childhood regardless. 'When we had a beef with someone, we'd meet up in the local park after school for a fist fight. *Fist fight*, mind you. No knives or guns. Ever. After that, it was all forgotten. No grudges. Play rugby together and share a bag of chips on the way home.' Thrusting both hands in his trouser pockets, he shook his head and moved on.

Opened in 2009, Cardiff Bay police station was little more than a stone's throw from the bustling multi-million-pound waterfront development. Comprised of a sand-coloured central tower, with two red-brick buildings sweeping away from it like aircraft wings, it stood at four storeys in height above the road.

Reece parked in his usual spot round the side and used the public entrance at the top of the steps off the main pavement to get in. 'Afternoon, George,' he said, marching through the empty foyer without stopping to chat. 'Thought you were cutting back this side of Christmas,' he called over his shoulder.

The desk sergeant looked surprised to see him. Checking his

waistline, he patted an ample belly. 'I'm down a full belt hole already, I'll have you know.'

'Yeah, yeah. Dream on.'

George watched him go past; dirty boots shedding wriggle-shaped worms of dry mud in their wake. 'You look like you've been down a hole.'

'On a roof,' Reece corrected, and sounded quite proud of himself.

'You?'

'And Yanto.'

'How is the miserable so and so?' George asked.

Reece spun a half-circle and raised his arms in the air. 'Happy as the proverbial pig when I saw him last.'

'Why do I find that hard to believe?' George chuckled to himself and made his way back behind the desk. Craning his neck through the hole in the glass he said, 'Seriously though, it's good to see you back. Did yourself proud at the Midnight Club.'

Waving, Reece disappeared into the stairwell with a squeak of its part-glazed door. Taking two stairs at a time, he spiralled upwards through the centre of the building, levelling off on the second-floor landing.

'Afternoon, all,' he said, passing through the open-plan space that was home to the Cardiff Bay Murder Squad. He checked his wristwatch and went through to his office in search of an overnight bag kept there for such occasions.

Morgan had made her own way back from the hospital in a pool car and was there at the station before him. 'Coffee's on your desk, boss.'

'Did you fly?' Reece asked with a deep frown. 'Or did Scotty beam you up?'

'All the lights were with me.' Morgan dropped behind her desk and raised the screen of her laptop. 'Oh, you remember

Ginge?' She nodded towards the lanky plain-clothes officer sat to her right. 'He's on a secondment to us.'

'Of course I remember him,' Reece said, rummaging through the contents of the travel bag. 'I was shot in the shoulder, not the head.'

Ginge leapt out of his seat and offered an eager hand in greeting. 'I'm working with the press department, sir. Putting some posters together to ID the dead man.'

'Sounds like fun,' Reece said, squeezing past the desk without shaking the outstretched hand. 'Mine are filthy.' He held one up as evidence and got as far as the door to the landing before turning to face the newbie. 'One thing I want you to know now you're on my squad: people here call me Reece, or boss, but never *sir*, you got that?' He was on his way again, headed for the showers and a change of clothes.

Thirty minutes later and Reece was sat at the head end of a long table, his team assembled for a major-crime briefing. 'Right,' he said, calling them to attention. 'All phones except mine should be off or on silent.' His gaze swept the room before settling on the paperwork in front of him. 'What we know so far, is that our victim is a white male in his early to mid-twenties. Identity as yet unknown. Stabbed once in the chest with what was likely to be a four-inch blade with a serrated edge.' Reece searched for Sioned Williams among the group. 'I'm guessing you still haven't found it?' When the CSM confirmed they hadn't, Reece went back to reading from the briefing sheet. 'The right side of the victim's heart was penetrated – full-thickness apparently – causing him to bleed out; but not before he managed to get to the other side of the road. That's where he collapsed and died.'

Someone said something that wasn't clear enough to hear.

'Poor sod,' said another.

Others mumbled in agreement.

'There were no defence wounds, or traces of the attacker found at post-mortem. No wristwatch, wallet, or phone either.' Reece glanced around the table. 'Maybe he doesn't carry them – I doubt it – but we need to know.'

'Robbed by the sound of it,' Ginge said authoritatively. Morgan clipped his ankle under the table, causing him to shift it quickly and wince. 'Sorry, boss. Getting ahead of myself.'

'Any CCTV we can get hold of needs to be looked at.' Reece stood, his phone vibrating on the desk in front of him. 'I want uniform knocking on doors with those photographs Ginge got done for us. Finding out who the victim is, is our number one priority.' He thumbed *Answer*. 'Reece.'

'Brân.' It was George, the desk sergeant. 'I've got an emotional lady down here. She says her husband's gone missing.'

'And?'

'She's asking for you by name. Won't speak to anyone else.'

'Did you tell her I only deal with the dead?'

'That's just it,' George said. 'She's convinced the man's been murdered.'

The woman caught Reece's eye as soon as he came through the door at the foot of the stairwell. She looked to be in her early-to mid-thirties, and would have been pretty had her face not been contorted with grief. 'Mrs Hall,' he said, extending a hand towards her. 'I'm DCI Reece.'

The woman stopped pacing and burst into tears almost immediately.

He contemplated giving her a hug. Looked to George for

help. The burly desk sergeant was busy dealing with an old lady reporting a missing cat, and so Reece found himself on his own. He patted the younger woman's shoulder – it was all he could manage – and led her to an empty restroom off the main foyer. 'What makes you think your husband has been murdered?' he asked, bringing two plastic cups of water to the table from a half-full dispenser situated to the side of the door. Setting one down, he took a sip from his own.

'Pete's been gone a full week,' Mrs Hall said, raising her head to look at him. 'He doesn't do that. Not ever.'

'Did you row before your husband left?'

'Pete didn't leave.' Her voice was raised. 'That man at the club had him killed.'

Reece shifted in his seat; his interest piqued. 'What man? Which club?'

'The Midnight Club in town,' Mrs Hall said without hesitation. 'Pete worked on the security system around Christmas time – told the owner that patching it in places was no good – that the entire thing needed to be gutted and started again from scratch.' She held her head in her hands and cleared her throat. 'But the owner was having none of it. Even accused Pete of trying to pull a fast one.'

'Are we talking about Billy Creed here?' Reece asked.

'I told Pete not to touch the place. "Don't get involved," I said. But he was convinced Creed would give him contracts on all his other businesses. "We'll be quids in," was how he saw it.'

Reece finished his water and got a refill. With his back to the visitor, he watched large bubbles of air glug noisily to the surface of the dispenser unit, and asked, 'How do you know it was Billy Creed?'

'I just do.'

'Not good enough. I'll need evidence.'

'Pete got a phone call a few days before he went missing. Something about having to pay for what happened to Denny.'

Reece shook his head. 'Too vague.'

'I read the newspapers.' The woman sounded angry when he pushed her for more. 'I know who Denny Cartwright was. How he died. And that Creed lost a knee in the shooting. You got hurt too,' she said more softly. 'That's why I asked for you, specifically. The reason I wouldn't speak to anyone else. That bastard had my husband killed, even if he didn't do it himself, it's still because of him. Help me, please.'

Reece held the cup to his mouth and nibbled at the rim. 'Okay. I'll see what I can do.'

5

The patient's condition was settling at last. A torrential haemorrhage stemmed by a pair of skilful hands and the application of a long-nosed arterial clamp. The surgeon peered over the top of his image-magnifying eye-loops, brow beaded with a silky sheen of perspiration. He nodded at the consultant anaesthetist. 'That was a close one.'

Dr Richard Wellman studied his monitor without reply. The woman's blood pressure was still a little on the low side. Heart rate galloping as her survival mechanisms compensated for the sudden and unexpected fluid loss. He opened a gate-clamp on the drip-set and let the transfusion speed through, noting that all parameters displayed on his screen were slowly returning to normal.

Back in his chair, he made a few entries on an anaesthetic record, his own heart not so much as skipping a beat during the entire fraught event.

The atmosphere in theatre lightened after that. A middle-aged man with a moderate scoliosis cracked morbid jokes as he transferred blood-soaked swabs from a metal floor bowl to a clear plastic bag. The surgeon called for someone to switch the radio on. 'Let It Bleed' by The Rolling Stones causing him to wax lyrical behind a light-blue face mask.

Wellman tutted under cover of a paper drape stretched taut between two drip stands at the head end of the patient. Such music only encouraged loutish behaviour and promiscuity, in his opinion.

He knew only too well. Wore the T-shirt to prove it. Metaphorically of course. He had, in all fact, never worn such a thing. Nor a vest-top, or whatever it was those hideous things were called. Jeans neither. He was strictly a suit and tie man – just as Aunt Freda had brought him up to be.

And then there were his colleagues. He despised those even more than he did their choice in music and dress. Many had previously spoken ill of him. Made trouble with the medical director. Particularly the flat-chested scrub nurse who reminded Wellman all too much of Coco the Clown. The others had recently given him a wide berth, most preferring instead to whisper conspiratorially in corridors and behind closed doors.

He caught fleeting glimpses of Coco counting clean swabs and used needles; flirting shamelessly with the professor while surgical instruments to and fro'd between them. What was the woman thinking, wearing all that ridiculous make-up at work? And what were *they* thinking, allowing her to do such an unprofessional thing?

She was flaunting her wares. Reminding him of Mother. Was close to selecting herself for the ultimate punishment.

But for the time being, at least, there were others who were far more deserving of his attention. Take that student nurse over in the corner, perhaps. She'd smiled at him twice. Came over to ask about his anaesthetic machine. She was egging him on. Would complain the very moment he dared reciprocate in kind.

Leaning forward in his chair, he couldn't quite make out what it said on her name badge.

Later then. When he had good reason to get closer.

Taking a newspaper from his satchel, he spread it over a crossed knee, trying all the while to ignore Mick Jagger's repeated offers to lean on him. Quickly disinterested in anything the broadsheet offered, Wellman reached for a copy of *Metro* from the shelf behind him.

He read that knife crime in the city was on the increase. No surprise there. It was a national pandemic almost – drug-crazed gangs running county lines – fighting for fresh territories like an invading army.

His own *plus one* hadn't helped the bleak statistics any.

The next page brought deep lines to his face. There had been more sightings of the stalker. *Still*, they misunderstood him. Had him labelled as a potential fiend up to no good. Several reports suggested he'd even been in two places at once.

If only...

But there was still nothing at all written about the dead girl. He'd got away with it. A confidence booster if ever he needed one.

Another glance at the beeping monitors had him reduce the concentration of volatile anaesthetic agent delivered to his young patient. Then a last entry made on the chart marked the conclusion of what had been a very complex procedure.

With that done, he took a peek over the top of the drape. The surgeons were busy closing the horizontal incision in the girl's lower abdomen, peritoneum and muscle coming together under the command of thick nylon sutures. Satisfied all was well, he chose his moment and stepped out to the anaesthetic room to liberate a full pack of Suxamethonium Chloride from the wall fridge. Back in theatre a few seconds later, he placed the glass vials in the fold of his newspaper, and *that*, into a side pocket of his leather satchel.

Another glance over the top of the drape showed the patient's wound fully closed, dressings applied, and the suction bottle on the drain compressed for use.

He looked for Smiler. Wanted to get proper sight of her name badge before going home for the evening. Could see her nowhere.

Lucky for her.

The short fabric strap hung like a stunted stalactite from the ceiling of the bus. Wellman gripped it tightly and pressed against the person in front of him when the vehicle rounded a bend in the road. The woman shifted position, turned, and would have seen a man dressed in expensive clothing. A man who apologised unreservedly and without delay. 'It's like a cattle market in here,' he said. 'Every person for themselves.'

She looked away with neither response nor complaint, moving a full two inches at the very most before a human wall blocked her way.

Leaning closer, Wellman breathed the scent of apple blossom in the woman's hair, and something that smelled like vanilla on the back of her neck. When she got off at the next stop, he watched through the condensation on the window – red curls rising and falling in concert with a wide and hurried stride.

She knew he was watching. He could tell. Even though she refused to look anywhere but straight ahead. He almost rang the bell when the bus prepared to pull away from the kerb. Contemplated getting off to follow her home.

Almost.

But random wasn't the way he'd chosen to do this.

Everything had its purpose; each move pre-planned to minimise omission and error. Even the minor hiccup with Harlan Miller had been dealt with efficiently.

The medical student shouldn't have used *that* laptop for the audit project. Nor gone browsing through his clinical supervisor's search history without asking. And should most definitely not have demanded a monthly 'expenses account' in order to 'keep this between you and me'.

Miller had paid for his greedy threats with his young life. His death made to look as though one of the city's many fuckwits had done for him in a drug deal gone wrong.

With the redhead out of sight, Wellman let his thoughts settle on the next chosen target. *Poppy.* What a pretty name. And so sad, some might say, that the petite blonde wouldn't get to see her twenty-fifth birthday.

Getting off at the next stop, he walked the rest of the way home without encountering another soul, and was met inside the front door by a draught coming from the far end of the narrow hallway. One bringing with it the noxious tang of meat turning bad. He'd have to deal with that. And quickly. Before some meddling neighbour called the environmental health team.

Or worse still, the police.

'I'm home, Mother,' he called into the darkness, and wiped his shoes on a mat that welcomed visitors in bold black lettering. 'How was your day?' Putting a hand to his ear, he listened for a reply he knew would never come.

Moving through to the kitchen, he rested his satchel against the legs of a wooden carver, his coat and scarf left draped over the chair's arched back. 'Tea?' he shouted at the underside of the ceiling and caught himself laughing at such a ridiculous suggestion.

The kettle got fresh water. A bone china cup, a strainer

heaped with aromatic green tea leaves. On the marble mantelpiece, a carriage clock announced the new hour with seven bright chimes, though Wellman didn't notice, his full attention focused on the satchel and its ill-gotten contents.

The muscle relaxant had proven to be the perfect choice of murder weapon, attracting no suspicion of foul play.

Using *the* laptop to load a Facebook *Profile Page* he'd previously viewed a dozen times or more, he reclined in a chair and sipped his tea.

He'd selected prospective victims by listening to loose coffee-room talk at work. Eyeballing name badges on the uniforms of the most boastful ones: pretty girls who made no secret of the fact they were playing the field. Pretty girls who thought nothing of snuffing out a man's hopes and dreams with a left swipe of a cruel finger.

And there were so many to choose from. On the general wards, labour ward, main theatres, day theatres. The supply was almost endless. And that didn't include students of medicine, of nursing, of physiotherapy.

All he required to get started was a name. Like Poppy Jones, for instance. Then input some '*Works at*' information on the Facebook page, and *voila*, there she was, the pretty and young midwife from labour ward. Wearing a short black dress, she held a glass of what would undoubtedly have been Prosecco. All her peers drank it, though Wellman couldn't for the life of him fathom why. Tasted like vinegar, in his opinion.

Poppy was at a party of sorts. Stood draped over the thick arm of some muscle-bound moron with dental veneers. Clicking on the *Photos* tab, Wellman stopped to check for new uploads, shaking his head when he came across the beach and bikini shots.

In the next photo, she wore a different dress; this one shorter than the previous example. Likewise, the replacement thick-armed moron.

Poppy was behaving like a whore. Would end up the same way as Mother if he didn't quickly intervene. Wellman tore his gaze away from the laptop images to stare at the underside of the ceiling. 'She's just like *you!*' he shouted through gritted teeth.

There were photographs of the girl's bedroom posted for all to see. As well as images of the layout of other parts of her home. None of it surprised him. Some women were foolish enough to pose right next to their front door: tits, thighs, and house number there to be found by all manner of deviants who should never be served such things on a plate.

'Mother, are you still asleep?' Of course she was. What the hell was he thinking? Leaning sideways in the chair, he scooped the satchel from the carpeted floor and dropped it onto the kitchen table in front of him. Unbuckling its leather straps with excited hands, he reached inside.

The yellow-and-white box was no bigger than a ten-pack of cigarettes, and was labelled Suxamethonium Chloride. He put it on the table and went rooting inside the satchel for a second time.

Sevoflurane, it said on the label of the fist-sized brown bottle. Used to incapacitate his victims long enough to position and inject them. He'd even made his own variant of a Schimmelbusch anaesthetic mask, by drilling dozens of small holes through the clear plastic surface of a standard one. The handheld device worked because the victim's own act of breathing drew air over a gauze wick system soaked with the volatile agent – picking it up in gaseous form – rendering the person asleep. The more the victim panicked, the faster they breathed, and the quicker the effect.

Wellman rolled the bottle in the palm of his hand, the air trapped within it forming a large bubble at its upper centre-point. Left and right the bubble went, and always in the opposite direction to the tilt of his hand.

What he had in front of him was sufficient to incapacitate and kill more than a dozen women.

Not nearly enough for what he had in mind.

6

It was the day Detective Sergeant Elan Jenkins had been dreading for almost three months. They'd suspended her on full pay following the Belle Gillighan case and arranged the disciplinary hearing stupidly fast.

In unprecedented time, even.

That must mean they want me back ASAP, she told herself during brief moments of positivity. *Or that they want you gone, and quickly*, the poisoned devil on her shoulder had teased. She didn't know either way. And no one would have enlightened her even if she'd asked.

But here it was: Judgement Day. The beginning of fresh opportunities. Or the premature end to something she'd worked so hard to achieve. It depended wholly on how she viewed the unfortunate situation she found herself in.

Holding her head in her hands, she sighed for the umpteenth time since coming downstairs for breakfast. A solitary croissant sat on a plate in front of her. An untouched cup of coffee steaming next to it. She wet the tip of a finger with her tongue and poked at a few wayward flakes of pastry. Brought the finger to her mouth before taking it away again, the flakes left untouched.

'You have to eat.' Cara Frost came to the table and took a seat next to her.

Jenkins didn't raise her head. 'Don't know why, but I seem to have lost my appetite this morning.'

'It's going to be okay,' Frost assured her. 'You're an excellent police officer, with an impeccable record. There's no way they'd do anything other than take you straight back.'

Jenkins squeezed her partner's hand. 'Thanks for the vote of confidence, but it's *them* I need to convince, not myself or you.'

Frost took a deep breath. 'Look–'

Jenkins beat her to it. 'What I did was indefensible.' She hung her head back and closed her eyes. 'I've no idea what I must have been thinking at the time.'

'You were under immense pressure and living with a manipulative individual,' Frost said. 'Besides, DCI Reece will give you a glowing character reference. He told me as much only yesterday.'

'Saw him, did you?' Jenkins levelled her head and looked away. 'Hasn't spoken a word to me in weeks.'

'He was at the mortuary, talking shop with Twm Pryce.'

'Back in work then.' Jenkins gave that some thought. 'Lucky him. Maybe that's why he's not responding to my calls – distancing himself from the pariah, as it were.'

'Nonsense.' Frost dragged her chair closer and poured herself another coffee. 'He's been preoccupied, that's all. Renovating the old cottage out at Brecon.' She remained still for a moment. Frozen in place like a child playing a game of *Statues*. 'Terrible – that thing about his wife.'

Jenkins didn't disagree, but wondered if Reece's presence at the hearing would do little more than hammer the last nail in her coffin. As far as she was concerned, the lid was already on;

all four corners screwed down nice and tight. Puffing her cheeks, she let the air out slowly. 'What if he gets all arsey with them and they take it out on muggins here?'

Frost leaned over and planted a soft kiss on top of Jenkins's head. 'He wouldn't do that to you.'

'You don't know him like I do. This PTSD thing has made him so unpredictable, it's scary.' She dabbed at the pastry flakes for a second time. More quickly, as though squashing an army of scurrying ants. 'As soon as they piss him off – and they will – he'll be lurching over that desk trying to chin one of them.'

Frost nibbled at a fingernail before speaking. 'Have you given any more thought to what I said yesterday?'

'I can't think about that right now.'

'We could sell this place and–'

'It's too soon, Cara.' Tapping the table with her hand, Jenkins whispered, 'Too soon.'

Frost checked her watch against the clock on the far wall. 'Shouldn't you be in the shower right now?'

Jenkins rose from the table, went to the counter opposite and disconnected her phone from its charger. 'I'm going to ring him,' she said, leaving the room. 'I can't risk him being there.'

She had no chance of getting through to Reece, off-grid as he was, pounding dirt track along the Taff Trail. So called because it followed the winding course of the river sharing its name, the full route stretched some fifty-five miles from Brecon to Cardiff Bay. He wasn't planning on doing it all – just a good five- or six-mile stretch – enough to clear a foggy head and a few annoying demons that hadn't yet pissed off and left him alone for the day.

The previous night had been a particularly bad one where sleep was concerned. For being alive, even. Lying there for hours on end before pacing the landing in search of a peace that refused to lend him its ear. And when eventually he drifted off, there they were again, waiting in his nightmares to taunt him with vivid images of his wife face down on the side of the road.

He'd woken up screaming her name, and in floods of tears. *Men don't cry*, he'd kept telling himself, hot water filling the bath while he'd felt for the pounding pulse at his wrist. The razor had marked his skin, but nothing more, only because of a promise made to a father in memory of his dead daughter. 'Damn you, Idris,' he'd said, smashing the heel of a fist against the bath surround. 'Why won't you let me die?'

And so he'd left the house well before dawn, a daily run better medicine than anything the shrinks could ever prescribe. It gave him time to think, to focus, and besides, Anwen was with him every step of the way. He could feel her presence. And if he listened to the wind – *really* listened, mind you – then he could hear her sweet voice the whole time he was out there.

He passed a man with a dog. Made way for a woman on a horse. And shared a tune with the earliest of birds.

He was crying again. Sobbing and laughing both at once.

Was glad to be alive, while hating every minute of it.

Nothing made sense anymore. Nothing. Not since Anwen had left him all alone.

And so he ran.

Ran to the beat of his own broken heart.

'I didn't see Reece's car out there,' Jenkins said as she and her Federation Rep passed through the front door of the County Hall building. She wondered if she should be any more or less nervous because of it.

Steve Merryman held the door open for someone coming in

behind them and nodded towards a reception desk a little way further along the foyer. 'Over there,' he said. 'We need to sign in and let them know we're here.'

Jenkins's insides were turning cartwheels. 'I said I didn't see DCI Reece out there.'

'Don't worry about that.' Merryman handed a letter to the woman sat behind the desk, following it up with the required items of ID.

Waiting in silence, Jenkins checked the windows for sight of her boss. She was so confused that she didn't know what she wanted. Turn up. Don't turn up. She really couldn't decide.

After what appeared to be little more than a cursory check, both the letter and ID were returned. 'You know where to go,' the woman said with a look of someone who expected a poor outcome. 'Usual room.'

Jenkins thanked her – not that she personally had any idea where the *usual room* might be – and followed Merryman towards a short flight of steps leading away from the reception area. At the top of the steps she stopped and got the woman's attention with the wave of a hand. 'I don't suppose DCI Reece has arrived yet?'

The woman shook her head and this time adopted a posture of denial. 'Hasn't confirmed his attendance despite two requests from us to do so.'

Merryman rested a hand on Jenkins's back, prompting her to descend the marble steps with him.

Reece had broken away from the main trail and was clambering up the steep slope of the mountainside as though chased by something that refused to let him be. Beyond the bare branches of overhanging trees were shades of purple heather, mountain streams, and steep drops into the valley below. Gripping handfuls of brittle ferns and sapling trees, he battled against the ruggedness of the land, the straps of a rucksack clawing at his shoulder as he rose and fell repeatedly.

His breath came in rapid bursts. Pulling with both arms, pushing with each leg, he dragged himself along on the flat of his belly when the terrain demanded it of him.

He was almost there.

Nearly at the summit.

Little over ten metres to go.

When at last he got there, he found himself sandwiched between mountaintop and the wettest of clouds. He rose against the wind, turning circles while screaming his dead wife's name.

'DS Jenkins.' The woman was tall and pale – Slavic in appearance – and wore the uniform and rank of a chief superintendent. 'Come this way please.'

Jenkins waited for Merryman to put paperwork away in his case and then gather a suit jacket from the back of a chair. 'Here goes,' she said, doubting her ability to survive the next few hours without throwing up.

The meeting room was smaller than she'd expected, with tables set out in a U shape. Lord Justice Vaughn sat opposite, on the bend, flanked by two other people. One was an independent member of the public. The second seat reserved for the vampiric chief superintendent.

Jenkins and Merryman were placed to the left of the panel, opposite the Force-appointed barrister and presenting officer.

Opening the buttons on the jacket of a black trouser suit, Jenkins took a deep breath to compose herself. It didn't help.

'Water?' Vampira again. The woman's eyes were an icy blue, making her all the scarier in Jenkins's opinion.

'Not for the moment, thank you, ma'am.'

Merryman took hold of the jug and poured a good measure for both of them. 'Take a sip,' he said for Jenkins's ears only.

After formal introductions and general housekeeping were out of the way, Lord Justice Vaughn read the charges.

Specifically:

'That you, Detective Sergeant Elan Jenkins, did, during the month of December last year, disclose sensitive and confidential information to an unauthorised third party...'

The judge continued, Jenkins listening to his every word as he levelled the charges against her.

'And that your conduct, as outlined above, is contrary to the standards expected of you as a South Wales police officer...'

Jenkins thought she might puke all over him. This was it. She was soon to be off to the shit-tip, no doubt about it.

'Do you accept or deny that the conduct amounts to gross misconduct on your part?'

'Elan.' Merryman nudged her. 'You have to answer.'

'I deny the charges, Your Honour.' The response was more forthright than she'd expected, leaving her concerned she might have overdone it.

'DS Jenkins was in a physically abusive relationship at the time in question,' Merryman said, handing out a fan of documents to support his claim.

'Are you submitting this as mitigation?' Lord Justice Vaughn asked.

'I am, Your Honour. For the record: DS Jenkins's ex-partner was an extremely manipulative and dangerous individual, who'd successfully deceived the prison service in the Republic of Ireland.' Merryman continued, 'DS Jenkins lived in constant fear of the woman, and any information divulged at the time would therefore have been as a result of extreme threat and duress.'

'Why then did she not report it?' the presenting officer asked. 'There are formal processes for such things.'

'She did.' Merryman again. 'To a DC Ken Ward – who unbeknown to DS Jenkins, was a corrupt officer in collusion with the woman in question.'

'To a senior officer I meant.'

The Federation Rep shrugged. 'DCI Reece was on forced leave. DI Adams unapproachable; his behaviour bordering on bullying. And Chief Superintendent Cable...'

And so it continued for the next hour or more. Question and answer. Claim and counterclaim. When they pushed for more detail, Jenkins became flustered and unable to recall key pieces of information. They wanted dates and times. 'No dates, no proof,' they told her.

'Fuck you!' she'd wanted to scream. And at one point almost got up and left. But that would have been tantamount to giving in. And whatever labels Elan Jenkins had picked up over the years, *quitter* wasn't one of them. She checked the clock on the wall opposite. Time was running out. *I need you here, Reece. I need you now, you mixed-up bastard.*

Then it came. A knock at the door. Vampira rose from the table and went to answer it.

Jenkins leaned to one side of her chair, unable to get clear sight of who was out there. Snippets of voice had her believe it might be the woman from the reception desk upstairs.

The door closed. Vampira returned, waiting on her feet a few moments longer before speaking. 'It appears Detective Chief Inspector Brân Reece has entered the building.' The woman lowered herself into her seat. 'Oh, boy.'

Jenkins gulped. *Oh, shit!*

7

Poppy Jones was down on both knees, forcing folds of thick cardboard into a clear recycling bag – bemoaning the fact that shit like this was always left to her – when a dark shape went past the side window of the kitchen. It made no sound, chose not to stop and knock at the door, was likely to be nothing more troublesome than her own overactive imagination doing its thing again.

That's what she told herself anyway, because that's what her housemates would have said had they been there with her.

But they were not; each out working the night shift at the local hospital.

All of them except Harlan Miller, that was. She hadn't clapped eyes on him since their half-drunken shag the night before last. And that stuff with his iPad – *Gawd*. What had she been thinking? Maybe he thought the same way and was choosing to ignore her from this point on. Was life in the household going to get any more awkward than it already was? Girls squabbling over men most of the time. It was fast becoming a right mess in there – her life included – all of them living in what she often referred to as *the goldfish bowl*.

Straightening, she pressed her face against the frosty glass of the window, saw nothing out of the ordinary, and opened the back door. 'Hello,' she called into a night that was as black as coal. 'Harlan, is that you?'

The garden gate squeaked a response, monotonously repeating itself on the command of a rising wind.

With the last of the bags knotted closed, and the back door left wide open, Poppy made off down the path, the cord of her dressing-gown trailing close behind on the wet flagstones.

The bin lid threw a small puddle of chilled water at her when she raised it, her right foot and its pink slipper catching most of the splash. She squealed and shook a leg like an old dog taking a pee. Lowered the plastic lid and bolted the gate closed, checking it again before turning away.

Who knows what first drew Poppy's attention to the bedroom window on the return trip up the path. What made her stop and stare. The curtains, perhaps? Had they not been fully open only a few moments earlier, when she'd stood at the gate and looked back at the house? Yes: no – she wasn't sure.

And that sliver of a gap between them. One just wide enough to let a person – a maniac – watch from the darkness beyond. She stabbed repeatedly at the air with a clenched fist. 'Eek, eek, eek,' she said, Hitchcock-style, and laughed at her own wicked sense of humour.

Back in the kitchen, annoyed with herself for letting the house get cold, Poppy engaged the Yale lock with a reassuring clunk of its heavy mechanism. *Maniacs* could stay the hell away tonight. It was time to finish that glass of chilled Prosecco and get stuck into a good book before a hot bath and then bed.

She frowned. Hadn't the glass rested on the table earlier, and not the draining board as it did now? The fluid level was the same. She'd obviously moved it before venturing out into the garden. That was it. That's what she must have done.

The floorboards creaked overhead. Always did at this time of night. But not usually in *that* way. 'Jordan, if that's you, I told you we're over. I'm not putting up with any more of your shit, okay.' She stared at the ceiling; eyes drawn slowly left to right in sync with the direction of movement. She ignored it – or did her best to – throwing herself onto the sofa to get stuck into a hardback book.

But there it was again. The noise. As loud as before, but this time right to left, and no less annoying. 'What's wrong with you?' she said, tossing the book to one side; inexplicably drawn to the door at the foot of the stairs. 'You know how this always pans out on the telly. Goes straight to shit, so it does. Lights out one and all.'

Pushing on the door, she stepped into the colder hallway, breath held deep within her chest. When the flick of a chrome light switch flooded everything around her in a soft yellow glow, she exhaled and let herself relax. 'A maniac would have cut the power,' she whispered for her own benefit, and was already more than halfway up the carpeted stairs. 'Harlan. Jordan. Come on, stop messing about.'

She knocked at the first door on the lower landing. Stood outside and waited. 'Suba, you home?' Silence but for the sound of her own heavy breathing. The same was true of the next three doors, leaving only the bathrooms, and her own room to check in what had once been the attic.

Inching towards the shower curtain, hand held outstretched, thoughts of Norman Bates *eek, eeking* loudly in her head, she got ready. 'One. Two. *Three,*' came as something of a muted squeal, the curtain swept aside to reveal nothing more improper than a worn bar of Imperial Leather soap, replete with a few dark pubic hairs sprouting out the top of it. Poppy made a mental note to remind Harlan that the girls didn't need to be dealing with such things every time they wanted to take a bath. She was rehearsing the forthcoming telling-off when something shifted in the mirror opposite. A smudge of dark colour that was gone in an instant. 'Jordan, I'm warning you. Come on, you're going too far, you're frightening me.'

And then she smelled it. Not aftershave, but a clinical odour that was vaguely familiar.

'It's time to die,' someone said. 'Are you ready?'

Before she could answer, a firm hand from behind pressed a face mask over her nose and mouth.

'Breathe. Make it easy on yourself.'

Poppy realised what that smell was. Recognised it from the hospital.

How could she have been so stupid?

There was a raucous celebration being held at the Rummer Tavern, opposite the castle. Built circa 1713, and until recently, a nostalgic pastiche of Tudor style, the pub was now one of a gazillion identical city sports bars.

'It *was* a whisky, wasn't it?' Ginge turned his back to the crowded bar and handed Brân Reece a drink over the heads of everyone else around them. 'There you go, boss.'

That got a nod from the DCI. 'Aye, Penderyn.'

'Sherrywood, right?' After making a fool of himself by jumping to conclusions at the briefing, Ginge was obviously keen to get off on a better foot. 'Sherrywood it is.'

'You'll go far,' Reece said, relieving him of the shorts glass. 'Cheers.'

Next was Ffion Morgan. Not waiting for thanks, Ginge passed a glass of tonic water, ice and slice to Elan Jenkins. 'You sure I can't get you anything stronger?' he asked. 'This piss-up's for you after all.'

'You know what that shit does to my brain,' Jenkins said, pulling a silly face. 'Alcohol's like poison to my system.'

'Wasn't aware that was a thing.'

'Take it from me, it is.'

'A final written warning then.' Reece came closer, pushed between the two of them and patted Jenkins on the back. 'That's my girl.'

'It's not something I'm proud of, boss.' She took a sip of her drink and suppressed a burp. 'It's all bubbles, this.'

Reece didn't reply, his eyes hunting for somewhere to sit. Giving up almost immediately, he said, 'Not worth the paper they're written on, those things. Makes the pen-pushers feel important, that's all.'

Jenkins didn't look convinced. 'I appreciate you coming today.' Reaching on tiptoe, she leaned to peck him on the cheek, quickly settling on the balls of her feet again when he moved out of reach. They both blushed.

'What did you expect me to do?' Reece said, ending the brief silence. 'You're going places, Elan. This episode won't hold you back none.'

'I won't be going anywhere for a while. They're holding a strategy meeting before I'm allowed back to work. And even then, there's no guarantee I won't be transferred elsewhere. As far as I see it, I'm done here in Cardiff.'

Reece's eyes widened. 'Over my dead body.'

'I wouldn't put that offer on the table if I were you, boss, they might just snap at the chance.'

'You're not wrong.' Reece looked preoccupied again. 'Where's Morgan?'

'Over there.' Jenkins pointed towards a rowdy gathering in the far corner of the room. 'Like a man-magnet as usual.'

'She's a good-looking girl,' Reece said, wondering if he

should go over and rescue her from the *roider* sporting an orange tan.

'*He's* getting friendly.'

'Hang on to this, will you,' Reece said, passing Jenkins his drink.

She caught his sleeve, not the glass. 'No need. Just watch.'

When Reece next got sight of Morgan, she had the man's face pinned tight against the wall, his bulky arm drawn up his spine, fingers pulled back in an agonising pose. People gathered around them, laughing; several using smartphones to film the event for their social media stories.

'You *do* know I used to practise Krav Maga?' Morgan said when Roider had been thrown out of the pub and all was well again. 'I'm thinking about going back to classes.'

Reece turned to Jenkins. 'Did you know we've got our very own Bruce Ffi on the squad?'

'Of course I did,' she said, laughing. 'That's why I told you to let her deal with it herself.' Jenkins and Morgan high-fived. 'Girl power.'

The DCI shook his head. 'Ginge, was I the only one left in the dark about this?'

'Looks that way, boss.'

Reece was about to respond when he caught the unmistakable reek of stale cigarettes close by. Someone reached through the crowd and pinched the flesh of his cheek between finger and thumb, tugging it playfully.

'And how's my favourite detective then?' Maggie Kavanagh: local reporter, Columbo-style mac, red lipstick, and five feet nothing, including the beehive hairstyle. 'Heard screaming when I went past,' she said with a wet cough, 'and knew you wouldn't be too far away.'

8

Reece stood on the threshold of the crowded bedroom, watching Dr Cara Frost examine the lifeless body. She had her back to him, and to Reece's mounting irritation, was being less than forthcoming with dialogue. He shifted to one side when a crime scene investigator approached carrying a large black case. Again, when a second CSI followed with a battery of photographic equipment. When he could take no more of the forensic pathologist's silence, he forced his head into the room and said, 'Find anything suspicious?'

Frost replied without turning to face him. 'Apart from the dead girl, and sheets stained with dry semen, you mean?'

The doorway dance continued as more people came and went. 'Are you telling me she was raped and murdered?'

'You're putting words in my mouth, Chief Inspector. That's not what I said.'

Reece wasn't one for games at the best of times, and drinking whisky well into the small hours was giving him little reason to change any of that. 'So why was I called to look at this?'

Frost was on her feet, putting things away in her doctors' bag. 'All I said to plod outside was that the evidence points to there being a second person present in this bedroom – a male specifically – before, or after that young woman died.' She smiled. Sort of. 'Either way, I thought it might be an idea to find and interview him.'

Reece's irritation needle was idling somewhere between amber and red. 'The uniform on the door called it in as a confirmed murder.'

'Must have been a misunderstanding.' Frost shrugged. 'You can't blame *me* for that.'

Stepping aside, he let her pass onto the landing; the floorboards creaking underfoot. 'Where's Twm?' he asked. 'Why isn't *he* here?'

'Dr Pryce is winding down into retirement, as you already well know.' Frost smiled a second time. Wider on this occasion. 'That means you'll be seeing a lot more of me from now on.' Pausing halfway down the stairs, she spoke through the gaps in a line of white spindles. 'Thank you for what you said at Elan's hearing yesterday. I'm told it was your testimony that swayed things in her favour.'

'And the post-mortem?' Reece asked.

'Should be able to get it done later today.'

He watched Frost disappear through the front door. Heard her heels clip-clopping on the pavement outside as she made her way along the street and back to a car parked at the far end. 'Right,' he shouted into the busy hallway, 'which one of you idiots got me out of bed earlier than I needed to this morning?'

No one owned up to the misdemeanour.

Morgan appeared at the foot of the stairs, dressed in a grey trouser suit over a black silk blouse. She didn't look half the worse for wear he did. 'Do you want to speak to the housemates, boss, or shall I crack on?'

Reece sat down on the top step and massaged both temples. 'Is there any point until we know it's foul play for sure?'

'One of them's got a fair bit to say for herself. Claims the dead girl's been followed home from work a few times lately.'

'By our stalker, no doubt.'

Maggie Kavanagh and the South Wales Herald had a lot to answer for. If her newspaper was to be believed, then half the women in Cardiff had experienced a recent encounter with the man. Half of those again, jamming the switchboards calling it in.

'On my way,' Reece said, getting up with a groan.

They were in the kitchen. Three housemates, two uniformed officers, and DC Morgan. The room smelled of toast and strong coffee, suggesting the cohabitants hadn't been up from bed for very long. There was a young woman sat alone at a large pine dining table. She was slight in stature and of south Asian origin. Indian, Reece decided. 'Any of that coffee going spare?' he asked, eyeballing a glass cafetière on one of the worktops.

'Help yourself,' the woman said with a dismissive flap of the hand.

'You don't mind?' He waved a piece of doorstop-thick toast at her. 'Didn't have time before I left the house.'

Morgan rested a hand on the woman's shoulder and took a seat on the other side of her. 'Suba, this is Detective Chief Inspector Reece.'

Pulling a chair opposite both women, Reece sat back to front on it. He took in the scene. The kitchen was plenty big enough, and almost square in shape. Tidy too. 'You the one who mentioned the stalker to my colleague?' he asked Suba.

'No, that was me.' There were two other women stood near an aluminium sink and draining board, both wearing bed hair and pyjamas. The one who introduced herself as Lowri lifted her gaze from an area of linoleum flooring. 'Just something I said to one of the police constables outside.'

Reece wiped butter from his lips with the back of a hand. 'Did Poppy get a description of the person who followed her?'

'No, but she insisted he was over there, next to the trees. She pointed no further than the kitchen wall. A man in a silver car.' Lowri glanced at the other woman. 'If we'd only believed her, then...' She didn't finish the sentence and broke down in floods of tears.

The other woman – Zoe – was strangling a bright-red tea towel one minute; using it to dry wine glasses the next. 'We weren't to know.'

'Those been looked at by Forensics?' Reece asked the uniforms. He told Zoe to put them down when neither officer could confirm either way.

'I'm sorry,' Zoe said when she knocked the taller flute over. It hit the floor and broke into a scattering of small pieces.

'Leave it there,' Reece said when she reached for a pan and brush. 'We might still get lucky if there's anything to be found on it.'

'Did Poppy have a boyfriend?' Morgan asked. 'Only, we found evidence of recent sexual activity on the bedsheets upstairs.'

'There was Jordan Patterson,' Lowri said. 'But they split up a few days back.'

Morgan penned the full name on a page in her pocketbook. 'Was there trouble between them?'

'Jordan's a total pain in the arse,' Zoe said. 'Best thing Poppy ever did was to get shot of him.'

Lowri came away from the sink. 'You never gave him a chance.'

'And *you* gave him a lot more than that,' Zoe retaliated. She spoke to Morgan. 'He's one of those possessive types – wants to know what you're doing, where you're going, who you're with – and all the other bullshit that comes with the territory.'

Lowri caught Reece's eye and mouthed, 'Not true.'

He turned to Suba. 'What did you think of him – this Patterson feller?'

She pushed her empty coffee mug to one side. 'He and Harlan have been arguing a lot lately.' She shrugged when the other women gave her looks of warning. '*What?*'

'Who's Harlan?' Reece asked, looking at each housemate in quick succession.

'Harlan Miller. He and I are medical students,' Suba said. 'Comes from Ohio I think.' A nod to herself. 'Yeah, Ohio.'

Morgan finished scribbling. 'What made them argue?'

'Poppy, usually. Jordan had it in his head there was something going on between her and Harlan.'

'Even accused her of shagging him,' Zoe said, sidestepping shards of broken glass. 'That's what had them break up in the end.'

'And had she?' Morgan again. 'Had she been sleeping with him?'

Suba shifted her attention to the voices and activity coming from beyond the level of the ceiling. 'I guess your people upstairs will tell you soon enough.'

Reece went and helped himself to more coffee. 'And where do we find this Harlan Miller?'

'Haven't seen him since the night before last,' Suba said.

'Would that be usual behaviour for him?' Morgan's pocketbook looked set for another entry. 'Did he often stay elsewhere?' she asked when her first question got no answer.

'Can't remember him doing it previously,' Zoe said. The other women agreed silently.

Reece came back to the table, coffee mug in hand. 'Do you have any idea where he might have gone?'

All three shook their heads in unison. Lowri answered, 'He's got no family over here. Not that he's ever mentioned.'

'We'll need a recent photograph if you have one,' Reece told them.

Lowri went to the door of the refrigerator and lifted a Volkswagen-Beetle-shaped magnet. 'Taken at Christmas,' she said, handing over the photo. 'You don't think he had anything to do with this, do you?'

Reece saw a dark-haired man wearing an ill-fitting reindeer jumper. 'Unlikely.' Holding it at arm's-length for Morgan to see, he said, 'Remind you of someone?'

'We've fallen on our feet there, boss.'

'Which one of those rooms upstairs is Harlan's?' Reece asked.

'Second door along the first landing.' Zoe followed him out of the kitchen. 'It's Jordan you want to be talking to, not Harlan.'

Suba was on her feet. 'Don't you need a warrant for that sort of thing, Chief Inspector?'

'We won't be going in there,' Reece assured her. 'Not until Forensics have taken the place apart.'

They were back at the station, Reece stood in front of the evidence board with two semi-circles of police officers and support staff facing him. Chief Superintendent Cable was at the front of the assembled group, in full regulation uniform minus the hat. Arms folded, she stopped talking and gave him the floor.

'Our victim's got a name at last,' Reece said, writing in red ink above the photograph of the man in the reindeer jumper. 'Harlan Miller: a twenty-three-year-old American studying medicine here in Cardiff.' He pinned a second photograph next to it and wrote Poppy Jones's name alongside. Pausing to tap the girl's photo with the end of the marker pen, he saw Cable's eyes narrow. 'Miller shared a student house with four women, ma'am. And this one here wound up dead last night.'

'Another stabbing?' Cable looked concerned. 'Why am I only just hearing about this?'

'Not a stabbing, ma'am.'

'What then?'

'I don't know yet.'

For a moment she stared at him with a look of bemusement. 'How can you not know?'

'Because we're waiting on the post-mortem to confirm cause of death. Look,' he said, pointing at each photograph in turn. 'Two youngsters living in the same house – one gets stabbed, and the other's found dead in bed a day later – you tell me that doesn't smell fishy.'

'We'll need to put a guard on the house,' Morgan said. 'They might all be targets.'

'That's a fair point,' Reece agreed. 'We'll need an ongoing uniform presence on the front and back doors, ma'am.'

Cable nodded. 'Okay. What else?'

'I want Jenkins back in work this week.'

'A conversation for another time and place,' Cable told him.

Reluctantly, Reece moved on, bringing all in the room up to speed with what he and Morgan had earlier learnt from the three housemates. 'Give me a sec,' he said, putting his phone on *speaker* when it rang. 'Sioned, what did you find in Miller's room?'

The crime scene manager's voice sounded tinny through the speakers of the small device, yet carried across the room nonetheless. 'Not a lot to be honest with you, Brân.' Just as well she couldn't see the look of disappointment on Reece's face. 'Got one thing that might be important though.'

'Go on.'

'If the iPad images are anything to go by, then there

definitely *was* something going on between Harlan Miller and Poppy Jones.'

'You've got photographs of them together?'

'Plenty,' Williams said. 'I'm no prude, but...'

'We going to match that semen to Miller, do you think?'

'Looks like.'

'Anything else?'

'Not as yet, but I'll let you know if that changes.'

'Okay, Sioned, thanks for your help.' Reece hung up. 'That certainly gives Patterson strong motive for killing them both.' He sought out the criminal intelligence analyst and said, 'Any luck with the phone companies now we've an ID and address for the victim?'

A frumpy-looking woman with round glasses, and hair that might have been parted with a hatchet, sprang to life with an enthusiastic nod. 'That phone's been on a few times today.' She turned the laptop towards the DCI. 'There's been activation of the telecommunications masts here, and again, here.'

'Which means the other end of Mermaid Quay in the bay,' Reece said, squinting at the screen. 'A stone's throw away.'

'Correct. But it looks like the user couldn't override the security PIN. There have been no calls or texts made from the device.'

'Good work. I want this person found and brought in,' Reece told his team. 'What's the door-to-door update for Miller?'

It was Ginge's turn. 'Allensbank Road is a decent area, boss. People living there tend to be tucked up in their beds and fast asleep that late at night.'

Reece gave scant thought to the hour in question. 'Lucky them.'

'There *was* one sighting of a car,' Ginge continued. 'By one of the locals letting her dog out for a wee. Something long, and light in colour.' He glanced at the DCI. 'She's an old lady, boss. That's the best she could do.'

'And the hospital CCTV,' Reece asked, 'did that show anything matching the description?'

Ginge grinned. 'Crime scene's just outside the boundary, so the pictures are pretty naff to be honest. But...' he said, pausing to play with the contrast and brightness settings, '...look at this.'

Morgan craned her neck. 'Definitely long, and light in colour.'

'My best guess from that distance would be a Volvo 740,' Ginge said. 'Plenty big enough to transport a casualty in, and then dump them near the hospital.'

'You know your cars?' Reece asked.

'My dad owned a garage when I was in my early teens. Made me wash everything on the forecourt for pocket money. Boring as hell, but I got to memorise all the makes and models.'

'A Volvo 740 it is then,' Reece said. 'Let's get looking at the city cameras and rule it out if it's innocent.'

Morgan's phone vibrated on the desk. She picked it up when Reece nodded. 'Uniform have found Jordan Patterson, boss. He's kicking off, but on the way in.'

9

'Take Ginge in there with you.' Reece was stood next to a one-way window in the wall of a small observation room, Jordan Patterson sitting alone at a desk on the other side. Patterson's pose was horizontal, almost; arms folded across the front of a tight-fitting white T-shirt, legs stretched out under the table. Twice, he looked up and over at the window to blow them a kiss, a thick link-chain round his neck glinting in the light thrown by the overhead energy-saving bulbs. 'You both happy with this?' Reece asked, taking a sip of hot coffee from a paper cup.

'Yep,' Morgan said, clutching a file against her chest. 'Come on then, Ginge, let's get this show on the road.'

Drawing a chair away from the wall on the other side of the room, Reece positioned it in front of the glass. 'Any news on Jenkins?' he asked once seated.

Chief Superintendent Cable remained on her feet. 'I've spoken with the ACC,' she said when they were alone.

'And?'

'He'll give your request due thought.'

Reece twisted in the chair, spilling a small amount of coffee on his trousers. 'Shit.' He stood and reached for a box of tissues on a nearby shelf. 'What's there to think about?' he asked, rubbing furiously at a damp thigh. 'Jenkins is off; Ken Ward's dead; and his replacement's as wet as a fish's bathing costume.'

'Owen is an experienced police constable.' Cable waited for Reece to get rid of the tissue and settle in his chair. 'And might I remind you, that it was *you* who okayed his secondment to the squad.'

Reece sighed deeply. '*Yes*, but I thought Jenkins would be back by now.'

'ACC Harris is making his decision first thing tomorrow morning.'

'That's good of him.'

'Look, Brân–'

Reece turned away. 'Shush, they're starting.'

On the other side of the glass, Morgan and Ginge had taken their seats; Morgan running through the preliminaries while Patterson watched on with both hands tucked down the front of his jogging bottoms. Pressing a red button on the digital recording device (DIR), she waited for the long *beeping* sound to cease before calling out the date and time. 'Present in the room are Detective Constable Ffion Morgan, and Detective Constable Owen Evans.'

Patterson sniggered and leaned towards Ginge. 'You sure you're old enough to be doing this, Owen?'

When Morgan finished, she took a photograph from an A4-sized envelope and slid it across the surface of the table. 'Do you recognise that woman?'

Patterson left it where it was and pressed his back against the upright of the seat, hands still fiddling with his privates. 'Yeah, that's Poppy.'

'Louder please. For the benefit of the recording.'

'It's Poppy. Poppy Jones.'

Morgan caught herself staring at the small port-wine stain birthmark on Patterson's right cheek. She did so only because her brother had one, and knew only too well how much it bugged him. 'Poppy used to be a girlfriend of yours.'

'She'll come round again.' Patterson looked away and sniffed. 'Always does. She can't resist me, you see,' he said with a leery smile.

Morgan shook her head. 'Not this time, I'm afraid.'

'Don't be so sure.' Patterson kept the smile going; for his benefit or theirs, it wasn't clear. 'Poppy needs her bit of rough. She'll be back.'

'Poppy Jones was found dead this morning.'

At first, Patterson stared at each police officer in turn, as though struggling to decide whether or not they were taking him for a ride. Then he shook his head, each movement more pronounced than the one before. 'No. No. No.' The denial came like rapid-fire gunshots.

'It's true.'

He was on his feet, all flailing arms and screaming obscenities. Ginge hit the alarm on the wall beside him, setting off a wailing siren. There was an almost-immediate sound of boots approaching in the corridor outside, followed by the interview room door swinging open to bang against the wall.

'It's okay.' Morgan got up; a hand outstretched in a *STOP* pose. 'Stand down,' she told the other officers. 'We're all right here, aren't we, Jordan?' She lowered herself slowly onto her seat. 'Jordan.'

Patterson did likewise. 'Dead?'

'You didn't know?'

He looked right through her. 'Of course I didn't.'

'Where were you last night?'

Patterson had the flat of his hands on the tabletop and looked like he was going to lurch out of his chair again.

'Just to eliminate you from our enquiries,' Morgan added.

'Down the snooker hall. The one on City Road.'

'Can anyone vouch for that?' Ginge asked, making a note in his pocketbook.

'Do they need to?'

'Just answer,' Morgan told him.

'Both snooker teams, and Big Babs on the till.' Patterson's mood lightened suddenly. '*Yeah*, Babs did the after-match chip butties, come to think of it. Gave me a right bollocking for nicking one before she'd put them out for us.'

'We'll need to check.'

Patterson was calmer. 'You do that.'

Morgan slid a second photograph towards him. 'Did this man come between you and Poppy?' She left the silence undisturbed for a short time. 'We know he did,' she said. 'And that you threatened to kill him only last week.'

'Slap! Not kill. I didn't say I'd kill him.'

'That's not what we heard.'

Forcing his head across the table, Patterson said, 'You heard wrong, then.'

Morgan didn't flinch. 'Give us your version of events.'

The *crown jewels* got another shakedown. 'Twat's always sniffing around her,' Patterson said, shaking his head. 'Wouldn't leave her alone. Was always interfering.'

'How did Poppy feel about that?'

He turned away, the look on his face worth a thousand words.

'You were jealous.'

'The fuck I was.'

'Hated him. Hated her,' Morgan said, positioning the photographs next to one another. 'There's no room for you in that relationship. Not anymore.'

'Is that what made you kill him?' Ginge asked. 'Start with Miller. Punish Poppy. Then kill her too.'

Patterson's hands broke free from his joggers. 'You're talking shit.' He banged a fist against the table. 'This has got nothing to do with me. Nothing at all.'

'Where were you the night before last?' Ginge again.

Patterson collapsed onto the table; head buried beneath his arms. 'Why do you keep asking me this shit?'

Morgan sat up and glanced at Ginge. 'Because looking at it from our point of view, you've got more motive than anyone else we can think of right now.'

Lifting his head, Patterson whispered, 'Motive?'

'You found out they'd had sex together, and that was more than you could bear.' Morgan pointed at him. 'That's why you killed them both. Come on, Jordan, make this easy for everyone.'

'Bullshit they did. Poppy wouldn't have shagged that scrote.'

'We've got forensic evidence suggesting she might have done. DNA checks are being run on it right now. Was that your semen on the sheets, Jordan? No, I didn't think so.' Morgan folded her arms across her chest. 'All the motive you need right there.'

'Fuck you!' Patterson was on his feet again. Leaning on the table towards them.

Morgan slapped Ginge's wrist when he reached for the alarm. 'Sit down,' she told Patterson. 'I said *park it!*'

'I need a break.'

'You'll get one soon enough.' She waited for him to settle. 'Do you see how this looks? Poppy Jones and Harlan Miller, both dead within twenty-four hours of one another, and the person with the strongest links to them, is you.'

· · ·

Reece and Cable were watching with interest from the other side of the glass. 'What do you think?' Cable asked. 'He sounded genuinely surprised when Ffion told him about the dead girl.'

Reece studied Patterson and didn't turn around when he answered. 'He's been in and out of places like this often enough to put on a good show.'

'But do you think he did it?'

'It's not what *I* think.' Reece got up. 'The CPS will have to decide on whether they think there's enough evidence to get a conviction.'

'Unlikely, I'd imagine,' Cable said. 'No murder weapon, and what sounds to be a cast-iron alibi for both nights. Not to mention the not-insignificant fact that we don't yet know if the girl was murdered.'

'As if by magic,' Reece said, thumbing the screen of his phone. 'Cara Frost's trying to get hold of me. Must be something to do with Poppy Jones's post-mortem examination.'

'What did she tell you?' Morgan asked as they accelerated off the roundabout. They were on their way to the hospital, Ginge sent over to the 'Chalk and Baize' snooker hall to check Patterson's alibi with the woman known as 'Big Babs'. The Cardiff City football stadium went by on their right; the air-dome of the 'House of Sport' on the opposite side of a busy road.

'Only that she didn't want to speak about it over the phone.'

'No clues?'

'Nope. None at all.'

Morgan pursed her lips. '*Mmm*, curious.'

Reece pointed to the glovebox. 'Pass me that screwdriver, will you. The short one with the black handle.' Someone beeped a horn behind them and got a sharp blast back in return for their protests. 'It's for the radio.'

She handed it to him. 'Jenks told me how you like to do this.'

'*Like* doesn't come into it,' Reece said, trying to keep his eyes on the road ahead. 'Got no choice, have I?'

Morgan gave the vehicle's shabby interior a slow once-over. 'You can get some superb deals on new cars at the moment.'

'What's wrong with the one I've got?' he said, plunging the metal end of the screwdriver deep into a hole marked *channel select*. He twisted the thing left and right until most of the hissing noise had disappeared. 'You like country music?' he asked, steering the car one-handed.

'I'm more of a modern Taylor Swift girl,' Morgan said, looking decidedly worried all of a sudden.

Reece handed back the screwdriver. 'Shame that, because country's all it wants to play today.'

Ginge couldn't see for cigarette smoke. 'This is illegal,' he said, waving a hand in front of his face.

The woman wore a stained vest-top, and judging by what was straining to get out of it, could only have been 'Big Babs'. 'Take it up with management. Mr Creed's office is over there.'

'It's you I came to see, not Billy.'

The woman shot a worried glance across the room. 'I don't know nothing about it,' she said, watching the office door.

'About what?'

'Whatever it is you're here for.' She picked up a duster and spray can of polish, and was off, rubbing down the wooden parts of the snooker tables.

Ginge followed, waving a photograph at her. 'Do you know this man?'

Babs tossed the duster onto the green baize. 'Already told you, I knows nothing.' She pointed towards the office. 'And if *he* gets sight of me talking to you, I'll be *good* for nothing.'

'I only want to know if this man was in here a few nights ago.'

Checking the door again, Babs grabbed the photo from the policeman and gave it a brief once-over. 'That's Jordan Patterson,' she said, quickly handing it back. 'He's in here most nights. Usually with some nerdy guy who's into computers.'

Ginge gave her the dates and times in question. 'And you're sure?'

'Like I said: he comes in almost every night.'

'Copper.' The voice was deep and came from the other side of the room. Big Babs was gone when Ginge next looked. The duster and polish likewise. Billy Creed came limping between the tables, flicking the polished cane out in front of him before planting it down again on the thin carpet. 'Thought I could smell a pig in the house.' He stopped in front of Ginge and blew cigar smoke at him.

'Mr Creed.'

Creed turned to Jimmy Chin. 'What's Copper doing here, Jimmy?'

'Must be lost, Billy. Wouldn't be stupid enough to come in here on his own.'

Creed leaned his full weight on the cane. 'I remember you,' he said, stopping to pick a speck of tobacco leaf off the tip of his tongue. 'You brought that blonde stripper to the Midnight Club. Came late for the Christmas curry. Yeah, that was you.'

'I'm finished here,' Ginge said, turning to go.

'Did you tell Copper he could do that, Jimmy?'

'Not me.'

Creed stepped closer still. 'Copper's gonna be staying a while longer.'

63

10

'It wasn't as obvious when I saw it back at the student house,' Dr Cara Frost said. 'Not that obvious even now.' Dressed in full cutting-room gear, she wore black scrubs, green plastic apron, and white clogs. She didn't look up and leaned on a counter, leafing through a mound of paperwork. 'If I'm right, then this is one clever killer you've got yourself.'

Reece stole a glance at Morgan, both eyebrows coming together to form one long line across his forehead. 'That's got to rule Patterson out of the equation for sure.'

'It's just a hunch at the moment,' Frost said, lowering the pen to give Reece her full attention. 'Stay with me on this until I've finished.'

Poppy Jones lay naked on the extraction table, legs extended, arms resting straight at her sides. Gravity had drawn her lifeblood to the lower levels of her body; a purple plimsoll line running full circle where skin touched metal. Her shoulder-length blonde hair had been combed away from a pretty face to reveal lips that looked stained by a full-bodied red wine. Beginning just above a folded white towel placed over the groin area, was a thick track of black stitching running up to the shoulders in a Y-shape. The skin was puckered tight against the suture material.

Morgan sighed. 'Such a waste of a life. So young.'

'Fit as a fiddle too,' Frost said, tapping a porcelain-white thigh with the back of a hand. 'Not a thing wrong with her that I could find.' She circled the table and helped herself to a pair of gloves from a rack on the wall. 'And that's what got me thinking about something one of my professors told us at university.' Pointing at a door to her left, she said, 'You'll have to come through to see properly.'

The smell was stronger on the other side of the glass. A clinical odour of pine disinfectant fused with the stench of human decay and excrement. And blood – that always hung about like a needy friend.

Reece didn't seem to notice. 'Show us what you've got then,' he said, getting close to the table and dead girl.

Frost took a pair of fine forceps and an even finer probe from a line-up of surgical instruments set out on a trolley. Using them to open up the track of Poppy's navel piercing, she leaned out of the way and said, 'See that there?'

Reece moved in closer, his head bobbing side-to-side. 'What is it I'm looking at?'

'Very difficult to see,' Frost said, checking the instruments hadn't moved and obscured the view. 'The piercing track itself is very well established; probably been there several years, I'd say. But this here alongside it,' – she opened it up a little further with the probe – 'is what I believe to be a more recent needle prick.'

'Recent, as in a day or so ago?'

'Yep. Definitely.'

Reece shifted his gaze. 'And by needle prick you mean an injection of some kind?'

'That's what I'm thinking, yes.'

'Could it be insulin?' Morgan asked from a position of not closer than five feet away. 'Was she a diabetic, maybe?'

'Blood glucose levels were within the normal range,' Frost said, coming away from the table to drop her gloves in a bin. 'The only abnormal parameter was the amount of potassium we found free in the blood. And *that* lends some weight to my hunch.'

When the pathologist said no more, Reece followed her into a side room and spoke to her back. 'Come on then, give it to me with both barrels.'

They'd left the mortuary only a few minutes earlier – Reece leading the way as usual – and had entered the main hospital building. 'Surely it's far too soon to be doing this?' Morgan was hurrying behind him and struggling to keep up. 'Dr Frost said it would take at least another day for the full tox reports to come back.'

'No harm in asking a few questions while we're here.' Reece marched along the corridor, pushing at doors with a firm hand. He stopped someone with a stethoscope draped round their neck. 'Where's the anaesthetic department?'

'Third floor. B-block.'

Reece thanked the man and headed for the stairs.

'*Really?*' Morgan said, rounding her shoulders like a moping teenager. 'We're on Lower Ground at the moment. There's got to be a lift somewhere nearby.'

'You don't want to go anywhere near the lifts in this place.' Reece spoke from experience. 'Not if you want to remain sane.'

They exited the stairwell on the third floor and turned left purely by chance. 'There it is,' Morgan said, looking pleased with herself. 'The Anaesthetic Department.' There was an office door next to the sign, with the outline of a person dressed in white on the other side of a frosted glass window. Morgan knocked on the wood surround and waited.

'Yes.' The man was tall. Powerful looking. With a face that suggested he'd spent a lifetime perfecting a frown.

'I'm Detective Chief Inspector Reece.' Producing his warrant card, the DCI added, 'And this is Detective Constable Morgan.'

'Is there a problem?' the man asked. 'I'm Dr Richard Wellman, Clinical Director for Anaesthetics.'

'We called in on the off-chance, truth be told,' Reece said, pointing to the sign near the door. 'And this looked like the right place to be getting started.'

Wellman stood there waiting. 'Started on what exactly?'

'Could we come in?' Reece asked with a glance up and down the corridor. 'It's not what I'd call private out here.'

'I'd normally insist you made an appointment with my secretary,' Wellman said. 'This is highly unusual, I'll have you know.'

'Two minutes and we'll be on our way,' Reece promised.

'At the most,' Morgan said.

The room was a tight fit for three people. 'I bet you've seen bigger prison cells.'

'I *was* expecting something a bit grander at your level,' Reece admitted. He took a fold of paper from his trouser pocket and held it close to Wellman's face. 'How do you say this?'

Wellman adjusted his position and read, 'Suxamethonium Chloride. What of it, Chief Inspector?'

'Am I right in thinking you can paralyse a person with this stuff; even stop them breathing?'

'Temporarily, yes.' Wellman leaned against his desk. 'We use it to secure an airway – place a breathing tube in the windpipe – prior to surgery. But I'd have to say its use is no longer as commonplace as it once was.'

'It wouldn't be available in these operating theatres, then?' Morgan asked, her pen hovering over her open pocketbook.

'Oh no, it's still in stock, and has its uses,' Wellman added.

Reece took in the contents of the office. Desk, chair, filing cabinet. And a smaller room leading off the back end of the main room. There were no photographs of a wife or children that he could see. And the place smelled. A cloying odour that hung in the air like a bad fart.

'It's the drains,' Wellman said. 'Something to do with the plumbing for the ward above us. They've had the ceiling tiles down more times than I care to remember.'

'Is it always like this?' Reece asked, turning his nose up at it.

'It'll disappear for a few weeks and then raise its ugly head again when you're least expecting it.'

'You could hide a decomposing corpse in here,' Morgan joked. 'No one would notice the difference.'

Wellman studied her before replying. 'I've already told you, most days it's nowhere near as bad.' Turning to Reece he said, 'Could we please get back to what we were talking about, Chief Inspector?'

Reece nodded. 'This Suxamethonium Chloride: it's kept where?'

'The fridges in each anaesthetic room.' Wellman looked irritated. 'Can I ask the point of your visit?'

'Not at the moment,' Reece said. 'And would it only be anaesthetists who'd have access to it?'

'No, not at all. Just about anybody working on the theatre suite could lay their hands on a box if they so wished.'

Reece concluded the summary of events and waited for Chief Superintendent Cable to react.

'I've never heard of such a thing,' she said, searching through a desk drawer until she'd found a bottle of aspirin. She and Reece were sat in her office at the Cardiff Bay police station. 'And it's still just a hunch of Cara's, is that right?'

'Until the tox screens are back,' Reece admitted. 'But Cara seemed confident we'd get a positive result.'

The pills were swallowed with two gulps of coffee. 'Sounds like something from a spy film.'

Reece stirred the contents of his mug with a pen and seemed happier with the taste when he next took a sip. 'The Novichok attack in Salisbury was for real,' he said, returning the Biro to a pot on the chief super's desk.

'Just put it in the bin, will you.' Cable rested her paper cup on the desk. 'Tell me what you know so far. I'll brief ACC Harris once we're done.'

'Make sure you remind him about Jenkins while you're at it.'

Cable looked up from her coffee and gave the DCI a look of warning. 'He's already said it's being dealt with.'

'Not quickly enough,' Reece said, letting his temper get the better of him. 'Two youngsters killed, and now this woman claiming Billy Creed's done her husband in.' He rose from his chair. 'I can't do it all myself, you know.'

'You don't go anywhere near him.' Cable pointed a finger in warning. 'Creed's lawyers are already threatening to sue us over our part in him getting shot.'

Reece was somewhere beyond agitated all of a sudden. 'I got a collapsed lung and a shoulder full of shrapnel – what if *I* sue you instead?'

'You got *yourself* shot. Wouldn't listen to a fucking word you were told, as usual.'

'Would you have let me go to the club if I'd stuck about and asked?' He watched her respond. 'Exactly. And that's why I went and sorted it out myself.'

Cable calmed herself with a series of deep breaths, allowing the tension in the room to ease off. 'You almost got yourself killed, Brân. What you did was bordering on reckless.'

'I got Jenkins out of there alive, which wouldn't have happened if I'd waited for the nod from you or Harris.'

That was certainly true. Cable took another deep breath. 'What were Cara Frost's exact words – so I can brief the ACC.' Reece was staring at her still. 'Okay, okay,' she said in defeat, 'I'll remind him about Jenkins.'

Reece lowered himself onto his chair and picked at the rolled lip of his paper cup while he spoke. 'When Cara was in training as a pathologist, she got one of those let-your-hair-down type lectures from one of the wackier professors. You know the type: the case you're never going to see in your career, but I'll tell you about it, anyway.'

Cable nodded and let him continue.

'Well, the professor talked about how this paralysing drug, Suxamethonium Chloride, was once thought to be the perfect murder weapon. Pathologists don't routinely screen for it at post-mortem examinations, and the entry wound is no larger than a fine needle prick. There's no outward evidence of foul play apparently, not unless you really look for it.'

'Sounds perfect to me.'

Reece shook his head. 'There's been only a handful of documented cases in the United States, dating from the early sixties up to the mid-nineties, I think. Deaths involving otherwise fit and healthy individuals like Poppy Jones. But what was common to all these cases was the occupations of the spouse. They were anaesthetists, intensive care nurses, even a friend of a veterinary surgeon in one case.' Reece lobbed the empty cup into a bin near the door before continuing. 'In each case, the police got lucky through *throwaway* comments made by workmates or neighbours, leading them to test for the drug.

And on each occasion, they secured a conviction. Frost remembers her professor saying – and it might have been from the newspapers, rather than something written in an official document – that there should be a push to consider screening for it when confronted with a case of similar circumstances.'

'But I'm guessing this isn't known in wider circles,' Cable said. 'Meaning other pathologists would have likely missed it?'

'Yeah, but I'm hoping ours is just a one-off example. Can you imagine having a serial killer loose in the city, injecting people with paralysing agents?'

Cable lifted the receiver off its cradle and hovered a finger over the keypad. 'If the tox reports on Poppy Jones confirm Cara's suspicions, then everyone in that student house becomes a suspect.'

11

Wellman listened to the late-evening news with a generous glass of his favourite Chateauneuf-du-Pape, and a rather good cheeseboard. He put Johannes Brahms on hold – but only for as long as it took the stupid woman on the television to update the principality on recent happenings.

There was nothing on there about the dead Poppy Jones. Not a mention of her at all, in fact. And the meddling Harlan Miller was already little more than a bad memory wrapped around greasy helpings of backstreet fish and chips.

But that police detective might become something of a problem. Turning up unannounced to ask questions about the drug, Sux.

Reece. Wasn't that his name? The man couldn't possibly know that Poppy's death was from anything other than natural causes. Wellman had been so careful to first incapacitate her with the Sevoflurane device. Breathed her down rapidly while holding her close so she couldn't injure herself by thrashing about. Once asleep, he'd taken her to her room – he knew which one thanks to good old Facebook – and undressed her before choosing an injection site that no one was likely to notice.

Though convenient, the body piercing had made him recoil with revulsion. Why was it that some women saw fit to spoil what was, in Poppy Jones's case at least, near-perfection?

Because they're whores. The very thought of it made him angry, the stem of the glass almost snapping in his hand. *That's why you chose her. She was playing the field. Had said so herself at work.*

What was it that counsellor had told him to do on such occasions of intense anger? Wellman took a series of slow measured breaths, relaxing his grip on the glass until he was somewhere near calm again.

His mind drifted back to Poppy and her demise. He knew that pathologists didn't routinely screen for such metabolites, having had a conversation with one of them only recently. Not a colleague from Cardiff, obviously. That might have raised suspicion given current circumstances. Professional conferences had many benefits, and not all of them for the greater good of the general public.

He'd have to be more careful now that Reece was snooping about. Lie low for a while, perhaps. Isn't that what they called it? Let things blow over, then start again another time. Another place, even?

But the urge to kill was getting ever more intense. Fuelled in part by a plentiful supply of whores who thought nothing of providing online running commentaries on their smutty indiscretions. *Breathe.* It was all he could think about for large parts of the day and night; the counselling sessions on Cathedral Road doing precious little to suppress it. *Breathe.*

'What was that, Mother?' he shouted at the underside of the ceiling. 'You'd like more music and wine.' Rising from the chair, he took the half-empty glass with him, turning up the volume on the old record player as he went past.

He tried to hold his breath at the top of the stairs, but couldn't.

On the landing, he turned the brass knob of the bedroom door, pushed on it and retched.

Inside, he said, 'Mother, you're beginning to smell like a dead cat.'

He went nearer the bed, tentatively at first, like a young child made to pay its last respects to a dead grandparent.

Like that six-year-old boy on Christmas morning, tugging at his father's cold feet.

Holding the glass above the corpse's head, he emptied its contents over the mottled face. 'Drink, whore.'

12

'Hey, look who it is.' Morgan tossed her bag onto the nearest desk and bounded towards Jenkins; arms open wide. 'Are you back?' she asked enthusiastically. 'Properly back?'

Jenkins ducked and dived under a flurry of hugs. 'Bloody hell, Ffi. Sort of, but it's a bit complicated.'

Morgan plonked herself down on the edge of the desk, her face still split in two by a broad grin. 'The boss has been giving Cable some right earache since the outcome of the hearing. Said they were to bring you back or else.'

'I've heard.' Jenkins was doing her utmost to resurrect a spiky fringe. Licking her fingers and pulling at it. 'The entire thing has been a bit of a whirlwind, to be honest with you.'

'Better that, than to have to hang around waiting the best part of nine to twelve months like most officers do.' The smile slipped away as quickly as it had appeared. 'I knew one copper who had to wait almost–'

'I'm not complaining,' Jenkins said, giving her fringe a welcome respite. 'Just knocked for six by the speed of it all.' Swinging on the back legs of the chair she asked, 'What have I missed lately? Any shenanigans with you know who?' She nodded in the direction of Reece's empty office.

'He's only just back to work himself. I'd say he was okay on the whole. One flashback I've seen.' Morgan told her senior colleague about the main case they were working on. About Poppy Jones and Harlan Miller. 'Looks like it could be a double murder. We're waiting on some tox screen results before bringing the rest of the household in for questioning.' She paused, her face suddenly lighting up again. 'How are things with you and Cara, by the way? She seems very nice. Clever, too. I got talking to her at the post-mortem.' Morgan leaned over and placed a hand on Jenkins's shoulder. 'The two of you will have to come round ours for a drink and nibbles sometime soon. Meet Josh. That will be nice, won't it?'

Jenkins promised they would. 'This Patterson feller; did he say much at interview?'

'Mostly that he didn't do it, obviously. And if your Cara's right, then the girl's murder is well beyond his capabilities, anyway.'

'Can we stop calling her that: "*Your Cara,*"' Jenkins said. 'Plain Cara, or Dr Frost, should be fine.'

Morgan slid off the edge of the desk. 'I meant nothing by it.'

'I know you didn't, but after what's just happened to me with Belle Gillighan, I'm nowhere near ready to be jumping feet-first into another relationship.'

'Whatever you say.'

'Ah Ffion, you're not pissed off with me now, are you?'

'No, not at all.' Morgan watched the first of the troops wander in and fuel themselves with early-morning coffee, and stale croissants left over from the previous day. 'The boss has called a briefing for quarter past,' she said. 'Wants a quick round-up of everything we've got so far.'

'Cool.' Jenkins stared at the empty desk opposite. It had,

until recently, belonged to their colleague, Ken Ward. 'That Ginge's now?'

Morgan twisted at the waist and nodded. 'Kenny had us all fooled, didn't he?'

'Hook, line, and sinker.'

'You must have been terrified down there in that basement. I know I would have been.'

'Strangulation is no way to go out of this world,' Jenkins said, putting a hand to the front of her neck. The scars had gone. The physical ones, at least. 'I can vouch for that.'

'The bastard.'

'I've called him far worse,' Jenkins admitted.

'Bet you have. Those upstairs arranged any counselling yet? You make sure they do.'

'Give 'em a chance, they're only just getting their heads around not sacking me.'

'You went way beyond the call of duty trying to sort that shitstorm out. They owe you big time for what you did there.'

Jenkins lowered her head. Her voice too. 'My actions contributed to the deaths of at least two people – let's not forget that – as well as almost getting the boss killed.'

'I got myself shot,' Reece said, entering the room from somewhere behind them. '*Me,* not you.' He stopped in his office doorway. 'That cleared up now?'

Jenkins didn't look at him. Sat staring at an imaginary point on the far wall. 'If you say so.'

'I do.' He closed the door, then opened it again not a moment later. 'Welcome back, by the way.'

Reece arrived for the briefing ten minutes later than everyone else. 'Apologies,' he said, looking down the length of a long table. 'I've been on the phone to the pathologist. All here?' After checking the room for absentees, he gave the usual instructions regarding mobile devices and other unnecessary interruptions. 'It's confirmed,' he said with a single twitch of the head. 'Poppy Jones was killed with the paralysing agent Suxamethonium Chloride.' There were surprised reactions all round. Lots of shrugging and other gesticulations which meant most people had no clue what he was talking about. 'Cara Frost found high levels of a chemical called choline in the brain, succinic acid in the tissue around the belly button, as well as the breakdown products of the drug itself in the urine.'

'Hats off to her.' Morgan glanced at Jenkins and then quickly away again. 'I'm well impressed.'

'It was a good shout,' Reece agreed. 'We've got ourselves two murders, and until known otherwise, we'll be treating them as connected.'

'What's your thinking on this?' Jenkins asked. 'A revenge killing by a jealous boyfriend?'

'That would be the most obvious,' Reece answered. 'Patterson's more than capable of stabbing someone – he's got previous for wounding with intent – but he'd need help to administer the drug, I'd imagine.'

'And he's a cleaner at the hospital,' Morgan chipped in. 'If the doctor is right, then Patterson would have no trouble at all getting his thieving hands on some.'

'Could it be one of the housemates?' Jenkins was reading from her briefing sheet. 'Says here they all have a medical background of one kind or another. Could one of them have helped him kill her, do you think?'

'There's definitely two camps in that house.' Reece looked to Morgan for her opinion.

'I agree. Particularly where Lowri and Zoe are concerned.'

'Go on.' The prompt was from Chief Superintendent Cable. 'Tell me what you mean by that.'

'Well,' Morgan said. 'I got the distinct impression that Lowri was pro-Jordan and anti-Harlan. Zoe the other way around.'

Reece nodded. 'There was also a throwaway comment made by Zoe, that Lowri and Patterson might have had a fling in the past.'

'She might still hold a candle for him,' Cable said, 'and be only too happy to help get rid of the competition, as it were.'

'True.' Reece had considered that already. It made the most sense, obviously. The pair had motive, means, and opportunity. People had spent lifetimes behind bars on far less evidence.

'And the Indian girl.' Cable again. 'Isn't she also a medical student?'

'She's the quietest of the bunch, ma'am.' Reece gave his head a good scratch. 'I'd be surprised if she had anything to do with this.'

Cable watched him over the upper rims of her glasses. 'You know what they say about the quiet ones.'

'Not this time, ma'am.'

'How does the drug affect a person?' Jenkins asked, putting the paperwork on the desk. 'And how does the killer get the victim to keep still long enough to inject it so precisely?'

Others at the table were asking the same question.

'Shush,' Reece told them, and leaned on his elbows. 'Ordinarily, it's injected into a vein before surgery, and about a minute or so later, you start twitching all over.' He stopped to look up at Morgan. 'What did Cara say the word for it was?'

Referring to her pocketbook Morgan said, 'Fasciculations,' and pronounced the word deliberately.

Reece nodded. 'After that, you're paralysed for somewhere up to ten minutes. Even the muscles used for breathing come to a complete standstill.'

'Christ,' somebody said. 'I'm not putting my name down for surgery any time soon. *Paralysed.* I never knew that.'

'You're given an anaesthetic beforehand,' another pointed out. 'You're asleep by the time it happens. I've had plenty for my knee, and can't remember a thing.'

'But getting the drug into her in the first place,' Jenkins repeated. 'How did he manage that when you said there were no injuries to suggest she'd been struck or assaulted in any way?'

'I don't know,' Reece had to admit. 'Suggestions anyone.'

Ginge's hand went up.

'Just shout it out,' Reece told him.

'Do you remember those old movies, boss? The ones where the spy soaked handfuls of old rag with chloroform and held it over the victim's nose until they were spark out.' He put a cupped hand to his face and pretended to lose consciousness. 'Maybe that's what the killer did.'

'If you can steal this *Sux* stuff so easily,' Morgan said, ignoring the newbie's theatrics, 'then chloroform is doable, I'd imagine.'

'Do they even use that anymore?' Jenkins asked.

'Find out,' Reece told her.

'If Ginge is right, then at least the poor girl would have been asleep throughout,' Cable said. 'There's *that* small mercy to hold on to, I guess.'

'No, Cara thinks Poppy was awake during most of it.' Reece turned to Ginge. 'I'm not saying the killer didn't use the method you've suggested, but it's got something to do with the amount of tissue fluid found in the girl's lungs. She'd been struggling to breathe against a blocked airway at some point.'

Cable shifted in her chair. 'My God.'

Reece didn't think *He* had anything to do with it, but said nothing, all the same.

'Any evidence of sexual assault?' Jenkins asked.

Reece shook his head. 'Doesn't look that way.'

'Does that lend weight to it being one of the girls?' Jenkins again. 'Lowri's looking more and more like a person of interest, if you ask me.'

'Agreed.' Reece sat back and checked his watch. 'Okay, let's go round the table and see what else we've got.'

'We've found Harlan Miller's phone,' one of the uniforms said. 'Homeless guy at the docks says he found it in the cemetery on Allensbank Road.'

'What was he doing there?' Reece asked.

'Buying a fix.'

'In a cemetery?'

'Unlikely to get robbed by the locals,' someone said to laughter all round.

Reece allowed himself the briefest of grins. 'Did you ask if he saw anything?'

'High as a kite, boss. Left him to sleep it off in the cells overnight.'

Turning to Morgan, Reece said, 'Once we're done here, you and Ginge go find out what he knows.'

Cable shifted. 'Jenkins can do that.'

Reece shook his head. 'I want her to go see the housemates. She might get more out of them than we did – especially from that Lowri character.'

'ACC Harris's orders are, and I quote almost verbatim, "DS Jenkins is to concentrate her efforts on the Harlan Miller case, and nothing else for now."'

'But–'

'It's the "nothing else for now," that makes it quite clear, don't you think?' Cable was on her feet. 'While I remember, the boy's parents are arriving later this afternoon. I want you around for that.'

Reece pulled a face. 'I'm going to be busy here. Why can't you do it?'

'Oh, I'll be there too,' she said, turning to leave. 'As will ACC Harris.'

'You're kidding me?'

'I'm not. They've got clout, this lot; the father used to be a–'

'I knew it.' Reece slammed his hand against the desk. Most in the room lowered their heads, not wanting to get involved. Several watched with one eye open. 'And Poppy was only a nurse, eh? What did her parents do – work in a factory, or something just as crap?'

Cable glared. 'That's not what I meant, and you know it.'

'And the CCTV guy,' Reece continued, unable to stop himself now he'd got started. 'What about that poor bastard? His family got any clout?'

'Just remember who you're speaking to, Chief Inspector. And you'll quit with the Billy Creed angle on that one, if you know what's good for you.'

Reece got up and followed her. 'Creed tried the scare tactics on Ginge yesterday. Didn't like us asking questions.'

Cable's eyes opened wide. 'You went round there?'

'*No*. Ginge did.'

'But *you* must have sent him?'

Reece shrugged. 'Nobody said I couldn't. It's *me* you've put the ban on. Not members of my team.'

The chief super clenched her fists, and for a moment looked like she might swing for him. 'I didn't stop you. It's the lawyers, for Christ's sake.'

'I was following up on a lead. Checking Jordan Patterson's alibi for the Miller murder, if you must know. You heard him say he was playing snooker that night.'

Cable relaxed. 'Mmm.'

'There we go then.' Reece stood his ground. 'Only, Creed turned up and got all defensive. Him and Jimmy Chin.'

'Boss.' Ginge was waving an arm overhead. 'Boss.'

'What?'

'I've been waiting for the staff rotas to come across from the hospital. Had to get Human Resources approval before they'd–'

'Just give me the punchline,' Reece said, still fuming after his altercation with the chief super.

Ginge blushed. 'When Lowri Hughes told us she's a nurse, she neglected to mention her speciality being anaesthetics.'

'You're joking.'

'Straight up, boss. And there's something else.' The newbie looked pleased with himself. 'The night Poppy Jones died – Lowri rang in sick for work.'

Reece looked to Jenkins. 'Get a car round there and bring her in.'

13

Reece had sent Ginge to explore the chloroform angle, deciding last minute to join Morgan in the interview room while awaiting the arrival of the Americans.

'None of your lot asked which department I worked in,' Lowri said with a look of bewilderment. She held a paper tissue in her hands and was busy tearing it to shreds. 'How was I supposed to know that was important?'

'And the others in the house?' Morgan was using a broken-ended Biro to doodle on a pad of yellow paper. 'Any of those routinely work with anaesthetic drugs?'

Lowri looked like she was trying to catch the detective's eye, but Morgan refused to lift her head, making things difficult. 'Zoe's a physiotherapist,' Lowri said, rolling the torn bits of tissue into compact balls; lining them up across the table in neat rows. 'She rotates every few months, but lately she's been doing stroke rehab, I think.' Lowri shook her head. 'You'd have to check with her to be sure though.'

'And Suba?'

'Cardiology block, and hating every minute of it last time we spoke.' Lowri fell silent while starting a third line of paper balls.

'Harlan was on an anaesthetic placement though. If you're asking: who else apart from me had access to drugs, then look no further than him.'

Reece shifted in his seat. 'Harlan Miller was recently on the theatre suite?'

Lowri had since turned her attention to picking at the veneered edge of the table, the paper balls strewn out over much of her side of it. 'Yeah, but why are you asking me this?'

Morgan hadn't stopped doodling on the yellow pad. 'What do you know about Suxamethonium Chloride?'

'What is this?' Lowri was still for the first time since she'd sat down. 'Why all the questions?'

'Just answer,' Reece told her. His voice was calm but firm in its tone.

'It's used to intubate patients. Whenever we need to do it quickly.'

Morgan lay the Biro flat on the yellow pad. 'You ever take any home with you?'

The woman's jaw opened wide. 'You're freaking me out now.'

'Did Jordan ever ask you to get him some from the hospital?'

'What?' Lowri bumped against the table, several paper balls falling to the floor.

'Where were you the night Poppy Jones died?' Reece asked.

Lowri was shaking. The head-to-toe proper kind. 'I already told the policeman back at the house, we were all at work that night.'

'Including you?'

'Yes. Including me.'

Morgan stared. Her latest doodle left unfinished. 'Let's try that again, shall we?'

'I was at work, okay.' Lowri looked towards the greyed-out window in the far wall and started crying. 'I was at work.'

Reece turned his file to face her. It was open to one of the pages sent over from the hospital. 'This here says you took the night off.'

After Chief Superintendent Cable had finished grilling her on some of the finer detail filtered down from the recent disciplinary hearing, Jenkins found Ginge on her way back to her desk. He was crouched over a blank laptop screen looking somewhat deflated.

'They don't use chloroform in hospitals anymore,' he'd said with a deep sigh. 'Not for years in this country, apparently.'

'Ah well,' she'd told him. 'It was worth a shot. Come on.' And that's how he'd ended up in the interview room with her.

The homeless man's name was Charles Rash, and despite his date of birth suggesting he was only fifty-two, he did in fact look older than dirt. 'Itchy, they calls me,' he said with a broad Cardiff accent and toothless grin. 'Itchy rash, get it?'

Jenkins did and considered the label wholly appropriate for a man who hadn't stopped scratching since he'd entered the interview room more than ten minutes earlier.

'It's a German surname,' Itchy said. 'On my father's side.' He turned his bloodshot eyes to Ginge. 'That's right, sonny, my grandfather was a Kraut.' He stood up suddenly and saluted. 'But *I* was in the British Army: C Company, 1st Battalion of the Staffordshire Regiment.' Saluting a second time, he stamped a foot. 'Saw action in the Gulf.' He went quiet then. Looked to be deep in thought and lowered himself onto his chair. There were tears in his eyes. 'Not all of us came home,' he said with a faltering voice.

Jenkins gave him time. Found a tissue and offered that too.

'I know what you're thinking: that I don't look like a soldier. Looks can be deceiving,' he said, brandishing a pair of fists, southpaw fashion. 'Regimental boxing champion, I was. And fully trained in hand-to-hand combat, I'll have you know.'

Jenkins had no idea how true that might be. Unlikely, was her best guess. 'How come you're living rough on the streets?'

Itchy looked sad again. 'Politicians send us to war. The same damn snakes who sell off our jobs when we try to make a future for ourselves.'

'What was it you did when you left the military?' Ginge asked.

'Steel works in Port Talbot, like my father before me.'

'Hard job that.'

'Good honest graft,' Itchy said. 'Loved every minute of it.'

'But they let you go?' Ginge again.

'Last in, first out.' Itchy took a sharp intake of breath. 'Job, house, and wife. In that order,' he said. 'Fourteen months start to finish.'

Jenkins shook her head. 'Where do you stay now?'

'Under one of the container units down the docks.' Itchy forced a smile. 'It's not as bad as it sounds. Keeps the rain off, anyways.'

Jenkins looked away, worried she might cry if she caught sight of him. When she'd composed herself, she said, 'I'm not having that. When we're done here, I'm making enquiries to the Veteran's Welfare Service to see what they can offer you.'

'You'd do that for me?'

'You bet your arse I will.'

Itchy puffed his chest and turned to Ginge. 'I like her. She's feisty.'

Once she'd stopped laughing, Jenkins pressed the red [Rec]

button on the DIR device and waited for the long beep to silence itself. 'Okay, Mr Rash,' she said when everything else was done. 'Let's make a start on what we're here for.'

'Itchy,' he corrected, and held the paper cup out in front of him. 'Can I get another one of these? More sugar this time.'

After waiting for the coffee to arrive, Jenkins started again. 'What if we call you Charles? That's much nicer, don't you think?'

'Charlie's better.'

'Okay, Charlie it is then.'

'I'm gasping for a fag.' Itchy hunched his shoulders and looked round the room, hopefully. 'Any chance of a couple of those too?'

'Not allowed, I'm afraid.'

Another check over his shoulder. 'Who'll know? There's only us in here.' He winked. 'I won't tell if you don't.'

Jenkins pointed to the camera overhead. Then at the window in the far wall. 'You wouldn't want me and Owen to get into hot water with our boss, would you?'

'Suppose not. You've been good to me so far.'

'Can I ask about the phone you were found with, Charlie?'

'It's mine.' The statement was forthright. Almost believable.

'We know it's registered to someone else,' Jenkins said. 'A murder victim.'

'I found it in the graveyard next to the hospital.' That came quicker than the ownership claim.

'That's better.'

'Can I keep it?' Itchy asked. 'They won't be needing it now they're dead, will they?'

Jenkins suppressed a grin. 'No can do, Charlie. Tell us what happened. What you saw while you were there.'

'I went to buy me a fix,' he said, scratching his side like a flea-ridden dog. He looked suddenly worried. 'You're not going to nick me for that, are you?'

'On what evidence?' Jenkins said.

That relaxed him enough to shift his attention to the opposite armpit. 'Minding my business was all I was doing. I weren't damaging nothing in there.'

'But did you see or hear anything?'

'*Felt,* more like.' Itchy put a finger to a nick in the pimply skin of his forehead. 'Landed right there it did.'

'The phone?'

'Aye. Heavy bugger it was too.'

'Did you see who threw it?'

'Course I did. Scared the shit out of me hanging on those railings, moaning like some zombie. Next thing I knew, he was down on the floor mumbling away to himself.'

'What did he say, Charlie? Did he give you a name?'

'Just kept saying, "*Doctor,*" over and over. Nothing else. Just that.'

'Why didn't you phone for one?'

Itchy looked everywhere except at the detectives on the other side of the table. 'Been on the streets long enough to know that you don't get involved in such things. Besides, he was a goner. I could tell as soon as I set eyes on him.'

'You took the phone and did a runner.'

'That's about the long and short of it.' He folded his arms in an indignant pose.

'Did you see anybody else?' Jenkins asked. 'Anyone at all.'

'Just a car driving in *that* direction.' Itchy pointed a finger to his right.

Ginge got his bearings. 'You mean away from the Maindy Barracks?'

'If you say so. I don't know the name of the road.'

Jenkins flipped a page or two in her pocketbook, searching for a space to write. 'Don't suppose you got a look at the number plate?'

Another scratch. This time somewhere south of the waistline. 'Nope. But I knows it was a silver Volvo.'

～

'I needed the money.' Lowri stared into a handful of wet tissues. 'How else was I supposed to keep my car on the road?'

Reece straightened his tie and got more comfortable in his chair. 'What is it you drive?'

'A Polo. Volkswagen.'

'Colour?'

'Navy blue. You're not going to tell them at the hospital, are you?' And then came more tears. 'I've seen them strike nurses off the register for doing this.'

'And *this* is?' Morgan asked.

'Phoning in sick, then working the night shift somewhere else.' Lowri dabbed her nose and sniffed. 'I'm not the only one who's done it, you know. Loads of nurses do. It's the only way to make ends meet.'

'Let's get this straight so I understand,' Reece said. 'You were supposed to work the night–'

'Day shift,' Lowri corrected before he could finish. 'That way you're fresh enough to do the night.'

'And you get paid for both shifts, presumably – sick leave from your employer, and enhanced rates, I'd imagine, from an agency?'

'My car failed its MOT, Friday of last week.' Lowri looked to the ceiling and threw her head back in resignation. 'One hundred and sixty quid they wanted to fix the brakes. Another fifty or so for the test.' She straightened and stared at Morgan.

'Where am *I* supposed to find that sort of money halfway through the month?'

'So you moonlighted?'

'The agency shift paid almost exactly what I needed. A no-brainer.'

'Couldn't anyone in the house help you out until payday?'

'There's five of us there for good reason,' Lowri said. 'We're all young and broke. Except for Harlan, that is; his parents are worth a fortune.'

'So why not ask him?'

'If it had been Poppy needing help, then yeah, I'm sure he'd have been only too keen.'

'But not you?'

'We didn't enjoy the same sort of relationship *they* did, if you catch my drift.'

'The two of you didn't get on?'

'He wasn't my type, that's all. A bit insipid.'

'Unlike Jordan.' Morgan was doodling again. '*He* more your thing?'

Lowri visibly stiffened. 'Let me guess. You've been talking to good ole Zoe.'

Reece counted eight people present, including himself, when he entered. Cooper and Vera Miller were the dead man's parents. Cable and Harris, he already knew. He vaguely recognised the two family liaison officers – FLOs – who went everywhere in pairs it seemed to him. And then there was a suited-and-booted man sat in front of a file containing paperwork. A lawyer was Reece's best guess. *Deputy Chief of Mission* at the American Embassy, he was told when he asked.

Ignoring Harris's look of disapproval, Reece helped himself

to coffee before joining them at an over-polished table. 'Condolences for your loss,' he said, taking a seat. 'Made all the more difficult by the fact it's happened abroad.'

Vera Miller didn't wait for the policeman to get comfortable. 'What are you doing to find our son's killer?' The accent was Midland American English. A couple of hours south of Lake Erie, Reece reckoned. He put the hot mug to rest on a sparkling glass coaster, and thought it nice the Assistant Chief Constable had made such an effort in welcoming the overseas guests. Perhaps there'd be a Welsh choir laid on in the foyer downstairs. A visit to the local Heritage Park thrown in for good measure. 'And what would *you* know of such things?' the woman continued.

There was no reason to not tell her, Reece decided. 'My wife was murdered in Rome just over eighteen months ago – on our honeymoon – stabbed and left to die on the road like your son.' He ignored Harris's fiery glare. 'That makes me the only other person in this room who knows first-hand what you and your husband are going through.'

Cooper Miller squeezed his wife's forearm. 'Condolences then to you also, Chief Inspector.'

'The Italians are no closer to catching Anwen's killer than they were on the day she died,' Reece said. 'No arrests. No leads. Nothing at all, in fact.'

'And that's supposed to make us feel better?' Cooper Miller looked to the other occupants of the room.

Harris shifted in his chair, preparing to say something.

'Not everyone likes me,' Reece said before the ACC could spout his usual drivel. 'And some might say I'm unconventional in my approach to policing.' His attention turned to Suited-and-Booted. 'Something of a maverick.' When he checked, he saw Cable's eyes close; screwed tight as she whispered something to herself. 'I'll catch your son's killer.' Reece paused to finish the dregs of his coffee before getting up. 'Harlan *will* get justice, Mr and Mrs Miller. You have my word on that.' Suited-and-Booted got another warning stare. 'All I'll ask is that you leave me and my team to do our jobs until this is over.'

14

Reece sat alone at the table in the press room, watching journalists circle like vultures eyeing up a carcass. Their crews were busy working through a battery of lighting measurements and sound checks before things properly got going. There were several television cameras, and miles of cabling running in all directions.

A few of the reporters were stood preening themselves in anything that offered a reflection. Rehearsing scripts and anchor-lines.

How can they be doing that when they don't know what we have to say yet? Reece had no idea, but did nothing to correct them.

There were brightly coloured microphones set out along the table in front of him, each belonging to one of several news channels in attendance. It looked more to him like the prep for a world sporting event than it did a call for potential witnesses to a particularly violent crime.

He unscrewed the lid from a bottle of sparkling water and checked the folded name cards either side of his own. ACC Harris was to sit on his right. *Sod that for a game of soldiers.* He leaned over and moved the Assistant Chief Constable up two places. He kept Cable where she was: to his immediate left.

Suited-and-Booted was placed at the far end of the table. No reason to change that, he decided. Wasn't as though he could get away with putting him in the men's bogs, now was it.

Aware of someone waving at him from a doorway in a recess out of sight of most people in the room, Reece twisted in his chair. It was Cable, calling for him to join the rest of them outside. 'I'm already here now,' he said, taking another drink. Turning away from her.

When at last they got started, the chief super did the housekeeping and introductions. Reece was to outline the crime associated with Harlan Miller and then appeal to the listening public for information. Miller's father would read a tribute to his son. There would be no questions taken on this occasion.

'*Someone* must have seen or heard something,' Reece said, finishing his bit. 'Or maybe you know of somebody in the area with a silver Volvo car. We're asking that you–'

'Ten-thousand pounds,' someone shouted from his left-hand side. 'Help us secure a conviction and the money's yours in cash.' It was Cooper Miller, Suited-and-Booted egging him on enthusiastically.

Reece leaned forward and shook his head just enough for both men to notice him.

Miller looked for the nearest active television camera, reached into his jacket pocket and deposited five white envelopes onto the desk in front of him. 'There it is. Two grand in each,' he said, tapping the pile. 'And there's plenty more where that came from.'

'Make him put the money away,' Reece told Cable. 'We never agreed to this.'

Cable whispered something to the American, who responded by raising an envelope to the camera. 'Ten thousand pounds,' he repeated. 'For information leading to the arrest and conviction of our son's killer.'

∾

'What the hell do you think you were doing out there?' Reece asked when they finally got back to the meeting room. He'd refused to take a seat, and was prowling. 'We'll have switchboard inundated with every crank caller who's ever wanted to win a jackpot.' He glared at Cooper Miller. 'I told you to leave things to me. It's not a game, you know.' He shifted his attention to Suited-and-Booted. 'This your idea?'

The man squared up to him. 'Where I come from, Detective–'

'You can do what the hell you want,' Reece said, interrupting. 'But you're not at home now. You're in my city. Where *I* know best.'

'Says you.' The man snorted before looking away.

'This kind of approach doesn't work,' Reece said, turning to Cooper Miller. Reece made a big effort to calm himself. The man had just lost a son, after all. 'People who genuinely want to help, do. And those who are purely after the money will make up any old bullshit in the hope they'll get lucky.' He sighed. 'But we're still obligated to follow up those leads, knowing full well we're wasting our time.'

Miller had stopped arguing at last and hugged his wife who was in floods of tears and unable to speak.

Suited-and-Booted – or Logan Johnson Jr III, to use a name that had, on first hearing it, left Reece wondering if the man had been named after an aircraft carrier – was now on his feet, rounding the table to comfort the parents. 'What lines of enquiry *are* you following?' He directed the question at ACC Harris, not Reece.

Reece watched Harris flounder. Let him do so for a short while longer. And when he could take no more of the man's babbling, said, 'There's reason to believe your son's death is connected to that of a girl he shared a house with.'

Cooper Miller straightened. 'You've got two murders there?'

Reece nodded. 'That's right.'

Miller raised both arms in the air. 'Well, Jesus H Christ.'

'Give me some good news. Anyone?' Reece said, marching through the incident room like he was looking for someone to punch. 'That lot upstairs are getting on my tits.' He slammed the door to his office and dropped into the squeaky swivel-chair. *Logan Johnson Jr III. For fuck's sake.*

There was a knock at the door, Ginge loitering the other side of it, turning repeatedly to look behind him.

'What?' Reece shouted through the glass. 'Open the bloody thing,' he said, pointing at the door.

'It's about the CPS, boss.'

Reece sat with his head tilted forward, a pair of clenched fists placed on the desk in front of him. 'Good news only, remember?'

Ginge looked suddenly flustered, as though wondering if he should go away and leave it for now.

'Tell me.'

'The CPS, boss.'

The fists tightened. 'We've done that bit already.'

Edging his way inside the office, Ginge looked behind him at least another twice before coming to a full stop.

'They won't let us charge him, will they?' Reece said, picking up on the telltale signs. 'They want us to let Patterson go.'

Ginge looked like a weight had been lifted off his shoulders. Relieved he hadn't needed to speak the words himself.

Reece had known it was unlikely all along. That without a murder weapon, or anything more tangible than rumour and counter-rumour to rely on, they'd be struggling where the CPS was concerned. 'Go on,' he said. 'Ask Ffion to show you how to get them both out of here.'

It was late afternoon; daylight getting ready to pack up and leave. Reece was stood outside the Cathedral Road offices of Dr Patricia Beven. Large spots of rain pebble-dashing the pavement battleship grey, as was usual at that time of year. He leaned beneath the overhang of the cast-iron guttering, sheltering from it, waiting all the while for the click of the door and an invitation to enter. When he reached for the bell-press a second time, the door opened without warning. 'Fancy seeing you here,' he said, stepping aside to let Dr Richard Wellman pass.

Wellman replied with little more than a cursory nod, and hurried through the small roadside garden without so much as a backward glance.

'Doctor, one minute.' Reece followed a few steps down the path, ignoring the rain that had started falling more heavily. 'Does the name Harlan Miller mean anything to you?'

A blank look. 'Should it?'

'He was a medical student on a recent anaesthetic placement. That would have put him in your department, presumably?'

'He and more than a hundred others during the course of any academic year.' Wellman raised his hands in defeat. 'I can't be expected to remember them all.' He turned and was quickly on his way again.

Reece watched until the doctor was on the pavement and out of sight, before entering a square hallway at the front of the building. The office door at the top of the carpeted stairs was ajar, the sound of teacups clinking against saucers coming from inside. He knocked and went through when invited. 'I'm a touch early,' he said, coming to a halt on a large rug that marked the centre of the room.

'Some might say, *late*,' Beven replied without looking at him. 'For the sessions you failed to attend,' she added for clarity.

'Snow.' Reece helped himself to a chair and got comfortable by straightening the sleeves of his suit jacket. 'Brecon gets a lot of it.' He nodded. 'Always snow around this time of year.'

Crossing the room to hand him his coffee, Beven said, 'And there's me thinking you were avoiding me.'

'Snow. Definitely.'

The counsellor took a seat opposite and waited for him to return the spoon to the saucer. 'Never mind, you're here now.'

Reece turned side-on to the door. 'The man who just left: he one of your patients?'

Beven gave him a look of surprise. 'You know I can't possibly tell you that.'

'I didn't ask why he was here.'

'My lips are sealed,' she said, drawing an imaginary zipper across her mouth.

'Could have been seeing his accountant in the office next door I suppose.' Reece watched for Beven's response.

'I'm saying nothing, Chief Inspector.'

He leaned to place his cup and saucer on a low table equidistant between both their armchairs. 'You've had your hair done.'

'Nice try.'

'It was a compliment.'

'We're still doing this,' she told him.

Checking his watch, he let out a long sigh. 'Let's get on with it then.'

'Okay, what went through your mind when you first entered that basement room at the Midnight Club?'

Shit, shoot from the hip, why don't you. The memory made him rub his shoulder. 'I didn't know what I'd find down there,' he said finally. 'Or *who*, to be perfectly honest with you.'

'What were you most in fear of finding?'

'Casualties of course.'

'Your partner, DS Jenkins in particular?'

Nodding, he said, 'Me not being in work at the time meant Elan had been taking up most of the slack in the department.'

'But there *was* another senior officer available to her.' Beven read from an open file on her lap. 'A DI Adams.'

'He's a complete dipshit. And the main reason I told her to go it alone.'

'And how would you have felt had that advice resulted in more serious injury to DS Jenkins?'

'Do I even have to answer that?'

Beven told him he didn't. 'The basement: what did you find there?' she asked, moving swiftly on.

'Denny Cartwright was already dead. Shot in the chest by Belle Gillighan when she'd found him throttling Jenkins.'

'And how did you react to meeting Belle again after all those years?'

Reece gave the question thought before answering. 'I don't know. There wasn't time for that sort of thing.'

'Did you still feel responsible for what happened to her?'

'Belle was pointing a gun at me. All I could think about was what might happen next.'

'But you knew she was there to kill Billy Creed and not you. Belle wanted closure. To serve up her own kind of justice.'

'Believe me, there's nothing I would have wanted more than

for her to have killed that bastard. To have put the gun between his beady eyes and blown his brains all over the back wall.' Reece slowed his breathing and looked away.

'But you threw yourself in front of him. Took the bullet and saved the life of the man you despised.'

Reece was quiet. Sat there staring into space.

'You knew what you were doing,' Beven said. 'And it wasn't for Billy Creed's benefit.'

Reece clawed at the leather arms of the chair. Wiped his mouth with the back of a hand. 'I don't know what you're talking about.'

'Yes you do, Chief Inspector. You saw a way out.'

15

Wellman pressed himself tight against the damp wall of the local park, hidden the whole time by the rear section of a concrete bus shelter. The recent rain shower had done little to wash away the fusion of human and cat pee, the wind lifting empty crisp packets from an overfilled bin; setting them off on their way down an otherwise empty street.

The wet pavement glowed orange under the weak light thrown by the overhead street lamp. Rain turned to drizzle, suspended in the night air like long strands of silver thread.

A car went past. Just the one at such a late hour. Receding further into the darkness, Wellman waited patiently for the red tail lights to follow the bend in the road and disappear out of sight.

With the car gone, there wasn't a soul to disturb him, except for the tabby cat pacing high on the wall above. Wellman tossed a small stone at it. Another when the first missed by a fair distance.

The stage was set. The leading lady on her way, heels tapping on the flagstones as she unknowingly approached what was soon to be her worst nightmare. She didn't see him hiding there when she went past. Nor hear the brief and unexpected release of excitement from his lips.

He watched her go by. Let her get a good ten to fifteen metres ahead of him so it didn't look too obvious when he stepped out and followed in the same direction. He moved, slowly at first, tools of the trade hanging from his shoulder in a small canvas rucksack.

Catching a waft of cheap perfume on the night air, he thought his head might explode, such was the excitement of the chase. This particular victim didn't fit the required profile in any shape or form. Couldn't in a million years compete with the likes of Poppy Jones, nor Smiler, the student nurse.

But she was on the list nevertheless. And for reasons all of her own doing. Her interference a risk to his well-thought-out plans.

The woman turned into a narrow street flanked both sides with parked cars and rubbish bins. Wellman ducked when she stole a brief look over her shoulder, losing his footing on a broken slab of kerbstone. He swung an arm, pirouetting in a violent attempt to stay upright, a wayward fist catching the wing mirror of a parked van.

He swore, but was thankful the impact hadn't set off the vehicle's anti-theft alarm. Licking his bleeding knuckles, he reached into a jacket pocket with the other hand to retrieve an open pair of surgical gloves, and slid them on.

There could be no risk of leaving DNA at the crime scene. Ruining things before he'd got properly started. He'd read extensively. Knew exactly what CSIs looked for, and how they found it.

The woman turned her head towards him with a swish of black-dyed hair, self-consciously pulling at the hem of her coat. He could hear her breathing heavily with the effort required to increase the shortening distance between them. That's what older women did when you pushed them hard. Panted like knackered dogs on their last legs. A stark contrast to his first two victims.

Poppy, in particular, had such beauty in life. Perfection almost. He'd lain with the young midwife when it was time for her to leave this world. Stared into her eyes so she knew she wasn't alone. She'd watched back, and had she been able, would have begged and screamed for more of his air. Would have offered him anything, as she undoubtedly had those men in the Facebook photographs.

But sex wasn't the motivating factor for what Wellman was doing. He could easily have taken her, but didn't. Eliminating such women, and in so doing, making the world a better place in which to live, was a far nobler act in his opinion.

He'd savoured the silence as she slipped away, the pulse in her swan-like neck shifting from racing to absent in a few short minutes.

Coco the Clown tottered ahead of him on heels that were too tall. In a dress and coat that were far too short. And the make-up. The fucking make-up!

He'd caught her talking about him again today. At least that's what he thought she was doing. *She* was the reason Smiler hadn't returned after her lunch break. Had to be. Coco must have told them to remove the girl. Kept her away for her own safety. That meant other people knew about him. And they'd have started talking too. *Everyone* was at it; gossip spreading like wildfire.

Or a cancer, even. One that needed to be cut out.

He clenched both sides of his head in his hands and squeezed tightly, trying to put a stop to the incessant chattering that went on up there.

Stood on a doorstep only three or four houses away from him, Coco was rummaging frantically through a gold-coloured handbag held close to the soft swell of her belly. He knew there was no point in her knocking on the door. She'd told the entire operating theatre team earlier in the day that her husband was working abroad – as a long-distance lorry driver – and wouldn't be home until the next day. They had no children. The opportunity had presented itself thus.

Coco was panicking. Looking up. Looking down. Not looking at Wellman. Fumbling with the key. Even from his current vantage point, he could tell she was unable to steady her hand anywhere near enough to unlock the door.

'Sandra.' He chose not to use her pet name. Thought she might consider that rude. 'Sandra, are you okay?'

'Dr Wellman.' The woman lowered her head and peered into the darkness, her facial features looking like they were painted onto some grotesque death mask. Apt under the circumstances. 'Jesus Christ. I thought it was that stalker-feller following me.' She laughed. Almost hysterically once she got going, clearing a smoker's throat with a series of hearty coughs.

'Just me,' he said, staring at smudges of mascara she'd somehow managed to wipe across both cheeks like warpaint. A nervous silence hung in the air after that. Followed by the offer of a hot drink. 'I suppose a coffee would warm me up while I wait for the taxi,' he said, not wanting to miss a gifted opportunity. This might be far simpler than he could ever have imagined.

The key slid in easily this time, the door opening to reveal home-made curry had been on the menu earlier that evening. 'You'll have to excuse the mess,' she said, leading the way inside. 'I'm a very untidy person.'

That didn't surprise him. 'Our lives are so busy these days.'

'You're telling me.' Coco tossed her wet coat over the back of the sofa. It slid to the floor. She left it where it was and led the way into a compact kitchen that looked as though a school cookery class had just finished in there. Pots, pans, and jars of ingredients covered most of the horizontal surfaces. 'Work, cook, clean. It never stops,' she said, making space for two mugs and a carton of milk. 'Bet you've got yourself a nice couple of young 'uns to do it all for you, eh?'

Wellman's eyes narrowed, his gloved hands forming tight fists in his pockets. *What does she know? She can't know.* He laughed, lightening an atmosphere that was on the verge of turning as sour as the milk. 'Nope. No such thing. I do it all myself, I'll have you know.'

'And Mrs Wellman; she just–'

'There *is* no Mrs Wellman,' he said, struggling to conceal his mounting anger. *She's asking questions. Trying to trick you. Stop her.*

'A big strong man like you never married? I don't believe it.'

He smelled alcohol and cigarette smoke on Coco's breath. Cringed when she lurched forward to squeeze his bicep. Heard her babbling away. Right up to the point when he lost all control and punched her hard and square in the face. The ferocity of the blow lifted the woman clean off her feet. Sent her stumbling backwards, arms flailing behind her as she sought something of substance to grab hold of. They glanced against the side of an armchair, doing nothing to prevent her fall to the carpeted floor. The left hand bent beneath the weight of her body, a loud snapping sound confirming a broken wrist.

'No!' he shouted. This wasn't supposed to happen. The woman had an obvious depressed fracture of the cheekbone. Not to mention a hand that now stuck out of her arm like the bottom end of a golf club. He threw his rucksack against the door of a kitchen cabinet. Then set about kicking the thing around the kitchen. He saw the knife on the worktop, discarded layers of onion and mushroom left alongside it.

Dropping on top of her, he straddled her chest while sorting through the contents of the rucksack. The bottle was broken. Useless. Sevoflurane seeping through the bag's material, filling the kitchen with a sweet and solvently smell. Hooking the collar of his sweatshirt over his nose, he took the pre-filled syringe of Suxamethonium Chloride and jabbed it straight into Coco's shoulder. She stirred. Tried to sit up, but couldn't under his weight.

Wellman watched the second hand make its way around the face of the plastic clock on the opposite wall, counting minutes that went by woefully slowly. 'Shut up,' he said when she tried to speak, and forced the pungent bag against her face. She began to fasciculate – all-over muscle twitches – the telltale sign that she was almost ready for what was coming next. 'Do you know what I call you?'

She didn't answer.

Couldn't answer.

He twisted and reached for the knife on the counter. 'That disgusting make-up,' he said, kneeling beside her, any intention of this looking innocent, now completely gone. He held the sharp blade to Coco's fractured cheek, spreading dark mascara in widening circles. He ran its blunt edge over her nose, lips, chin, then throat. 'Makes you look like the whore you are.'

16

Reece had given up all hope of sleep after four in the morning, and had then resorted to wandering the cold living room downstairs, trying to make sense of what he knew of the case so far. He was as sure as he could be that the two murders were in some way linked. Likely to have been committed by the same person. Or for the same motive, even though the methods used to kill Harlan and Poppy were different in each case.

He pulled the sweatshirt over his head. Went through to the kitchen and flicked the manual override switch for the central heating system. The house would hopefully be toasty-warm by the time he got back for a shower.

Lowri and Jordan acting together – Jordan stabbing Harlan Miller, Lowri injecting Poppy with a paralysing agent – was an idea that could still go somewhere, Reece supposed. He hadn't discounted that angle altogether; convoluted and unlikely as it was.

As he'd previously pointed out at the briefing: there was definitely means, motive, and opportunity where that pair were concerned. Jordan, spurned by Poppy, kills Miller in an attempt to win back his ex-girlfriend. Then Lowri, still carrying a flame for Jordan, does away with Poppy so that *she* can have him instead. But then maybe the pair had unknowingly acted independently of one another, rather than as a duo.

Either angle is possible, Reece decided, tying the laces of his running shoes. He pulled the front door closed behind him, dragged the woollen hat down over his ears, and started the timer on his sports watch.

The first few breaths penetrated his airways like icy fingers poking their way deep into his lungs. With his teeth aching under the onslaught, he closed his mouth and drew air in through his nose instead. And when he settled into his rhythm, he moved with a graceful and economical motion that belied his fifty-something years on this earth.

On the road, hills, and mountains, there was a peace he experienced nowhere else. He loved it there. Glancing left, he crossed the wide expanse of highway, speeding up as the first of the early morning commuters rounded the bend some twenty or so metres away. A thought struck him suddenly: *Had he really tried to get himself killed at the Midnight Club?* That's what Dr Patricia Beven had him close to admitting in a moment of weakness on his part. Pushed him into a corner until he was on the verge of saying almost anything just to be let out of her office. He'd been trying to preserve life when he'd thrown himself in front of the bullet meant for Billy Creed.

That's what he'd told himself.

Dr Beven had been close to putting words in his mouth.

Reece quickly decided that it was far too early in the morning to be going there; to be delving into the darkness of his messed-up mind, and went back to thinking about the case instead.

Dr Richard Wellman. Something just didn't sit right there. Reece had learnt quickly to judge other people in the course of his work. To push, prod, and test them – observing their reaction to the pressure he put them under. Whether they deserved it or not, he'd done it anyway.

Emotionless was the adjective that came to mind when he pictured Wellman. And the fact the man hadn't asked many questions about why he and Morgan were there to talk with him, was odd in itself. *Most people would have done under similar circumstances.*

Squeezing through a narrow gap in the rusted railings, Reece set off across a frost-covered field that crunched beneath his striding feet. Even in the weak dawn lighting, he could make out the imposing silhouette of Llandaff Cathedral rising high above the surrounding oaks.

Built in the eleven hundreds, on the site of an earlier church, the cathedral had been extensively damaged in the fifteenth century when Owain Glyndwr had rebelled against the parliamentarian troops during the English Civil War. Then, in circa 1703, *The Great Storm* – an extratropical cyclone – had caused such extensive damage to the building, that what was left of the cathedral was almost taken down and abandoned.

Positioning himself on the dead-ball line of the rugby field, Reece did ten sprints to the twenty-two-metre markings, with a slow jog back on each length. He bent at the waist when done, coughing, and listening to the traffic multiply in number on the adjacent road.

Following two full circuits of the outer perimeter of the field, he was on his way home again, thoughts of Dr Richard Wellman still niggling at him.

Reece had wondered what his first visit, post shooting, would be like. As he pulled up in the alleyway behind the Midnight Club, he felt somewhat numb to the situation now he was there. He vaguely remembered standing outside, talking to the Polish cleaning lady when the first shot had sounded from deep inside the building. He'd gone running in unarmed with Ffion Morgan calling for him to wait until backup arrived.

Had there been a second shot? He couldn't remember, but knew he'd followed the sounds of voices until he reached the place Billy Creed called his *Games Room*.

The scene when he got there had shocked him. He didn't mind admitting it. Denny Cartwright was lying dead against the bars of a cage normally used to parade half-naked women. While Jenkins was hunched on all fours in front of the big-man, red welts on her neck, gasping for breath.

And Belle Gillighan: she was stood somewhere off to one side of everyone, psychotic, and waving a handgun at anything that moved.

Reece pressed the buzzer next to the security camera and saw it had been fixed since his previous visit.

'What the fuck do you want, Copper?' It was Billy Creed. His usual charming self.

'Open the door.'

'You're not allowed round here, Copper. Not supposed to come anywhere near me.'

'Stop whining, Billy.' Reece pressed again. Three sharp bursts' worth.

'My lawyer's already drawing up papers to have you directing traffic.'

'If I come back, it'll be with a warrant,' Reece promised. The door clicked open a moment later. He remembered the smell: cheap booze and disinfectant. There had been a blonde woman lying flat on her back on the day of the shooting. Near the bar. Mumbling incoherently, mostly. Strange how he'd forgotten her until now. She'd been the one to send him down to the basement. He couldn't remember her name. Someone outside would have taken that for the record.

There was a metal staircase ahead of him, rising from behind the DJ's station, up to a mezzanine level and Billy Creed's office. At the top of the stairs stood a man who dwarfed him. A man whose jaw looked like it might have been fashioned from the same steel girders as those preventing the office crashing to the ground below. 'Step aside,' Reece said.

Jimmy Chin shifted an inch or two, but not far enough for Reece to get past.

'Stop being a twat, Jimmy.'

'Or what?'

'It's okay.' Creed's voice came from somewhere within the room. 'Let Copper in. We can compare war wounds.'

Chin retreated a half-step only, both men practising their *I'm the bigger dog* stare as Reece pushed past.

The room smelled of cigar smoke and patchouli oil. Creed was sat on a leather sofa opposite the door, his leg stretched out in front of him on a low stool. There was no one else there. 'Take a pew,' he said, offering a chair near the door.

Reece took it only after making sure Chin hadn't moved any closer.

Creed smiled. 'Jimmy won't hurt you. He's on a short leash today.'

Chin howled like a wolf. Turned in circles and panted.

'And that's the best replacement you could find for Cartwright?' Reece jerked his head in the general direction of the stairs. 'You've been dragging the bottom of the pond, Billy.'

Creed's grin slipped away slowly. 'Don't underestimate him, Copper. Jimmy comes with a public health warning.'

'So does the pox,' Reece said, turning again, this time to make sure Chin had caught his every word. Reece faced the front when sure the man had. 'I see the security cameras are up and running.' He didn't miss Creed's eyes narrowing a fraction. Others might not have noticed. But Reece did. 'Who did you use this time? Couldn't have been Pete Hall.'

The eyes again. *Guilty as sin.* 'Denny took care of all that before he was taken from us.' Shrugging, Creed said, 'The big-man wasn't one for paperwork as you already know.'

'You'll have bank statements, I'm sure?'

'All done with cash from the safe.' Creed hooked a thumb over his shoulder, pointing it at the back wall of the office.

'Convenient.'

'It's the way I works,' the gangster said, reverting to Cardiff dialect. 'Why'd you come here today?' He patted the sofa all around him, and dry-smoked a thick Cuban when he found it.

'Pete Hall.'

'This some sort of name-game, Copper?' Creed caught Chin's attention. 'Your turn next.'

'Idris Kneath,' Chin said.

Reece tensed at the mention of his father-in-law.

'They *can* be dead, can't they?' Chin asked with a smirk.

Creed struck a match and held it to the air, its orange flame dancing wildly in the draught from the open doorway. 'My turn now. Let's do boy:girl.'

There was the sound of a scooter passing in the alleyway beneath them. Reece pulled at his collar, not daring to check outside the window for the arrival of that big black cloud. *You utter her name and I'll kill you both.* He swallowed hard and fought to control his breathing.

'Gabby Logan.'

Reece got the feeling Creed had repeated the name several times. 'What?' he said, unable to fully shake off the remnants of the daydream.

'Gabby Logan,' Creed said. 'Bet you've given her some thought, what with you being single all this time.'

Reece's eyes darted around the room. He was in Billy Creed's office, covered in sweat, not sure how he'd got there. And why was the man talking to him about a sports presenter? He took a deep breath and rebooted his brain. 'Pete Hall fixed your security system, Christmastime.' He was back online.

'Fucked.' Creed peered through a cloud of clearing smoke. 'Fucked my security system, more like.'

'Is that why you killed him?'

'Copper's poking his nose where it don't belong.'

'You look nervous, Billy. Something to hide?'

'Copper knows nothing.'

Reece *knew* he had the measure of the man. 'Copper's going to put you away.'

Creed moved the conversation on. 'Thought my lawyer made it clear to your boss that you're not welcome round here?'

Reece went through his pockets. 'While we're on the subject of lawyers, Billy, you're going to need a good one this time.' He leaned over and handed the gangster a scrap of paper. 'Where were you on that date?'

Copper wasn't long gone, Creed left to his nagging thoughts, and a daily physiotherapy session for a ruined knee. He was walking straight lines on the dance floor – the stopping to turn at either end of the room, the most difficult part of the whole exercise. Leaning on a cane, he caught his breath. 'I want the old lock-up in the docks cleared out,' he told Kyle Cartwright and his dreadlocked sidekick, Albino Ron. 'Torch the van some place quiet. You understand me?'

Denny's younger brother waited for the gangster to stop wincing with pain. 'You expecting trouble, Billy?'

'Just tying up loose ends. Copper's sniffing about again. Can't help himself.' Bending at the waist, Creed pushed a finger beneath the Velcro strap of the knee brace when it bit into his skin. 'Give the place a good once-over before you leave, I want nothing left there.'

'You got it, Billy.'

Creed shifted his weight and used a finger on the strap again, still not satisfied with the position of it. 'There'll be someone coming for the keys in the morning – posh twat with a wad of cash. Just make sure one of you is down there to meet him.'

'You want him done over?' Cartwright asked.

Creed moved in closer and put an arm around the younger man's shoulder, pulling him uncomfortably tight against his body. 'Just take the money and let him go.'

Cartwright's cogs turned slowly. 'You setting him up?'

Creed gave Cartwright a playful slap across the back of the head. 'Getting myself an insurance policy.'

17

'There's been a murder, boss.' It was Elan Jenkins on the other end of the phone. 'Nurse at the hospital again. Killed last night by the looks of it.'

Reece had just settled in his seat and was preparing to reverse down the narrow lane away from the Midnight Club. He braked to a full stop and put the car in neutral. 'Same MO as the other girl?'

'Not really. And she's older by a fair margin, I'd say. There's something else.'

'Go on,' he said, when at first Jenkins didn't elaborate.

'This one's got the word WHORE carved across her chest in capital letters.'

'You're kidding me.'

'Only wish I was.'

'Text me the address,' Reece said before putting the handset away.

When he got there, he saw a single white van, two patrol cars, and an ambulance waiting outside a row of terraced houses. The emergency vehicles had their lights flashing but were silent. CSIs were in and out of the property, several metres of blue-and-white crime scene tape stretched like party bunting from one lamp post to another. Jenkins was waiting in the doorway, and waved as he pulled up further along the road. 'Pathologist here yet?' Reece asked once he'd joined her in the usual protective gear.

'On her way.' Jenkins looked up and down the street as though checking. 'Where've you been?' she asked him, looking one last time before going in through the open door. 'Took a fair few go's getting hold of you earlier.'

'I was paying Billy Creed a visit.' Reece did his best to ignore her look of disapproval. 'I promised the wife I would.'

'And you promised Chief Superintendent Cable you wouldn't.'

'Did I?' He shrugged. 'Must have had one of those amnesia things the counsellor keeps telling me about.'

'Bullshit you did.' Jenkins had her arms folded and eyes wide.

Reece couldn't match her stare when he tried. 'Who teaches women to look at a man like that?' He shook his head and turned his back on her in the end. 'Must be something you're all born with.'

Following down the short hallway, Jenkins said, 'You don't really believe Creed killed that guy just because the security system failed?'

'Creed lost Denny Cartwright and a knee in that shooting.' Reece came to a halt in the living room, twisting and turning to take in the full scene. 'He's killed people for a lot less than that.'

'I suppose.'

'Who's in the kitchen?' Reece stuck his head through to see for himself. 'Sioned, how you doing?'

'Good. And you?' The CSM stopped brushing the handles of

two full mugs. 'Looks like the victim knew her attacker. Even made him coffee.'

'Who found her?' Reece asked, casting an eye over the dead body. Sandra Cole lay face up, and in a somewhat awkward pose on the kitchen floor. Her legs were bent at the knee, and drawn slightly over to her left, causing the hip on that side to be raised an inch or so off the ground. Even as a non-medical man, Reece could tell there was something seriously awry with the dead woman's face. Right wrist as well. He wasn't exactly sure what he'd expected to see after Jenkins had told him about the chest carving. Not something this crude, that's for sure. The blade had ripped through the skin rather than slice it. Had torn a nipple half-off, leaving ragged edges of raw flesh in its wake.

'The husband,' Jenkins said. 'Came back from Toulouse this morning to find her like this.'

'France. What was he doing there?'

'Picking up aircraft parts. It's his job.'

Reece looked but couldn't see the man. 'Where is he?'

Jenkins moved for someone to get past. 'A few doors up at a neighbour's house.' She pointed to her left. 'I've sent a couple of uniforms to stay with him.'

'And you've got someone checking his alibi, presumably?'

'Done. All his paperwork is dated and stamped for the journey back to the UK.'

'Good.' Reece went into the kitchen and noted the mess. 'A break-in?'

Sioned Williams shook her head. 'Has all the signs so far of the victim letting her attacker in before the assault began.'

'Not our stalker then,' one of the other CSIs said, coming in on the tail end of it.

'Why?' Jenkins asked. 'Who's to say he hasn't moved up a notch this time.' She glanced at Reece. 'It's what they often do, isn't it? Start with something like stalking. Then, once they've gained more confidence with that, they'll enter a property and physically assault their first victim – with escalating levels of violence, usually.'

'True,' Reece said. 'But it's also sexually motivated in most instances. Poppy wasn't interfered with. We know that for sure.'

Williams looked up from what she was doing. 'And apart from the blouse and bra, *this* woman's clothing is intact, including her knickers.'

'Maybe sex isn't his primary motivation,' Jenkins continued. 'Or maybe he's not yet ready for that sort of thing.'

Reece scratched his head. '*Yet?*'

Jenkins moved again, the room crawling with people. 'I don't think he'll be able to help himself once he's more established.'

'You sound like an expert on the subject.' They all turned when Cara Frost entered the kitchen.

Reece saw her wink at Jenkins. 'I want you to run the same tox screens you did on Poppy Jones,' he said before the Home Office Forensic Pathologist had a chance to get anything of a handover.

'You sure about that?' Frost tilted her head to read the writing on Sandra Cole's chest. 'This one looks way different at first glance.'

'Another nurse,' Reece said, proceeding to tell her what they knew so far.

'Okay. I'll get the screens done once we have her back at base. That knife do this?' Frost pointed to one that was bagged and labelled on the kitchen counter.

'There was what looked to be skin and fat tissue on the serrated edge,' Williams said, showing it to her. 'I'm as confident as I can be that it did.'

At the neighbour's house, Reece saw a man stood in front of a gas fire. He looked tired, unshaven, and traumatised by events he neither understood nor had control over. 'I'm DCI Reece.' The tone was gentle. Delivered by someone who knew first-hand what it was like to lose a spouse under similar circumstances. 'I'm very sorry for your loss, Mr Cole.' The man burst into tears almost immediately and searched for somewhere to sit. Reece took his elbow and walked him to the empty sofa.

A middle-aged woman appeared in the kitchen doorway carrying a tray of steaming mugs. 'Oh,' she said. 'Now there's two more of you.'

Jenkins told her she and Reece were fine. 'Do you live here?'

'I've been friends with Ian and Sandra for years. Terrible thing this,' the woman said, setting the tray down on a glass table. 'Such a shock.' She took a mug over to the man on the sofa, hovered there a while when he made no attempt to relieve her of it, and took it away again, shaking her head at the police officers.

'Had your wife mentioned anyone following her recently?' Reece asked.

The man named Ian looked up and wiped the back of a hand across his nose. He sniffed. 'I saw what was written on her chest. What twisted bastard would do that to a woman?'

'Did she say anything?' Reece pushed. 'About being followed.'

'Not to me.' To the neighbour, Ian said, 'What about you?'

The woman shook her head. 'I'd have remembered something like that, for sure.'

Reece lowered himself into an armchair opposite and rested both hands on his knees. 'Can you think of anyone who might have wanted to harm your wife? Anyone at all. Any arguments recently – particularly at work?'

'*At work*. You think someone from the hospital could have done that to her?'

'It's one line of enquiry,' Reece admitted. He checked his watch, but needn't have. It had gone dark outside while they were talking.

'It's not true, you know. What was written on my Sandra's chest. Not true at all.'

Reece had no way to be sure, but knew the man had suffered enough. He kept it simple and nodded.

'What happens now?'

'We'll need to confirm cause of death.'

'Cut her open?' Ian Cole balled his fists. 'Hasn't she suffered enough?'

Reece spoke with a sympathetic tone. 'It'll help us catch the killer.'

The husband looked away and didn't argue. 'And when will I be able to bury her?'

'Things are more complicated in a murder investigation,' Jenkins told him. 'But we'll do everything we can to make sure you don't have to wait any longer than is absolutely necessary.'

They'd stopped for pizza on the way back to the station, Reece wanting to organise his thoughts before letting the team escape home for the evening. 'I'll have anything except the one with pineapple,' he said, tossing his jacket onto the desk in his office. 'Which one of you heathens ordered it anyway?' he asked, cocking his nose up at the unopened box.

No one admitted responsibility for such a dirty deed.

Jenkins was having a hard time working her way through the contents of the boxes with nothing sharper than a plastic knife.

'Does anyone mind if I use my fingers to tear them apart? Be here all night otherwise.'

'Fine by me,' Reece said, loosening his tie. 'Make sure I don't get pineapple on mine.'

Jenkins stopped what she was doing to look at him. 'I heard you the *first* twenty times.'

Ginge was loitering like a family dog waiting for scraps. 'I don't mind what I have.'

'Give *him* the pineapple,' Reece said from the other side of the room.

'He's messing with you,' Jenkins said when she saw the newbie's reaction. 'Help yourself to whatever you want.'

He did, and lots of it. 'Thanks for this, boss.'

Reece waved in acknowledgment of the comment, sat back and let his team tuck in first.

Ginge poked his tongue out, head arched backwards as the pizza slice bent towards him. Using a finger to support the end of it, he took an enormous bite. 'This is stonking.'

'Look!' Reece said when at last the feeding-frenzy had finished and everyone moved out of the way. 'Bloody pineapple is all that's left.'

'Pick the bits off,' Jenkins told him. 'The other stuff is ham.'

'You can have *this* if you want,' Ginge said, offering the rest of a half-eaten slice. 'Meat feast, boss.'

Reece circled the table. 'Any garlic bread left?'

Ginge stopped playing limbo with his food and searched through the boxes. 'Just the crusts by the looks of things.' He laughed. 'You should have got stuck in like the rest of...' He left it there when he saw the pissed-off look on the DCI's face.

Reece piled bits of pineapple on the tabletop and searched

for somewhere to wipe his fingers. 'Anything new to report while we were out?'

'Got a sighting of the silver Volvo on the night Harlan Miller was murdered,' Ginge told him. 'Elderly guy walking his dog. Wouldn't leave his name. Wasn't interested in the money either.'

'Did he get anything of the number plate?'

'Part of it,' Ginge said, using a paperclip as an improvised toothpick. 'But only because it reminded him of his late wife, Molly. M followed by some numbers he couldn't recall. Then OLL as the end part.' Ginge went over to his desk and came back with a notepad. 'Belongs to this lady,' he said, handing over the address. 'A local named Molly Gantry.'

'Okay,' Reece said. 'You and Ffion go over there first thing in the morning; see what this Gantry woman has to say for herself. And find out if anyone else has access to that car.'

Ginge checked over his shoulder. 'I haven't seen Ffion all afternoon, boss. Thought she must have been with the two of you.'

Reece frowned at Jenkins. 'You know where she is?'

'Nope. You want me to give her a ring?'

'It can wait until we're finished here.'

Jenkins put her phone away without dialling. 'She *was* acting a bit mopey this morning, come to think of it.'

'Yeah, snapped at me once or twice,' Ginge agreed. 'I thought it must have been her time of the month.'

'Oi.' Jenkins threw a short length of pizza crust at him. 'Cut it out.'

18

'I've got cancer.' Those were not the words Jenkins was expecting to hear when she'd called Morgan straight after the briefing. Not in a million years. 'Had a bit of a freak-out, and couldn't talk to Ginge about it,' Morgan said.

That wasn't the type of conversation you had on the phone. Not with a friend. Not with anyone, really. And so Jenkins had gone straight round there on the way home to find out what the hell was going on.

They'd hugged and cried on the doorstep. Again, when they moved silently to the living room. Josh was there too – Morgan's boyfriend – sat on the sofa opposite the television, red-eyed and puffy-faced. He said hello, but little more than that.

'What happened?' Jenkins asked, unsure if it was the right time for such questions. 'How do you know?'

Morgan dropped onto the sofa next to Josh and squeezed his hand, her other pointing to her chest. 'I found a lump just over a week ago. Thought it was related to my cycle at first. Told Josh I'd keep an eye on it.'

Not wanting to sit any distance away from the couple, Jenkins rested on her knees in front of the sofa.

'I checked it every day. A hundred or more times a day, in fact,' Morgan said with a poor attempt at a laugh. 'But it was still there, and didn't feel like any of the usual lumps you get during the month.'

'That's when I made her go see about it,' Josh said. 'It's what they tell you to do, isn't it?'

'Absolutely.' Jenkins took Morgan's hand in hers and found herself tapping it gently. She stopped, but didn't let go. 'You *went* to see a doctor?'

'I made a private appointment for lunchtime.' Morgan looked suddenly sheepish. Like she'd committed an unthinkable sin. 'We're lucky Josh gets paid well.'

'Don't apologise,' Jenkins said. 'It's the way I'd go, if I had the money.'

Morgan nodded. 'Get down there, I thought. In and out, and then back to work in time to help Ginge sort through all those calls we've been getting.' She started crying again, and took a while to compose herself. 'But I could tell the moment the doctor put her hand on it. The look on her face, the way she went back to it and examined it again and again. I knew, Jenks. I knew.'

Jenkins willed herself to be strong. 'But they can't know for sure. Not without tests, surely?'

'They've already taken bloods and booked me in for some scans and a biopsy.'

'When?'

'Tomorrow.' Morgan leaned forward. 'Will you speak to the boss? I don't think I can.'

'Yes, of course,' Jenkins said. 'Look, there's every chance the results will come back as all-clear.'

Morgan blew her nose in a paper hanky. 'My mother died of breast cancer when she was thirty-seven.' The hanky got another bashing. 'I'm thirty-two, Jenks. I can't die yet.' She collapsed into Josh's arms.

Jenkins willed herself to be strong, to not break down, if only until she was home at her own place.

Kyle Cartwright drove the van away from the Cardiff Docklands, turned right on the roundabout, and headed north up Rover Way. Albino Ron was in the van with him. Sat in the passenger seat watching porn on a mobile phone.

The usual suspects were out and about. All hoodies and baggy trousers. Loitering on street corners, racing one another on stolen shopping trolleys. Some had gone a step further than that; wheel-spinning cars that looked unroadworthy on sunken suspension systems, their cannon-sized exhaust pipes producing almost deafening sounds. One of the onlookers threw a can of something into the middle of the road, a spray of white foam doing circles on the broken tarmac when the van hit it.

None of this was anything out of the ordinary for Cartwright. This was home. Where he'd grown up on a diet of fights, cider, and anything else he could get his hands on for free. His big brother, Denny, had been his only father figure, teaching him all he needed to survive in a dog-eat-dog environment.

Kyle hit his hand hard against the horn, giving the onlookers a loud salute as he went racing by. Someone shouted his name. Others gestured *wanker.* All laughed hysterically. Including him.

It started raining. Heavy as it slammed against the windscreen. Loud on the roof of the van. Cartwright took his foot off the accelerator, not only because he could no longer see where he was going, but mostly because he'd had an annoying thought. 'How the fuck do we get home, Ron?' Billy Creed hadn't mentioned that. Only to get the van shot from the lock-up and torch it. He pulled over onto the side of the road and twisted in his seat.

'Taxi,' Ron said, mesmerised by whatever was happening on his phone.

'You got money then?' Cartwright asked over the sounds of deep-throated moaning. 'And put that fucking thing away,' he said, knocking the handset out of Ron's hands and somewhere into the dark wheel well.

'Ah shit, man, it was coming to the best bit an' all.' Ron pointed between his feet. 'You should see the way this bird–'

'Leave it!' Cartwright wound the window down and stuck out an arm. 'We're going to get soaked.'

Ron reached a hand towards his phone, dirty-white dreads hanging like tentacles well past his knees. The woman wasn't getting any quieter. 'I'm calling Jimmy,' he said defensively when Cartwright looked set to lamp him one. 'I'll tell him to send someone round to pick us up.'

'We'll be on that bit of waste ground behind the water works.' Cartwright sat back and listened to what little he could of the telephone conversation. At least the on-screen blonde had been given some downtime. Poor woman must have been knackered. 'What did he say?' Cartwright asked once Ron was finished.

'He's sending one of Billy's cabs. An unmarked one. And it won't be coming anywhere near this place, so we'll have to leg it back down to the roundabout and wait.'

'Fucking hell.'

On they went, along the coastal road, past industrial buildings that looked more suited to the set of a George Orwell movie. Tall. Sprawling. Most having long lengths of ducting that reached across the wide expanses of concrete yard.

Cartwright turned the headlights off, slowing to what was little more than a crawl. There were no buildings further out, only broken chain-link fence and the sound of the sea crashing against the rocks. He drove the van up and over the pavement; the vehicle leaning left, then right, shaking and banging. The hole in the fence was just about big enough; fresh scratches in the paintwork nothing to worry about given the circumstances. He put the window down again and had a good look at the place. 'Shouldn't be anyone this far out from the water works,' he said.

Albino Ron agreed. 'Security's probably asleep.'

'Keep your eye out, in case,' Cartwright said, opening the van door. He went round the back and emptied the entire contents of a jerrycan over the floor of the vehicle. A second can used on the front seats and steering wheel. The door handles got a dousing of their own. All lit with a single match.

The heat was immediately intense. Face-drying hot. The whole surrounding area lit up in shifting shades of orange and yellow.

'Oi, you!' It came from behind them and belonged to one of two men stood waving a torch beam in their direction.

'Run,' Cartwright said, and heard one of the security guards tell the other to get an extinguisher from the back of their van.

Reece reached for the Blueridge acoustic guitar and strummed a few open chords while sat on a stool in his kitchen. The sound the instrument made was rich and warm. Full and pleasing. He'd known as soon as he'd picked it up and played it in that old shop in Rome, that this was the one he'd spent close on a lifetime searching for.

When Anwen had realised that too, she'd pretended to be looking the other way. Paying no interest to what conversations her new husband was having with the store's owner. And when she'd left him browsing the showroom of a Maserati dealership – on the pretence of calling into the shop next door – she had in fact gone back to put a holding deposit down on the guitar.

Reece had only found that out when the storekeeper rang Anwen's phone to ask why she hadn't yet picked the instrument up.

She was already dead.

Reece hadn't wanted it then. Could think of nothing but her.

The storekeeper had insisted Reece take the guitar home, telling him that whenever he played it, Anwen's spirit would be there with him. The man had left the instrument at the hotel reception desk one morning together with a condolence card – no further payment necessary.

Reece thought about her now, guitar resting on his knee, playing sweet melodies they'd loved to sing together.

'She had the voice of an angel,' her father, Idris, used to say. Reece couldn't argue with that.

He put the guitar to one side for the night and went to a jumper folded over the back of the sofa in the living room. Raising the soft fabric to his nose, he inhaled what remained of Anwen's scent and began the lonely walk upstairs.

19

It was a good thing Dr Richard Wellman had been watching the televised press briefings. Monitoring the local rags. Especially the stuff about the sightings of a silver Volvo in the area. That had given him a useful heads-up on what leads the police were now following.

And had it been sheer coincidence, or divine intervention perhaps, that he'd come across the advert for the lock-up in the evening newspaper when he'd needed one most? As a devout Christian, he'd quickly decided on the second of the two available options.

Using the mobile telephone number supplied with the advert, he'd spoken with an unsavoury character. The man asked no questions regarding his plans for the place. Had wanted to deal in cash only. And insisted on there being no paperwork to exchange between them. For a modest sum of money, and little effort on his own part, the lock-up now belonged to him.

And that hadn't been the luckiest break of all where adverts were concerned. The card in the window of the local post office

– a few weeks earlier – had trumped the advert in the newspaper by some distance.

He'd gone to buy a car. A silver Volvo. *The* silver Volvo. Something big enough to transport victims when he got to that level, and found his biological mother in the process.

He'd known instantly who she was. Couldn't explain it, but knew the moment she'd opened the door.

She'd flashed a disingenuous smile with well-practised ease. Made small talk. Led him on. And all for the purpose of getting what she wanted. Mother hadn't changed her ways, and never would.

He gave thought to how different things might have been had she thrown her arms open wide and hugged him. Had she taken him inside her home and poured her heart out, apologising for tearing their young family apart all those years earlier. For driving a good man to suicide. Not to mention leaving a six-year-old child, to all intents and purposes, an orphan.

It's just as well your sister, Freda, showed me more charity. Took me into her home and brought me up as her own.

When he'd entered the Gantry woman's house – Mother's house – he'd told her who he was almost immediately. Couldn't help but do so. Blurted it out.

She hadn't listened. Turned him away again, unwilling to fulfil her responsibilities even after the passing of so much time.

He'd cried. Wept in her presence and laid himself bare.

But still she refused to acknowledge it, insisting he was mistaken, even though he gave her every opportunity to end the cruel charade and tell the truth.

Even when he reached for the wrinkled skin of her neck. Closed both hands around it and squeezed. Even then, the whore refused to repent.

He'd cleaned the house. Even the rooms he hadn't set foot in before then. Got rid of all traces of himself, claiming the Volvo for his own use. When he bumped into one of the neighbours at the bottom of the drive, he'd told the man he'd been working abroad; that he'd already taken Mother to stay with him for a few months, and had returned only to collect the car.

Mother was in the boot. Curled up and very much dead.

The man had wished him well – said he rarely, if ever, saw her – and asked if they wanted the mail forwarded to any particular address. Wellman told him there would be no need, that he'd be back from time to time to make sure the house was okay.

It was just before dawn when he squeezed the Volvo down a narrow lane in the docks area of the city, looking for the lock-up. So far, so good. No blue lights nor loud sirens on his tail. If they'd picked the car up on their ANPR – automatic number plate recognition system – then there was no evidence of it as yet. And once the vehicle was stored away under cover, then that's where it would stay for the foreseeable future, his ongoing plans needing to be modified somewhat.

A figure stepped out in front of him, the man's eyes shining white in the light thrown by the headlamps of the vehicle. Wellman braked hard, and despite the slow speed, lurched forward in his seat. When he checked the rear-view mirror, he saw another man stood behind the car; this one's face hidden behind a curtain of dreadlocks.

The muscular man in front tapped the bonnet. His cue for the driver to kill the engine and get out. Wellman did. There were no handshakes or pleasantries exchanged between them. They were there to do business, neither party having any interest in the other's intentions beyond that.

'It's all there,' Wellman said, handing over a supermarket carrier bag that was folded over. The two men counted the money, regardless. He thought the pair smelled of smoke and accelerant, but knew better than to ask.

'I don't fancy your chances of getting out of this place alive,' the bigger of the two said with a crooked grin.

Dreadlocks took a step closer.

Wellman's hand hovered next to his jacket pocket. He had one pre-made syringe only, and decided its contents would be for the more powerful looking of the two, should things get out of hand. 'I've given you the money.'

'Not us.' Muscles laughed and turned away. 'Even the rats are shit-scared of coming down here.'

That sounded perfect to Wellman. He couldn't have chosen a better hideaway. 'I'll take my chances,' he said, heading on foot towards the lock-up door.

When he next looked, both men were gone.

Reece had swapped things around a bit. Sent Ginge over to attend Sandra Cole's post-mortem while he and Jenkins paid the owner of the silver Volvo a visit. Besides, she'd said she needed to talk, and this way, they could do both at the same time.

Jenkins stared out the side window of the car. 'And that's why Ffion went AWOL yesterday afternoon.'

'Shit,' Reece said, pulling away from the traffic lights. 'Is there anything I can do to help? I know a couple of people who wouldn't mind me calling them.'

'She's gone private,' Jenkins said. 'Most of what needs to be done at this stage should be over by the end of today.'

Reece glanced at her, the main focus of his attention being a trio of cyclists behaving like dicks; using the full width of their side of the road. 'If she needs help with any of that, then I've got some money put away.'

Jenkins patted his knee. 'Josh's got it sorted.'

'Even so, you tell her,' Reece said, trying to get past the trio for the umpteenth time.

'I will.'

'Get over, you fucking idiots!' he shouted in Jenkins's right ear.

'Boss!'

'They're doing it to piss me off, can't you tell?'

'Don't go round them,' she squealed, screwing both eyes closed. 'There isn't *roooom...*'

'Single file!' He accelerated hard, hand gestures giving as good as he got.

Jenkins sank in her seat, hands covering her face, terrified and embarrassed all at the same time. 'I can't believe you did that.'

'Wankers, the lot of them,' Reece said, not looking at her. He sensed her staring. One of those, *I'm well pissed off with you* types of looks. 'Come on,' he said, risking a peek. 'You name me any man worth his salt who goes about parading his ball-bag in pink Lycra.'

She tried not to laugh. Held on to the urge for as long as she could before creasing up.

'It's not funny,' he said. 'They should make dressing up like that illegal. Scares kids and old people.' He double-took. 'What's wrong?'

'You. Just you.'

For a while there was nothing but silence between them. Reece ducked as they went past the castle. The griffin was there, high above one of the castellated towers, watching over the people of Cardiff from its vantage point. A right turn at the next junction took them past the museum, then the Redwood Building that belonged to the university's School of Pharmacology.

Jenkins was first to speak. 'Ffion's got that breast cancer

gene you hear about on the radio. Told me most of the women on her mother's side of the family went on to have mastectomies.' She paused, composing herself. 'Imagine that: waiting for the day you've always dreaded, but know is coming.'

'I wouldn't want to know.'

'Really? Not even if there was something you might be able to do about it?'

'I don't know.' He couldn't comprehend it, truth be known. 'Those women are far braver than I'd ever be, that's for sure.'

They were clear of the city and headed for one of the more affluent suburbs. 'Nice houses,' Jenkins said, watching double-fronted detached properties go by on both sides. 'Jesus, you could play tennis on that lawn.'

Reece slowed for a speed camera. Sped up again once out of its range. 'Bet this lot keep the local golf and bridge clubs going.'

'This is it,' Jenkins said, tapping him with the back of a hand. 'That one there with the gravel drive.'

'You sure?'

'Said so on a post at the side of the road.'

Reece stopped, and reversed a short distance. 'You're right. Come on, we'll walk up and have a nosey on the way.'

Jenkins got out and followed him. 'How are we going to play this?' she asked, breaking into a trot to keep up.

'We knock the door and ask whoever answers if they drive a silver Volvo.'

'Simple as that?'

'Why would you want to make it any more difficult?'

They'd reached the brow of the rising drive and were confronted with a garage one side and the house just ahead. The property itself wasn't as large as the others in the area and looked somewhat tired; green mould growing on its walls where sunlight hadn't penetrated the encroaching treeline.

'Could do with a lick of paint,' Reece said, knocking on the front door.

'Looks like no one's done anything to it for years.'

After knocking a second time, he went to one of two front windows, put his hand between head and glass and peered inside. 'Looks like they're out,' he said, passing behind her to get to the window on the other side. 'Let's go round the back.' Before they got there, he stopped and did a detour over to the garage. When he twisted and pulled at the handle, the door lifted up-and-over with a high-pitched squeal.

'Boss, you really shouldn't be doing that. There's no reason to be going in there.'

'Who's going to know?' Reece said, stepping inside. There wasn't much to be found: mostly piles of old stick drying for a night on the log burner.

'*He* might,' Jenkins said, nodding at a man who was marching up the drive towards them.

'Can I help you?' the man shouted. He slowed down, as though unnerved by what he might have got himself into.

Reece held up his warrant card and pointed towards the house. 'You live here, sir?'

The man indicated a neighbouring property. 'Over there,' he said, looking decidedly more confident. 'This one is Mrs Gantry's house.'

'She's not in,' Reece said, closing the garage door with another squeal of its aged mechanism. 'And the car's gone.' There were tyre tracks in the soil beneath his shoes.

The man stood wringing warmth into his hands, a green woollen tank-top with matching check shirt not nearly enough to keep out the chills of the cold March morning. 'Her son took it a couple of weeks ago.'

Jenkins joined in. 'Son?'

'Home from working abroad, apparently. Came for his mum first; the car a few days after that.'

'Did he leave a name, or forwarding address?' Jenkins asked hopefully.

'Afraid not. He was very much like his mother. Not much of a talker, to be honest with you.'

'What about a description?' Reece asked. 'You must have got a good look at him?'

'Not really. He never got out of the car. Window was only down an inch or so, and what with the trees blocking out most of the light.' The man shrugged. 'Sorry.'

'But you saw the car?' Jenkins asked.

'Old Volvo estate.'

'Colour?'

'Light. Silver. Yeah, silver.' The man looked suddenly worried. 'Is everything all right. Nothing's happened to Mrs Gantry, has it?'

Reece ignored the question. 'Was she in the habit of going out late at night?'

'Hardly went out at all, as far as I know.'

'Thanks for your help,' Reece said before leading the way back down the drive.

Reece hovered over Ginge's desk. 'Tell me about the post-mortem.'

The newbie handed him a copy of the interim report. 'Sandra Cole had enough coronary artery disease to kill her within the next five years.'

'Heart attack brought on by the shock of the assault?' Reece asked. He hadn't got to that part yet.

Ginge shook his head. 'Dr Frost is still waiting on the results of more tox reports, to be sure and all that, but the urine has already tested positive for the metabolites of Suxamethonium Chloride.' He waited. 'Says so on the last page.'

Reece pushed off the desk and straightened. 'I knew it. Same killer, different approach that's all.'

'Any luck with the car?' Ginge asked. 'You know it was picked up by ANPR last night?'

Reece lowered the report. 'Where?'

Ginge gave him an overview of the route once it had been spotted. 'And then it vanishes.'

'But it was heading towards the docks at the time?'

'Looks that way, boss. I've already asked a couple of the patrols to swing by the area on their way back to the station.'

'Good man.' Reece finished his reading and dropped the file onto the desk. 'I've got another job for you,' he said, dragging a seat up alongside. 'I seem to recall from the Belle Gillighan case that you're a dab hand at finding information on people who fly below the radar.'

'I know my way around a fair few databases.'

Reece tapped him on the back and stood. 'You've got until the other side of the weekend then, to find me everything you can on Molly Gantry's son.'

20

'Jenkins will lead things while I'm away for the weekend,' Reece said, scratching his chin. 'I'm off to Brecon for the Wales-England game. No way I'm missing that one.'

Chief Superintendent Cable peered over the rims of her spectacles before removing them altogether. Folding their arms first, she lay them on the desk in front of her. 'DS Jenkins is supposed to be concentrating on the Harlan Miller case. Did you not listen to anything ACC Harris or I've had to say?'

Reece stared over Cable's shoulder. Out the window and way off into the grey distance beyond. 'I heard you all right. But I still don't see why Miller's case should get any more time spent on it than Poppy Jones or Sandra Cole.'

Cable leaned her elbows on the desk and sat there massaging her temples. 'The Americans are threatening to ask for another force to come in and investigate their son's murder.'

'Who do they think they are?' Reece waved a dismissive hand at her. 'They've got no chance.'

'*Money* is what they've got. And with that comes influence.' Cable hunted through the drawers of her desk, opening each one in the order of top to bottom. 'Don't underestimate the clout of either.'

'I don't give a shit who or what they've got in their pockets.' Reece tapped his chest with a finger. 'I, for one, won't be dancing to their tune, okay.'

'I'm not getting into another fight with you.' Cable put a bottle of aspirin next to the spectacles. 'Not today.'

'Who's fighting?' Reece had both hands on his hips, suit jacket swept back behind them. 'I'm just telling it like it is.'

The last desk drawer closed with a firmer shove than was necessary. 'What can I tell them?'

'Apart from *fuck off and leave me alone*, you mean?'

'Chief Inspector!'

Reece's attention was drawn outside the window again. This time by a pair of seagulls dancing on the wind. For some strange reason, the image reminded him of his wedding day, and Anwen's father:daughter dance with Idris. Snapping out of it, Reece said, 'You can tell them these cases are all related.'

Cable groaned and sank further into her seat. 'Brân, don't you think you might be clutching at straws here?' She counted the points off on her fingers: 'Miller was stabbed in the chest. Poppy Jones killed by what appears to be very sophisticated methods. And poor Sandra Cole; well, she was viciously assaulted. I'll be frank and admit I don't follow your logic.'

'I'm telling you,' Reece said, his eyes screwed tight shut. 'Cole has tested positive for that paralysing drug in her urine, linking her death directly to that of Poppy's.' He gave Cable a moment to get onto the same page as him. 'And as we've already agreed at the briefings – Poppy and Harlan Miller's deaths being nothing but coincidence – is codswallop.'

'And you remain satisfied that none of this has anything to do with the ex-boyfriend?' Cable sifted through the paperwork, looking for the name. 'Jordan Patterson.'

'I'm not going to rule him out of the stabbing just yet,' Reece said, 'but the injections are way beyond his capabilities.' He saw the chief super's eyes narrow. 'I know it's possible he could have managed it with help from one of the others in the house, but I think it's unlikely.'

'What else can I tell Miller's parents?' Cable gave him a look of warning.

Reece sighed. 'That we're following fresh leads on the Volvo. We now know who it belongs to, and I've got Ginge tracking down the son of the owner.'

'Well, that's brilliant.' Cable broke into what might have been her first smile of the day so far. 'Why didn't you tell me any of this earlier?'

Reece stared at her and said nothing.

'Sit down, Brân.'

He pointed to the office door. 'I was just going to–'

'Sit.'

'Will it take long?' he asked, reluctantly accepting the seat.

'I've been speaking to Dr Beven about your sessions.'

He'd been waiting for this moment since the counsellor had tricked him into talking about the shooting. Trapped and made him say things that weren't true. He kicked himself for having let his guard down. Promised he wouldn't do that a second time. 'They're a waste of time and money in my opinion,' he said.

'Patricia disagrees. Says you're making progress at long last.'

Another trap. Don't utter a word.

'Did you hear me?'

He nodded. *They're probably in it together like a pair of witches.*

'So that's good, isn't it?'

Another nod.

'Are *you* feeling all right?' Cable asked. 'You're acting awfully strange.'

'I'm fine.'

'You keep saying.'

Leaning forward in his seat, Reece said, 'Ah, but now I've got the shrink saying the same thing.'

'"*Making progress*," is what Patricia actually said. Let's not get too far ahead of ourselves.'

'Can I go now?'

Cable nodded. 'Oh, there *is* one other thing before you do. The hospital wants you over there for a chat with the Board. Reassurance that their staff are safe coming and going from work.'

'When?'

'This afternoon. Three o'clock to be exact.'

Reece's shoulders rounded. 'Can't you do it? I was hoping to knock off early today.'

'Believe me, I would if I could, but I've got this serious crime audit meeting to attend.'

'And there's no one else?'

'You're leading the investigation,' she told him.

He got up, muttering obscenities, this time allowed as far as the office door before she stopped him.

Cable put the bottle of aspirin to her lips and shook a couple out onto her tongue. 'Please Brân – best behaviour.'

'It's been a mixed bag tracing the son,' Ginge said when Reece got back to the incident room. 'Mrs Gantry had only one child, by the looks of things: a boy born in nineteen sixty-two at the Cardiff Royal Infirmary. Six years later, he's put up for adoption. The records are a bit shaky. Non-existent in some respects. No servers to store it on back then in the Dark Ages.'

'I know,' Reece said. 'Having lived through them myself.'

'Sorry, boss.' Ginge went back to his screen, turning it for the

DCI to see the list of dates and comments made by several social workers at the time. 'Looks like the boy was in and out of foster homes for a while. Again, some records are missing. Others not fully completed. Never settled, it seems. And there might be something here to suggest he was eventually taken in by another family member.'

Jenkins came away from her desk to join them. 'Keep digging. If it's true, then whoever that relative was, they might just lead us to him.'

Ginge frowned. 'Unless they've died after all this time.'

'How long ago do you think the sixties were?' Reece asked, swiping a hand at the ducking newbie. He turned to Jenkins. 'Abandonment as a child might make him resentful of women now he's grown up, I suppose?'

She didn't look at all convinced. 'But what's his beef with the likes of Poppy?'

'I don't know,' Reece said, loosening the knot of his tie. 'I'm just throwing it out there for discussion.'

'Did the child keep the Gantry name?'

'Up to here.' Ginge pointed to the last line of entries on his screen. 'And then it's as if he disappears at the age of twenty.'

'Or changed his name,' Jenkins said.

'No record of it in any of the registers I had access to.'

'Keep looking.' She watched Reece go to his office and pick up his car keys. 'Where are you going?'

Checking his watch, he said, 'I've got an appointment over at the hospital. You go find a magistrate and get us a search warrant for the mother's place.'

'On what grounds?'

'I don't know. Lie if you have to.'

'Boss!' Jenkins shook her head at him. 'I'm on a final written warning as it is.'

'Tell them we're worried about Molly Gantry. That her life

might be in danger. Embellish it, for God's sake, you know how it goes.'

~

Reece sat in a hospital boardroom that smelled of polish and musty old men. There was a table running along the room's centre; a pull-down projector screen hanging from the ceiling at one end of it. He stirred his coffee, listening to the chairman express sorrow over the tragic "*passing*" of three of the organisation's employees.

Others present in the room included the Executive Director of Nursing, the Medical Director, and a stern-looking woman from the Deanery. On Reece's insistence, Dr Richard Wellman was there in the capacity of Clinical Director for Anaesthetics.

'This has been truly terrible for all concerned,' the medical director said. Dr Simon Underdown was a short, plump man with a rosy complexion. Reece had him pegged as something of a drinker. Probably something of an eater as well.

The nursing director, on the other hand, was a thin stick of a woman. Slightly kyphotic, and in dire need of a makeover. 'Chief Inspector, how do you propose to keep our staff safe while you're hunting this beastly man?'

Reece put the thumb end of a closed fist to his mouth and tried not to laugh at the woman's pretentious manner. 'We've a patrol car passing through the site several times a day, as well as a doubling of our usual on-foot activity.'

'And you consider that enough, under the circumstances?'

'It's all I'm going to get,' Reece said curtly, 'given current budget restrictions.'

'And what about further afield?' the chairman asked. 'The two nurses were killed at their homes, after all.' He looked round the table as though seeking confirmation of his claim.

Reece nodded with the rest of them. 'Staff should be encouraged to travel in pairs. Larger groups, if able.'

'Do you have any idea who you're looking for?' Underdown asked. 'I read you've been trying to trace the owner of a silver Volvo.'

'We're following up leads and getting closer,' Reece said, letting his gaze settle on each of them in turn. 'I'm willing to believe the killer works here at the hospital.'

The director of nursing almost slid off her seat. 'Good Lord. You can't be serious?'

'You've a problem with security of drugs on that theatre suite,' Reece said. 'Both women were injected with the paralysing agent, Suxamethonium Chloride. We think they were then left to asphyxiate and die.'

'There was nothing in the press about that.' The chairman's brow furrowed like ripple marks left in wet sand.

'And that's how it's to stay,' Reece said. 'Kept within these four walls for now.'

'Yes, of course, we understand.'

Turning to Wellman, the chairman said, 'Richard – your opinion on this?'

Wellman was calm in his response. 'I've previously spoken to the chief inspector, explaining why certain drugs need to remain available to the end-user throughout the entire course of a surgical list.' He shrugged. 'Besides, you can't know for sure that the Sux came from our suite. Any more than it did from a neighbouring hospital, or veterinary practice for that matter.'

'Fair point.' The medical director looked decidedly less troubled with that. 'It could quite easily have come from anywhere.'

'Not quite *anywhere*,' Reece insisted. 'From a handful of places at most, and I'm sticking with my gut feeling.'

'But Harlan Miller was stabbed, not drugged.' The woman from the Deanery opened a file on the table in front of her.

'I can't go into the specifics of each individual case,' Reece said, 'other than to say we've every reason to believe all three deaths are connected.'

'Miller was doing audit work for *you* it says here.' The woman leaned to look down the table at Wellman. 'Did he mention anything about being mixed up in something unsavoury?'

Reece was on his feet. He rounded the table and stopped only when he got behind Wellman's chair. 'You told me you'd never heard of Harlan Miller.'

'You caught me on the street, Chief Inspector, and in passing barked a name.' Wellman didn't turn around. Stared straight ahead as he spoke. 'Had you shown me a photograph, then perhaps I'd have had a fighting chance of placing him.'

'*So?*'

'So what?' Wellman asked.

'Now we've jogged your memory, is there anything else you want to tell me?'

'Nothing at all.'

'You sure about that?'

'Are you calling me a liar?'

Reece got closer and whispered in the man's ear. 'What's your date of birth?'

21

Jenkins had positioned a pair of uniforms in the field behind Mrs Gantry's house. The other side of the thick treeline. 'In case someone makes a run for it,' she'd said. With her in the unmarked car was Ginge, and two constables who looked like they'd rather be in bed at such an early hour. It was still a few minutes before six, the day after she'd embellished the shit out of her story at the local magistrate's court.

In the car behind them were four more uniforms; all wearing protective over-vests and BWVs – body-worn video cameras.

The vehicles sped up the gravel drive on Jenkins's command, spewing chippings into the untended flower borders. When they slid to a halt outside the house, Jenkins was first to get out. She marched towards the front door, Ginge in close pursuit. This part of the job always gave her such a buzz. The uncertainty of what might happen next was exhilarating to say the least.

Banging on the front door, she shouted, 'Police', identifying them to potential occupants and threats alike. 'Open up.' Peering through a small panel of frosted glass, she saw no movement. The door took another hammering. She shouted again, only this time, louder. One of the waiting uniforms was summoned forward. 'Time for the *Big Red Key*,' Jenkins said – meaning that the man was now authorised to smash through the door with the heavy length of steel he carried two-handed.

Metal struck against wood three times. Metal coming off victorious, as was almost always the case.

They were greeted in the cold hallway by air that carried an odd odour. At first, Jenkins didn't recognise it. She sniffed, trying to call on memory to help her out. It wasn't from cooking. No, something else altogether. 'You take upstairs,' she told Ginge. 'I'll start down here.'

At the end of the hallway was a glass door that opened into a narrow living room, which itself was divided into two distinct areas. The bit near the front window was more formal. Contained a reading chair, lamp, and writing bureau. Whereas the opposite end of the room had a television, sofa, and a small dining table and chairs.

Jenkins put on blue latex-free gloves and started over by the window. Checked behind the reading chair. Lifted its cushioned seat and found nothing. The front of the bureau lowered like a medieval drawbridge to reveal a red-leather writing surface lined like a road map from years of use. Running a hand over it, she wondered what stories the indentations might share if able. Leaving the red leather to its secrets, she moved on to a neat letter rack and checked the address on each envelope before carefully removing the contents to skim read. They were bills, mostly. A television licence and an overdue reminder for an appointment with an optometrist.

On the wall above the bureau was a large print of a hunting scene. A man dressed in a green tunic with matching hat stood in the stirrups of his giant steed, blowing into a long and curved horn. A pack of dogs were already unleashed, keen on the scent of the fleeing hare. Jenkins found herself instantly despising the man, and all that he and his kind represented.

In the magazine rack next to the log-burner, was a copy of the *Radio Times* and a couple of newspapers. She checked the date on the most recent one.

The tiled mantelpiece was free of both clutter and dust. Everything in the room had the appearance of having been cleaned meticulously. She frowned, her detective mind working overtime.

In the kitchen, the kettle was empty and cold. Not a pot or dish out of place. No teaspoon or butter knife sat alone in the aluminium sink. *Weird. It's like the place has been forensically cleansed.* The cupboards contained half-sized cans of beans, and corned beef, among other things. In the drawers were tea towels, and instruction booklets for the white goods on show.

'Ginge.' Jenkins was stood at the bottom of the stairs now. 'You found anything up there?'

'Not a sausage.' She went up and joined him on the landing. 'Doesn't look a bit like my gaff,' he said. 'Tidier than a show home, this.'

'That's what I thought.'

'That bother you?'

'Can't you smell it?'

'Bleach.' Ginge sniffed the air. 'Weak but you can definitely tell it's there.'

Jenkins paced the landing. 'Everything in this house has been cleaned to within an inch of its life.'

'Like someone trying to hide something.'

She nodded. 'Goes well beyond the realms of the owner being house proud.'

Ginge watched her. 'What now?'

Jenkins had already made her decision. 'Get on to Sioned

Williams, will you, and tell her I want this place gone over with a fine-toothed comb.'

~

Reece hung up once Jenkins had filled him in on the search of the Gantry house. He'd told her she was right to have called for a forensics sweep. That he had every confidence in her. Why wouldn't he, she was a bloody good detective.

But the case was a frustrating one for sure: all teasers and not a lot of hard evidence to go on as yet.

He had his suspicions though.

Knew who to keep his eye on.

Just needed more time before playing his final hand.

On entering the pub in Brecon, he could hear, rather than see, his friend Yanto – shouting at the television in the back room. Reece went over to the bar and returned to put a tall glass on the table in front of his friend. 'Afternoon.'

The farmer shifted position, looked past him and said nothing.

'Still not talking to me, you miserable sod?' Reece gave the other man's foot a playful kick.

'Shouldn't have left me on that roof,' Yanto said, shaking his head. He ran a spade of a hand through a mop of tight black curls. 'That was taking the piss, that was.'

Reece tried not to laugh. 'I got called back to Cardiff, didn't I. There's been a few murders there. You must have seen it on the news?'

'You want to sort your priorities out.' Yanto wagged a finger at him. 'Half the fucking week it took me to finish that roof off for you.'

'And I'm very grateful. Look, I've even bought you a pint.'

'Half the week.' Yanto took the glass and downed a good two-thirds of its contents in one gulp. 'The sheep have been running riot with me gone – turning cartwheels they are, up in that top field.'

Reece could hold back no longer, and belly-laughed. 'Ah, Yanto, I love you,' he said when able. 'Best mate I ever had.'

The farmer-cum-builders' merchant sank back in his chair. 'Fuck off.'

'I mean it.'

'And I do.'

Reece stood. 'Another pint?'

'You're buying all afternoon,' Yanto told him. '*All* afternoon, I said.'

'We going to do it then?' Reece asked when he got back with the drinks, and two packets of crisps dangling from his teeth.

'It's the Grand Slam.' Yanto pumped the air with a fist. 'And against the English an' all.'

'We're up against a decent team though,' Reece said.

Yanto leaned forward in his seat, eyes boring holes through the policeman. 'It's the *Grand Slam*.' The last two words came as a deep growl. 'It's ours.' He was on his feet, climbing onto a chair, arms held high above his head. 'Oggy. Oggy. Oggy!' he shouted.

'Oi. Oi. Oi,' came the resounding reply.

'Yanto, get down.' The woman behind the bar was making her way towards the hinged door in the countertop. 'If I have to come over there,' she warned.

He was back on his arse without uttering a word in protest.

Despite Yanto being the hardest man Reece had ever known, he still wouldn't have been foolish enough to bet on him in a one-on-one with his wife, Ceirios. 'How much do I owe you for the roof?' he asked once Ceirios had gone back to what she'd been doing.

Yanto shook his head and waved an arm.

'I mean it,' Reece said. 'Let me pay you a few days' labour at the very least.'

The farmer looked horrified. 'Butties don't pay for helping each other out.' He finished what was left of the first pint, and sank half the second in one go. 'You've gone soft now you're a city boy. Forgotten your roots, you have.'

'What do you mean?'

'You have, haven't you? Suits and ties messing with your head. You think you're one of them.'

Reece checked to be absolutely sure. He was wearing a rugby shirt and faded jeans like most other people in the pub. 'Huh?'

Yanto leaned forward in his chair and pointed to a panelled window opposite. 'Remember when we were little kids playing on those mountains out there – rain, sunshine, or snow – it didn't matter to us. That was our garden. Our playground, so to speak.'

Reece shook his head. 'Have you been smoking something again?'

Yanto sat back. 'They've got Paras and SAS training on it now. *Fucking SAS*,' he repeated in a higher tone.

'Meaning?'

'We're made of tougher stuff round here, Brân. City people are soft. Got everything handed to 'em on a plate.' He paused; sermon almost complete. 'Give 'em to me, they want to. I'd whip the lazy bastards into shape.'

'I'm sure you would.'

'I'm telling you. There's–'

'Hang on,' Reece said, silencing him. 'I need to take this.'

Yanto hung his head. 'Here we go again.'

'No, really, I need to take this call.' Reece crossed the pub, pushing through hordes of people singing 'Mae Hen Wlad Fy Nhadau' – 'Old Land of My Fathers'. He had no chance of hearing anything else until he got to the car park outside. And then a fair distance beyond that. 'Colonel,' he said, near breathless with palpitations.

'Chief Inspector. Buongiorno – good afternoon – to you.'

'You got something to tell me?' Reece asked, unable to contain himself.

Colonel Gianfranco Totti of the Carabinieri, in Rome, cleared his throat. 'There have been developments in the case regarding your late wife.'

'Just tell me,' Reece snapped. 'You got him? You found my Anwen's killer?' He felt like he was in a dream after that. Not the usual one where his life was getting flushed fast down the pan. This was a good dream. One in which the Italian police were bringing the whole terrible event to something near closure. 'And you're sure it's the right man?' he asked once the colonel was finished.

After confirming they had every reason to believe it was, Colonel Totti went on to explain the legal process of his country.

'Your equivalent of our Magistrates' Court after the weekend then?' Reece said.

With the telephone conversation complete, he'd walked out of the pub car park in a daze, not at all sure of where he was going. He had no idea how long he'd been gone, or from which direction he'd returned. Re-entering the pub, his arm was grabbed by someone who spun him around while they danced a jig.

'We won the Grand Slam!' Yanto kept shouting at him. 'Where've you been?'

'Outside.' Reece pointed. 'I've been on the phone.'

'For two hours? Thought you'd gone back to Cardiff again.'

Reece checked his watch against the one on the wall above

the widescreen television. Two hours, right enough. 'They've got him.' He was shaking. 'The Italians have caught Anwen's killer.'

~

Reece woke up in a bathtub. There was no water in there with him. And he wasn't at all sure where *there* might have been. He let his eyes get used to the dark. But that didn't help any, either. His mouth was dry; head pounding. 'Where am I?' He could hear snoring. 'Yanto, is that you?'

'Huh?'

'Where the hell are we?'

Yanto sat up suddenly and struck his head against the underside of the wash basin. After a fair amount of loud swearing, he got up and opened the blinds. 'My bathroom,' he said, looking confused.

'What am I doing here?' Reece asked.

'Did we win the Grand Slam yesterday?' Yanto was slowly piecing things together. He put his mouth under the cold water tap and took a long drink.

Reece watched him. 'Did I get a phone call from Rome, or was that a dream?'

'I don't think we were dreaming,' Yanto said. 'Did we stay on for the lock-in?'

Reece swallowed, fighting the urge to throw up. 'I think we might have done.'

There was the sound of pans knocking against the stove downstairs. 'What time is it?' Yanto asked, reaching for the handle of the bathroom door.

'Twenty-five past ten.'

'In the *morning?*'

'Of course it's in the morning.'

'Aw bollocks, I was supposed to be taking Ceirios shopping by nine.'

'She'll be all right.' Reece stepped out of the bathtub. He grabbed for the wall, his legs objecting to a night of being tucked under him.

Yanto held the door open. 'You go down first and butter her up.'

'You make her sound like a piece of toast.'

'Tell her it was all your idea. She likes *you*.'

Reece shook his head. 'Look who's gone soft now.'

22

Yanto took Reece home to the cottage in a white Land Rover Defender that shook and rattled along the tramlines of churned dirt track. It was almost noon. Sunday in the middle of March. 'What you going to do with yourself this afternoon?' he asked with a wide yawn. 'Sleep off that thick head of yours, I bet.'

Reece looked beyond the windscreen. Towards the mountains. 'I've got something to tell Anwen and Idris.'

'You're not going up Pen y Fan in this,' the farmer said, flicking the windscreen wipers to full-on. 'It's blowing a gale out there.'

'I'll be careful. I know the place like the back of my hand.'

'Brân–'

'Look, I'm not one of the weekend warriors,' Reece told him. 'I'll be all right up there.'

'I'm coming with you then.'

'No, you're not.'

'Brân, I–'

'Yanto!' Reece lay his hand down heavy on the other man's knee. 'I'll be fine. Stop fussing.'

They drove another mile or so in silence, except for the noise of rain drumming on the roof, and the grunt of the Defender's engine as its wheels spun in the mud before getting traction, propelling them onward again.

'Look at this rain,' Yanto said, still sounding seriously concerned. 'The cloud base is right down low.'

'SAS kids, remember?' Reece replied with a gentle voice. 'Built of tougher stuff, and all that.'

'I mean it, Brân. You're gonna get yourself killed. Why not wait until tomorrow?'

Reece got out and held on to a door that fought to pull away from him. 'No can do. I'm back in Cardiff.' And with a wave of thanks, he was headed for the plant pot on the front porch.

Jenkins opened the iron gate and let Cara Frost go first. 'Can't believe you've never been to Roath Park,' she said, raising the umbrella over both of them.

Frost ducked and waited for her to unsnag it from the top of the railings. 'I've only been in Cardiff six months or so. And never at all before that.'

'It's a lovely city,' Jenkins said, turning to keep the boating lake on their left as they set off on a circuit around it.

'First impressions are positive,' Frost replied, looping their arms together. 'Looks like it has everything I need right here.'

'What was Guernsey like to grow up in?' Jenkins asked. 'Sounds very posh. I used to watch re-runs of that detective series when I was a kid. Years ago. Oh, what was it called?' She snapped her fingers, trying to remember.

'*Bergerac?*'

'Yeah, that's the one.'

Frost shook her head. 'That was set on Jersey.'

'Ah, I remember now. Blue seas and summer all year long.'

'Not all year.' Frost repositioned the umbrella so they could catch sight of the way ahead. 'And *you* grew up here in sunny Cardiff.'

Jenkins smiled, happy for the first time in a long while. 'I'm an Ely girl,' she said sheepishly. 'But don't let that put you off.'

'You'll need to educate me. I've not had much to do with the area as yet.'

'Ely's not like Guernsey, for sure.' Jenkins paused for thought. 'A person can go one of two ways coming from my neck of the woods.' She paused a second time. 'But I suppose that's true wherever they come from.'

'Ah, I see. I'm getting the picture now. You saw the light and chose the police over the dark side.'

'Can't remember ever wanting to do anything else.'

'Something you saw, shape you that way?'

Jenkins slowed to a halt close to the edge of the water, toeing a small stone before tapping it over the side with a *plink* sound. She looked for another. 'My father was a policeman back in Jamaica. He told me stories – censored for his little girl obviously – and that had me sold from a young age.' *Plink.*

'He still there now?'

A shake of the head. 'Came to Cardiff in the seventies. Met my mum, and had *me*.' Jenkins raised both arms skywards. 'Da-da.'

Frost smiled. 'And did he join the South Wales Police when he got here?'

Jenkins sighed deeply. Could find no more stones. 'Diabetes did for Dad's toes, and so he became a lay preacher instead.' She paused to watch a pair of swans approach. Looked across to the boathouse on the other side of the lake, to where the pigeons were doing their dance on the roof. She put all thoughts of Amy Hosty, or Belle Gillighan – or whoever the hell that woman was

– out of her mind. 'He thought it was God's sign to follow another path.'

'Didn't have you down as a secret God-botherer,' Frost said.

'I'm not.' Jenkins looked offended. 'I went along with it for his sake. No point in shitting on someone else's beliefs, not unless there's good reason to be doing so. Each to their own, I always say.'

'Very noble of you.' Frost leaned closer and planted a kiss on Jenkins's temple.

Jenkins went back to watching the birds. Couldn't help herself. Thought she could hear someone calling her name. She saw a woman stood on the other side of the lake, looking their way. She squinted, but it helped none. Something tugged at her arm. 'What?' she said, turning to face Cara Frost.

'I asked if he was still working in the church. Your father?'

Jenkins looked over her shoulder. The woman was gone. Jenkins checked up and down the lake – across to the memorial lighthouse, but could find her nowhere. 'He's dead. Heart attack a few years back. Mum still helps out there a couple of days a week. It's good for her to get out.'

Frost raised the collar of her coat and tightened the top button. 'Do you see her much?'

'Not as often as I should.' Not since Jenkins had been back at work. Had she even told her mother that she *was* back? She couldn't remember and made a firm promise to herself to do it that night.

'I'm enjoying this,' Frost said. 'Getting to know you better.' She steered them to an empty bench and took some paper tissues from her bag to wipe it down before they sat. 'We've seen one another only a handful of times since this began.'

Jenkins lowered her head. 'It's me. I know it's me.' She picked at the edge of a thumbnail. 'Belle left scars.'

'Sure. There's no rush.' Frost looked away.

It was brief, but Jenkins saw it all the same. She said nothing. Not yet, anyway. 'Come on.' She extended an arm. 'I know a place up the road that does a fantastic carvery.'

Yanto hadn't been at all wrong in his assessment of the day's weather. Just getting from the cottage to the foot of the mountain had been an astonishing feat of endurance in itself. Pounding mud and marsh, Reece had been mid-shin, and a lot deeper at times. He pulled at handfuls of bracken. Gripped and used anything he could to make his way through the battering wind.

When the hail emptied from the plum-coloured sky like a bucketload of glass marbles, he lay himself next to a boulder, curling into the foetal position while ice struck rock with the clinking sound of a hundred or more stone masons' chisels.

His wet-weather gear was doing a sterling job of keeping him dry and warm, though a bit more beard coverage would have been a good thing. He waited for the worst of it to pass before setting off again, zigzagging as though negotiating a field of scattered land mines.

At times, he sought to duck beneath the wind. Others, he let it push him on his way, directing him to the foot of the arduous climb.

Heading south-west, he passed the Cwar Mawr quarry a short distance in. He knew he had, even though he couldn't see it very well. The rain had eased. Or was it a case of him getting used to it? His trail shoes gripped the silty ground, slipping only when they contacted a flat and well-trod rock on the winding path.

Pushing on, and bent at the waist, he couldn't wait to give Anwen and Idris the news, and found himself rehearsing the speech over and over in his head. Should he build up to it slowly, adding an air of suspense to the situation? Or was it better to blurt it out? Did it matter, the important thing was they'd caught him. They'd actually gone and arrested Anwen's killer after all this time.

It wasn't his imagination. Further on, the weather was definitely easing. Things changed so quickly up there on the mountain, and today it was shifting from awful to something much better than that. It was a sign. He'd tell Dr Beven at their next counselling session that he was all cured now, and no longer in need of her expensive shrinkery-dinkery. He didn't think she'd believe a word of it, but decided to tell her as much, regardless.

When he arrived at the summit, he instantly forgot most of the words he'd practised on the way. Threw himself to the ground in a flood of tears. 'They've got him,' he said, clawing at the hard earth with gloved hands. 'Anwen. Idris. Do you hear me?' They spoke for a long while; Reece in their mother tongue; *they*, as whispers brought on the air currents that swirled around him. He knew they were there. Could even see their faces in the softer clouds that passed on the upper level winds.

If he looked hard, he could see Llyn Cwm Llwch – Dust Valley Lake – way off in the distance. But no matter how he tried, there was no sign of the fairies said to inhabit the mythical island at the lake's mid-point.

He made his way over the other side of the summit; along Corn Du – Pen y Fan's slightly shorter sister – and down to where the Tommy Jones obelisk stood alone. Reece stopped to pay his respects to the dead five-year-old. Removed his woolly hat and read the tribute carved in the rock, as he always did. 'Sleep tight, little-un,' he said before continuing down the mountain.

≈

It was just after 9.30pm when Reece heard the sound of the car's engine. Then a few seconds after that, its wheels clawing at the gravel outside the front window of the cottage. He rose from the chair and leaned to pull the curtain open enough to see what was going on out there. At first, the stark white light from the headlights blinded him. The driver quickly shut them off, leaving halos of a softer glow hanging in the air before all went dark again.

When the car door opened and the occupant got out, Reece recognised the man immediately. Tapping the window, he indicated that the visitor should make his way around to the kitchen entrance at the side of the building.

'Twm, what are you doing here?'

The pathologist looked troubled, and entered the small kitchen without answering. Reece shut the door behind them and followed him in. 'You've been baking.'

'Having a go at some bread,' Reece said, nodding at a notebook lying on the kitchen table. 'Tried my hand at a potato and leek soup as well.' He stepped aside to let Pryce see the pan resting on the Aga behind him. 'Anwen had recipes for all sorts. Are you hungry?'

'Not really,' Pryce said, removing his jacket and driving gloves.

Reece could tell the man was famished. 'I was about to have another bowl,' he lied. 'Be nice to have some company for once.'

Pryce took a seat at the table. 'A small one then.'

'What's this about?' Reece asked, serving a full bowl of soup to the pathologist. 'Surprised you found the place in the dark.'

'Satnav.'

Reece nodded. 'Jenkins tells me I've got it on my phone somewhere.'

Pryce chuckled. 'And if you only spent some of your money instead of hoarding it all, then you'd also have satnav in the dashboard of your car.'

'My car's fine as it is. Got miles left in it yet.'

The pathologist raised a bushy eyebrow and blew on his soup. 'I fear I might have missed something recently,' he said, leaving his spoon to support itself in the thick mix of steaming liquid. 'During a post-mortem on a young girl.'

Reece was busy scraping the black bits off the dole of a loaf of bread, his interpretation of Anwen's timing instructions not yet mastered. He stopped what he was doing and listened.

Pryce rescued the drowning spoon and stirred his evening meal. 'She was a young woman. Twenty-three, and not a single thing wrong with her that I could find.' The spoon ran another few circuits of the bowl. Licking juice from his fingers, he added, 'And a nurse at the hospital.'

'When?' Reece folded his arms. The wooden chair creaked beneath him as he shifted position. '*Recently?*'

'A couple of weeks ago. Few days more than that, maybe.'

Reece smelled blood. 'And?'

'I did all the usual tox screens, of course. But nothing for Suxamethonium Chloride, or any of its metabolites. I mean, why would I?' Pryce looked to the policeman for reassurance.

'But now you're thinking you should have done?'

Pryce nodded. 'Cara told me about the cases she's been working on.' He took a deep breath and wriggled in the chair, unable to get comfortable. 'And that got me thinking.'

'Thinking what?' Reece asked. 'Come on, Twm. Spit it out.'

23

Reece finished and sat there waiting for a response. He didn't need to wait long.

'Not a hope in hell.' Chief Superintendent Cable watched him from the other side of the desk, a look on her face that was somewhere between the realms of complete disbelief and horror. 'You'd have to be bonkers to think I'd see it any other way.' She massaged her temples and dropped her chin onto her chest. 'Can you even imagine what ACC Harris would have to say about this if I dared mention it to him?'

Reece didn't give a shit what the man thought, and was on his feet, refusing to sit down again when told to do so. 'We'll just leave her there to rot then. Not know how she died. Is that what you want?'

Cable poked her head halfway across the desk. 'And you think that's any worse than us digging her up in front of the family to find we're wrong?'

He was like a guard on patrol; marching back and forth. 'We're not wrong. I know we're not. This girl is one of his victims, I'm telling you she is.'

'You can't *know* that.' Cable's voice was raised enough to

attract the attention of her personal assistant outside. 'For Christ's sake, Reece. Not for sure, anyway.'

'We will if we exhume her,' Reece argued. He put both hands on the desk and leaned on them. 'What I'm saying is: we can't leave her there in that grave and wonder. We owe it to the girl and parents to get justice for them.'

Cable pinched the bridge of her nose between finger and thumb. 'You've given me a nosebleed. Look,' she said, using a paper tissue to dab at spots on the desk.

'You should put your head back. Pinch your nose just there.' He demonstrated.

She glared at him.

He took that as a signal to carry on. 'She was in her twenties. Little more than a kid when you stop to think about it.'

Closing her eyes, Cable said, 'You're going to be the death of me, I swear.'

Reece straightened. 'You're doing it then?' He watched her reach for the telephone and pushed it a few inches nearer her. 'You're going to ring and let Harris know?'

Cable turned the swivel chair one hundred and eighty degrees so she couldn't see him. Jammed a finger in her free ear so she couldn't hear him either. 'They warned me about you before I came here. Even back home in London they know who you are.'

Reece pulled a face.

'Most said I was crazy to consider coming anywhere near this place. Anywhere near *you*, especially.'

He didn't pass comment. Sat there making *talk-talk* hand gestures to the back of the chief super's head.

'ACC Harris, it's Rachel Cable...'

Reece shrugged. 'What?'

The chief super had turned in her seat to glare and mouth obscenities at him throughout her brief and almost career-ending phone call to the Assistant Chief Constable. 'Billy Creed,' she said, awaiting the DCI's response.

'What about him?'

'His lawyer has been on to the Executive Office. It appears my phoning ACC Harris saved him a telephone call.'

'Creed murdered a man. What did you expect me to do?'

'Change the record, Reece. Who've you got him down for this time?'

'Pete Hall.'

'Who?'

'The CCTV guy from the Midnight Club. *The Belle Gillighan case*,' he added for clarity.

Cable sat back and folded her arms while he told her about the visit from Hall's distressed wife. 'And you've got proof of this?'

'Not yet,' he admitted.

Cable was still staring at him. 'So why go there without it?'

'To get some.'

'But I told you not to. I did say that – not to go within a mile of the man – didn't I?'

Reece turned away, refusing to look at her.

'What did you say?'

'Nothing.'

'You're treading on thin ice, Chief Inspector.'

He was on his feet again. 'And *you're* preventing me from doing my job.'

Cable slapped the tabletop so firmly that the photo of her pet Labradoodle toppled over, cracking the glass. 'His lawyer is–'

'A bigger fucking crook than Creed himself.' Reece took a gulp of air. 'Look–'

'No! *You* look,' Cable said, wiping new spots of blood from the lapels of her white blouse. 'If you're incapable of obeying orders, then I'll have you cuffed to one of those desks out there until you draw your pension.' She got up and grabbed at the door, swung it open, and pointed the way out. 'And Creed's got an alibi for the date you gave him. His lawyer says they were both with his accountant.'

'The exhumation?'

'*Out!*'

Reece rolled his eyes. 'Pinch it just there,' he said holding his nose as he went past.

'I could tell as soon as I set eyes on her,' Wellman said. 'The very moment she opened the front door and looked me up and down, in fact.' He leaned forward in his chair and returned the cup to its china saucer. 'Wasn't that utterly remarkable after all these years?'

Whatever her view on the matter, Dr Patricia Beven's face gave nothing away. 'And did your mother recognise you – as you did her?'

'I think she did, you know.' Nodding, he straightened a red bow tie. 'Yes, I believe she did.'

The counsellor took a sip of tea. 'Then why do you think she gave no firm indication of that being so?'

Wellman looked away, his mood souring in an instant. *Because she was being a bitch. It's what whores like her do to men.* Composing himself, he said, 'I don't know. But she knew all right.'

'You sound very confident. Don't you think there might be a possibility that–'

She's not listening. They never do. 'I've already said I could tell.'

His tone had changed, the words forced. When he next paid the counsellor any attention, he did so with a stony stare. Beven half-smiled. He could see her lips trembling. *She's scared.* The experience was new and excited him. The others had been given no time to exhibit such overt signs of being frightened; a hefty dose of Suxamethonium Chloride preventing all ability to do that.

This was different.

It was turning him on.

But then, *Patricia* was different. She was well dressed, with no chest or thighs on show. No flaunting her wares in public, as it were. He studied her hands; the fourth finger on the left one specifically. She was married. Had no Facebook account. He'd already checked of course. *I'll let you live, my sweet Patricia. But do be careful to never tease me like that again, won't you.*

'And when you went inside your mother's house, did her attitude towards you change?'

You mean when I throttled her so hard her eyes almost popped out of her head like they were on springs? He took a moment before answering. 'There was no change at all. Business chit-chat mostly. About how reliable a Volvo is. That you could fit a dining table in the back if need be. And that I was getting it for well under its market value.'

'That must have hurt. Must have made you feel almost insignificant as a person.'

She's getting off on my misery. She IS a whore, just like the rest of them. Be careful, Doctor. Be very careful. 'Yes, it hurt.'

'Describe those feelings. Vocalise them if you will.'

She's doing it on purpose. Pushing me in a direction that she alone has chosen to go. 'I hated Mother for it.'

'Just your mother, or women in general?'

Oh, you're good. Very fucking good. The bow tie got another pull and prod. 'I don't hate women. Not per se. Only those who act like whores.' He stopped himself. *Did I say too much then? Should I have used that word – whore? Did they put that in the newspaper?* He couldn't remember reading they had. *She's staring now. I know what she's thinking.*

Beven blinked, then stood and collected their cups and saucers. 'I think we'll bring today's session to an end.'

He caught her hand as she reached for his teacup, held it tight and wouldn't let go. He let his eyes linger on her tight waist. Her pert chest. Something was changing within him and he had to admit he liked it.

'Doctor. Dr Wellman.'

He let go. Watched her rub a red circle at her wrist.

She distanced herself from him, turning away as though preparing to say something that wouldn't sound too contrived or nervy. 'Please leave.' She walked two sides of the room, keeping close to the wall. Maintaining maximum separation.

Getting to his feet, he followed, polished shoes making slow, yet loud, impressions on the wooden floor. He flexed his fingers while looking for a suitable squeeze-point on the woman's slim neck. 'But we're nowhere near finished,' he said, almost within an arm's-length of her.

A sudden knock at the door made them both jump. Beven checked her watch. 'My twelve o'clock appointment is early,' she said with ill-disguised relief.

'Next time it is then,' Wellman replied with the coldest of goodbyes. As he descended the stairs of the building, he was still aroused. *Time to look up Smiler, the student nurse. I've got something new for that one.*

'Who let *you* in here?' Reece said, entering his office to find Maggie Kavanagh sat behind his desk, filing her nails. He was still seething after his telling-off upstairs.

She looked up; hands held out in front of her like those of a praying mantis. 'Charming. Is that any way to behave when an old friend comes to pay you a visit?'

'You've been smoking.' He went to the window and opened it. 'Jesus, Maggie.'

'Might have had a cheeky one. But I did leave the door open, so no harm done, lovie.'

'Ginge.' Reece poked his head into the incident room. '*Ginge!*'

'Yes, boss.'

'This any of your doing?' He pointed at the reporter.

Ginge looked like he wasn't at all sure what to say. He stayed where he was, glancing first one way, and then the other. When Kavanagh nodded at him, he said, 'Maggie told me she had an appointment with you, boss.'

Reece spun in the doorway. 'Appointment. What appointment?'

Kavanagh grimaced, and shrugged an apology. 'More of an open invitation.'

'When?' Reece asked. He shooed her from behind the desk but didn't take the seat himself.

'In the pub the other night,' she told him. 'Jenkins's drinks. You said pop round any time I wanted.'

'Bollocks, I did.'

'Come on, Brân, you did well to hide the death of that first girl. Poppy Jones, wasn't it? But Sandra Cole...'

'How do you know about that?' He looked to Ginge, who immediately shook his head.

'Wasn't him,' Kavanagh said. 'I got it from one of the older woman's neighbours, and then made the link myself.'

'Did you indeed.'

Kavanagh pulled a chair away from the far wall. She dragged it across to the desk and sat. 'I was piecing it together anyway. What the neighbour told me only sped things up a little.'

Reece got them a coffee each. He shut the office door on his return and dropped into his seat. 'What do you want from me?'

'What do I always want?' Kavanagh said with a wet cough. 'A story.'

'There's nothing to say.'

'Throw an old dog a bone, won't you?' She took a cigarette from its packet and dry-smoked it. 'You've got three dead hospital staff on your case files and reports of a stalker singling out nurses before that. Last weekend, you raided a Mrs Molly Gantry's house looking for her son in connection with that silver Volvo.'

Reece's mouth opened wide. 'How the...'

'Money talks, Brân. You know how it is.'

He shifted in his chair, loosening his tie. 'If it's anyone at this station, they'll have me to deal with.'

'Dry your powder,' she told him. 'I can get you more on the Gantry woman. Everything you want to know in fact.'

'Ginge is more than capable of doing that himself.'

Kavanagh inhaled deeply on the unlit cigarette. 'Two heads are better than one.'

Reece leaned an elbow on the armrest of the chair and put his knuckles to his teeth. 'Okay,' he said with a deep sigh. 'But *these* are going to be the rules we play by.'

24

Wellman found Smiler in the smaller of two coffee rooms on the Main Theatre corridor. Sat opposite one of the anaesthetic trainees, twirling a curl of raven-black hair with a finger.

The trainee stood as soon as the clinical director entered. Made his excuses and left without so much as a backward glance for his admirer.

Smiler watched the trainee leave, then turned her attention to the new arrival. Even went back to playing with her hair. 'Hello, Dr Wellman,' she said with a voice that had a sexy rasp to it.

See how easily she shifts from one to the other of us. There's no doubt that this one is a bona fide whore. 'I didn't catch your name last time,' he said, craning his neck to get a better look.

Raising the name badge towards him, she said, 'Skye.'

She made me look at her breast. Could easily have told me without doing that. 'What a lovely name.'

'Thank you. Can I get you a coffee?' she asked. 'I was about to make one.'

She wants to keep me here. Doesn't want me racing off like that trainee did. 'Stay where you are, I'll do it,' Wellman said. 'Milk and sugar?'

'Just milk, thanks.' People came and went. But not Skye.

He checked the time. 'I thought they let you students out long before now?'

'I'm going soon,' Skye told him. 'Psyching myself up first.'

Wellman frowned. 'For what?'

'The long trudge across that field back to the car.' She glanced at the windows and the impenetrable darkness beyond. 'A few of us do it together usually.' She twisted in her seat, facing him. 'But I'm the only student on duty this evening, and what with that stalker out there and everything that's been happening lately...'

'Tell you what.' Wellman waved his coffee mug at her. 'I'll chaperon you round there, and then perhaps you'd be kind enough to drop me back at my car. It's in the multi-storey.'

'*You?*'

'Look at the size of me,' he said, rising to well over six feet in height. 'No stalker is going to want to mess with this.'

'Definitely not.' Smiler was smiling.

'One condition though.' Wellman raised a finger to his lips. 'You don't mention this to anyone who might come in here while I pop over to my office.'

Skye looked suddenly confused, the smile almost gone completely.

'I've a reputation for being something of a miserable so-and-so.' He leaned close and whispered, 'I'd rather like to keep it that way, if it's all the same with you.'

'Oh, right. Yes, of course,' she said, tapping her nose. 'I understand.'

You'd be the first. Even the counsellor can't work me out. But she will soon enough.

· · ·

They'd met up again near the lifts; once Skye had changed out of her theatre scrubs, and Wellman had collected whatever it was he needed from his office. And now they were pushing through a hole in the chain-link fence that led into a wooded area just short of the field. It was very dark in there. Silent apart from the sound of their feet churning leaves and bits of fallen stick.

'I still can't believe you're doing this,' Skye said, ducking beneath a low-hanging branch. 'I'll have to come up with something nice in return, as a thank you.'

She's offering herself on a plate. 'The pleasure's all mine.' He hoped that hadn't sounded too sleazy. The girl didn't appear to be offended. Was acting as she had only moments earlier. *She's used to dirty talk.*

'And your secret about us doing this together is safe with me, don't you worry.'

Why would I worry? You'll never speak to another person again. In fact, you should get as much talking done as you possibly can, right now, and before it's too late.

'Dr Wellman?'

He was gone.

Skye turned in all directions. 'Don't do that, please. Don't scare me.'

He'd already prepared his wares – the time spent in his office – and took the needle and syringe from his coat pocket, holding them out of sight behind his back. 'Sorry about that,' he said, stepping from behind the trunk of a towering oak. 'Not as easy to get under these low-hanging limbs when you're my height. You were saying.'

'For a minute then I thought – *Ouch!*' Skye pulled a face and put a hand to her shoulder.

'What's the matter? Are you okay?'

She was rubbing the area with a circular motion. 'Feels like I was stung by a bee.'

'Not at this time of night. Not at this time of year, in fact.' Wellman shook his head. 'Do you think a thorn or something might have got inside your coat when you pushed through those bushes back there?'

'Something did.' Her hand hovered in mid-air. 'I feel a bit weird, actually.'

He hadn't brought the Schimmelbusch mask with him this time. Hadn't yet replaced the bottle of Sevoflurane broken at Coco the Clown's place. Couldn't therefore breathe his current victim down and make it easy for himself. He had to keep her walking. Occupy her until he saw the final telltale signs. 'How is it now?'

'It's not painful anymore. I just don't feel right.'

'Are you allergic to anything you know of?' he asked, sounding concerned.

'Not that I'm aware. Shit.' She was slurring her words. Swaying on her feet. 'Doctor: that bee?'

'It wasn't a bee sting.' His voice had changed; concern quickly replaced by a tone more associated with contempt. The whore had gone into the woods at night, all alone with a man more than twice her age. That was tantamount to signing her own death warrant. He showed her the syringe. Held it between finger and thumb, letting it swing by the needle in front of her pretty face.

'What have you done?' That's what she tried to say.

He understood her. Filled in the blanks. 'I'm making you a better person. Not that you'll understand, of course.'

'*You* killed those women.' She attempted a scream but didn't manage it.

He'd timed the revelation perfectly. Was counting down the minutes in his head. Only a matter of seconds now. 'Can you outrun me?' he asked. 'A young slip of a thing like you should be able to.'

'*Please,*' was the last word she spoke.

'I'll give you a ten-second head start,' he said, prodding her in the small of the back with a finger. 'One.' He watched her stagger off into the darkness, two steps forward for every one she took sideways. He closed his eyes and listened. Knew she wouldn't get far. When he heard her fall to the ground, he followed like a viper locating its prey. When he got there, he stood astride her twitching body and undid the front of his trousers. 'I *definitely* have something a bit different for you.'

25

'We need to stop meeting like this.' Jenkins was stood next to the naked corpse of a twenty-something woman. 'People are going to start talking.' It was a lame opening line, but then again, gallows humour was what got a murder squad detective through a harrowing day. 'Same killer,' she said, noting the crude chest carving.

'No doubt about it.' Sioned Williams got up off the floor, circles of black mud staining the knees of her coveralls like the rings around a Panda Bear's eyes. 'He raped her this time,' she said, pointing to smears of blood on the woman's inner thigh. 'Looks like you were right about the level of violence escalating with each attack.' Williams wrote something on the outside of an evidence bag before handing it to another member of her team. 'What the hell is he going to do to his next victim?'

Jenkins had no idea. Didn't want to think that far ahead. 'Did he leave a specimen?'

'Used a condom by the looks of things,' Williams said, 'and took it with him as far as I can tell.'

Jenkins's eyes wandered from the familiar breast-carving, to more red lettering, this time on the young woman's bare abdomen. 'What does it say?' she asked, angling her head both ways to get a better look.

Williams squatted. 'There's a number four. *Here*,' she said, using a finger to write in the air above the carving. 'And that's an *OF*, I think.'

Jenkins moved side-on to the body and squinted to see if that helped. 'And the last bit; the squiggly thing?'

'I'd say it was a question mark. Meaning – *four of how many*, perhaps?'

'What was that?' Reece poked his head through the flap of the tent, his gaze passing from the victim to the two women and then back again. The corpse's limbs were perfectly straight – not like she'd fallen to the floor in an untidy heap – but as though she had been carefully positioned after death. Some of her clothing was scattered next to her body. A shoe. Underwear. And a coat. He'd seen other items on the wet grass outside, guarded by numbered yellow cones.

'He's messing with us now, boss.' Jenkins waited for the DCI to enter before pointing out the additional carving in the flesh of the abdomen. 'Only thing is: it says four, not three.'

'There *are* four.' Reece told them about Twm Pryce's recent visit to the cottage. About the pathologist not screening for the metabolites of Suxamethonium Chloride. The request to exhume Megan Lewis, and ACC Harris's point-blank refusal to even entertain the idea. He took a deep breath and exhaled slowly, acutely aware that both Jenkins and Williams were watching. Not wanting a repeat performance of his reaction to the Harlan Miller crime scene, he took another breath and counted from five back to one before letting it out, as Patricia Beven had taught him. He reached beneath his coveralls in search of his phone, patting both hips front and back until he found it.

'What are you going to do now?' Jenkins asked. 'This means Twm's right, doesn't it?'

Reece turned his back on them, and when Chief Superintendent Cable answered, went at her without warning; about how ACC Harris was wrong, and that she should ring him again and insist they get the exhumation request started without further delay.

'What did she say?' Jenkins asked when he'd finished. 'Did she go for it?'

'Fucking idiots.' Reece looked for somewhere to hurl the handset, then thought better of it. He put a gloved hand to his forehead and counted five back to one, a second time.

Sioned Williams moved away, looking busy again.

'You two finish up here,' Reece said, using his free hand to sweep back the flap at the front of the tent.

Jenkins followed a few steps. 'And you're going where?'

He didn't stop or turn around to face her. 'It's probably best you don't get involved.'

Reece sat in his car outside a red-brick bungalow with matching garage door. On a rectangular plate next to the front window it read, *1 Park Place,* the address Twm Pryce had given him the other night. He'd just finished speaking with the coroner – hadn't bothered checking with Chief Superintendent Cable, or ACC Harris – and had news for the dead girl's family.

With a great deal of apprehension, he got out of the car and made his way up the crazy-paved garden path towards the front door.

He didn't need to knock when he got there; two sad faces on

the other side of the window watching every step he took towards them. One disappeared suddenly, only to reappear in the doorway a few moments later.

With introductions over, Reece went inside. But once there wasn't at all sure how to get started with such a grim tale. How to tell the grieving parents that *this* would happen with or without their consent. Life as they'd previously known it was over, and what news he'd brought with him would undoubtedly make things ten times worse for them.

Friends and family members would already have been encouraging the parents to move on; telling them that Megan wouldn't have wanted them grieving this way. The do-gooders, that is. The know-it-alls. The fucking experts. People who'd never been through anything this terrible. People who thought you could snap out of your deepest nightmares as easily as you could a hypnotic trance.

But Reece knew only too well that no matter how loud the finger-click, the nightmare was next to impossible to escape. He cursed himself for not having the forethought to bring the Family Liaison Officers with him. Those FLOs were worth their weight in gold at times like these.

'There's sugar in the bowl.' Mrs Lewis put a plastic tray on the kitchen table. It looked like the type you'd find in a school canteen, or motorway service station – dark brown and devoid of any pattern. 'Biscuits there,' she said, pointing to a small plate. The woman's eyes looked as though she'd recently been attacked with pepper-spray, her hands shaking enough to spill a small amount of coffee from two of the three floral mugs.

Reece rescued his from the puddle and stirred in two sugars. He took a sip and began. 'There's no easy way to say this, I'm afraid.' Putting the mug down, he reached for Mrs Lewis's hand. 'But I've every reason to believe that Megan was murdered.' He tightened his grip when the woman tried to pull away. Stood and put an arm around her shoulder when she fell apart. If he cried with her, he knew he wouldn't stop. 'I'll catch him,' he said, composing himself. 'You have my word on that.' He went back to his chair and sat down. 'But I need you to work with me on this.'

'No. No way,' Mr Lewis said when Reece had finished telling them about his conversation with the coroner. 'Not my Meg. Not that.'

'I can imagine—'

'No, you can't,' the woman said, reaching for another handful of paper tissues. 'You're trained to say such things. You have no idea how we feel.'

Reece let it pass. No point in him going over the same old ground every time someone said something similar. It never helped any when he did. 'The coroner had to be informed of the new findings – about the paralysing agent found in the tissue of the other victims. There was no choice. We *had* to tell him about Megan.'

'Get out of our house.' Mr Lewis stood, his chair toppling over onto the tiled floor. He made no effort to reach for it, and stopped Reece when he tried.

'Did Megan ever mention being followed home from work?'

'Out!'

'She's waiting for you upstairs,' George, the desk sergeant, said. 'And spitting piss when I saw her last.'

Reece slowed as he walked through the foyer of the police station. 'Who is?'

'Chief Superintendent Cable. Not just her, but the ACC went up there a little while ago.' The desk sergeant rolled his eyes. 'What've you been up to this time, Brân?'

'*Me?*' Reece said when he got to the door at the foot of the stairs. They both laughed. And then he was gone, taking the steps two at a time as always.

'The chief super wants to see you,' Ginge said on first sight of him. 'She looked a bit miffed, to tell the truth.'

'Did she now.'

Ginge studied the ceiling tiles with one eye closed. 'Seething. That's a better word for it. Yeah, she was *seething*.'

'Is that coffee fresh?' Reece asked, swilling a mug under the hot tap. 'And where's Jenks?'

'Said she's gone to get some stuff for tomorrow's briefing. Did you hear me, boss? The chief super's waiting upstairs.'

'I did, Ginge. But that doesn't mean I have to go sprinting up there like some first-year at school.'

'Right you are, boss.'

'They're not like us, that lot,' Reece said, settling on the edge of the newbie's desk. He plunged a finger in his coffee and chased something around the surface of it. 'Not proper coppers.'

'I don't get you?'

'*Degrees*. They've all got degrees. Like that's something to be proud of.'

Ginge looked like he might still not be following. 'I've got a degree,' he said. 'In History and Fine Art.'

'And I bet Billy Creed and his kind are shitting themselves because of that.' Reece put the mug and its drowning fly to one side and got up off the desk. 'Upstairs you said?'

Ginge nodded and watched him leave.

When Reece got there, he could see them through the glass of Cable's office window. Her, sat leaning on elbows. Harris, prowling nearby like an overfed lion. 'Mary, how's it going?' Reece said, passing the PA's desk.

'Oh, you can't go in there yet,' the woman said on sight of

him. 'Chief Superintendent Cable asked that you take a seat over there when you arrived.' She pointed towards a line-up of what might have been IKEA furniture, in greys and oranges mostly.

Reece didn't stop. 'It'll save wear and tear on the upholstery if I go straight in.'

The PA stood and chased after him.

Catching hold of the door handle and opening it all in one noisy movement, Reece entered while Harris was still in mid-flow. 'Afternoon, both.'

Cable looked up from where she was, then at the woman who was now stood tugging at the DCI's sleeve. 'You were told to wait outside until we were ready for you.'

'Wasn't her fault,' Reece said.

'It's okay, Mary,' Cable told the flustered PA. 'That will be all, thank you.'

'Close the door,' Harris said, 'and sit down.'

'I'd rather stand, if it's all the same with you, sir.'

The ACC ran a hand over his Brylcreemed mullet. 'I don't give a fuck what you'd rather do. Get your arse on that chair. Now!'

Reece sat; took a pen from his pocket and tapped out a tune on his knee. Harris glared at him, insisting he stop. The pen was put away in the jacket pocket of his suit. 'I'm sensing a problem.'

Although the comment was mostly directed at Cable, it was ACC Harris who answered. 'Oh, there's a problem all right.' He came closer, shaking with rage, bent at the waist and stared deep into Reece's eyes. 'And I'm looking at it.'

Reece studied an unruly monobrow, wondering why it was the man had so far done nothing about it. 'This got anything to do with the exhumation order?'

'You know damn well it has,' Harris said, still invading the DCI's personal space. 'Didn't I already make it perfectly clear that we were doing no such thing? That there's no reason to exhume that poor girl. Mostly, because she's already had a post-mortem carried out by the most senior forensic pathologist we have available to this force.'

Reece nodded. 'The very same man who came out to Brecon on the weekend to tell me he thought he'd made a mistake. That's right,' he said when Harris glanced at Cable. 'Twm Pryce wants this second post-mortem as much as I do.'

'What?' Harris straightened and took a step or two rearwards.

'The chief super told you this already, sir. I was here in this very office when she made the call.' The ACC moved about the room as though in a daze. 'But I think you were more interested in bollocking me over the Billy Creed thing,' Reece said. 'Maybe you didn't hear what she was saying?'

The combover got more attention. The area in front of Cable's desk walked in both directions. 'But an exhumation of all things...'

'I have to agree with my officer,' Cable said, getting up. 'With the case developing so rapidly, DCI Reece was right to inform the coroner and family.'

Harris snatched his service hat from a hook on the wall. 'Sort this mess out,' he said without looking at either of them.

When at last they were alone, Reece whistled through his teeth. 'Thanks for that. I'm grateful for your support.'

'Oh, don't be,' Cable said, swinging the office door closed with a loud bang. 'I haven't even *started* on you yet.'

26

Ffion Morgan was sat in one of the hospital's waiting rooms. Though not there to witness a post-mortem examination on this occasion, she could still have done with a vomit bowl wedged between her knees. She was shaking and couldn't stop. Even Josh's strong arm around her shoulders did little to make her feel safe. She'd have swapped this for anything, including a day downstairs with the dead. The thought sent her mind into sudden overdrive. *The Dead.*

Wasn't that going to be *her* anytime soon? Another statistic. Another helpless victim of the dreaded BRCA gene.

She listened to names being called out by a short nurse dressed in green scrubs; women vacating their seats with the same look of dread on their faces as Morgan did. Some came back to wait for who only knew what. Others, she never set eyes on again.

When they called her name, her legs refused to move at first. She looked to Josh for help. Where the hell was that vomit bowl? And what on Earth was she doing in a place like this?

She'd made this walk so many times before. But only in the darkest of nightmares. She'd get to the consulting room, where the doctor would do his best to smile and put her at ease. But try as he might, she always knew what he was about to say. He'd pass a death sentence. Tell her how little time she had left. That she should get her life affairs in order. Then he'd say he was sorry, that it was nobody's fault; not even her mother's, or *hers* before that.

Some people just got dealt a bad deck.

'You don't have to come,' she told Josh. 'It's not fair. There's no need for you to listen to this.'

He held her tight and kissed her before speaking. 'This is you and me together. Soulmates, remember.'

A nurse took them into a room that was smaller than Morgan had expected. It was very white in there, except for a black examination couch pushed against the far wall. The doctor was sat side-on to a wooden desk, no doubt rehearsing his awkward speech.

When Morgan looked, she saw no box of tissues waiting. And neither doctor nor nurse were avoiding eye contact.

'Take a seat,' the doctor said after checking who Josh was. He wasted no time and hit her with it, ready or not. 'It's good news,' he said with a wide smile. 'All clear.'

'What? I'm okay?'

He nodded. 'The biopsies showed no sign of malignancy.'

Morgan didn't hear much more than that, bent at the waist as she was, sobbing. Josh wasn't much better. She sat up straight, suddenly worried again. 'Are you sure you've got the right patient? I mean you read about this sort of thing all the time, don't you? About how they give a patient their results and then–'

The doctor reached a hand and put it on hers. 'You don't have breast cancer.'

Morgan got up and walked about. Everything was a blur. 'Oh my God.' She laughed. Then cried. Vomiting came last of the three.

'Someone's gonna sleep well tonight,' the health care assistant said before leaving in search of a mop and bucket.

'The forensic sweep on the Gantry house came up empty,' Jenkins said. She'd waited for Reece to return from his outing upstairs before feeding back the news to the rest of the team. She didn't dare ask how it had gone up there, but given the look on the DCI's face, it'd quite obviously been an experience he'd rather avoid in future.

He accepted the lukewarm coffee that was waiting for him, but didn't as yet take a sip. 'And you found no correspondence from the son. No letters, photographs, nothing?'

'Zilch,' she told him. 'Other than a diary that Ginge has been checking through this morning.'

'Find anything?' Reece asked over his shoulder.

'Might be nothing,' Ginge replied, 'but the initials FB crop up in it from time-to-time. Could be some reference to Facebook, I suppose.' He shrugged, looking like he knew he was clutching at straws.

'Just the initials. No message?'

'Nothing more than that, boss.'

'Okay, I want Molly Gantry's name and image splashed across all media outlets,' Reece said. 'Television, newspapers. Even get the local radio stations involved. Someone might well recognise this woman if she's been out and about with him.'

'If she's alive, that is,' Jenkins said. 'There's nothing to say she's in any way involved in this, and might well be a victim herself. Especially if childhood abandonment was a motive.'

Reece knew there was every possibility that might be true. 'Okay, let's move on,' he said, checking his watch. 'Did you get a match on those rogue fibres you found on Sandra Cole's clothing?'

Sioned Williams shook her head. 'Only that they came from a black jogging suit. Bad news is, those garments are common to a dozen or more supermarket outlets you could take your pick from. And there were no prints on the knife, or anywhere else we tested for that matter. I'm thinking we might have run a blank on this one.'

'He's one careful so-and-so,' Reece said. 'Even at the rape scene, we got nothing.'

Williams nodded slowly. 'Meticulous and very organised, I'd say.'

'What does that tell us about him, Agent Starling?' Reece's question was aimed at Jenkins; a response to her previous admission of interest in profiling techniques.

She shot him her best *sod-off* look, but answered anyway. 'That our killer is likely to be a high-functioning individual.'

'Employed?'

'Look, boss, I've no formal training in any of this, and could be completely *off-piste* with everything I'm saying.'

'Humour me,' Reece said. 'Do you think he's employed?'

Jenkins took a deep breath. 'I'd imagine so. Able to mix in professional circles, although awkwardly around women in all probability. And that might spill over into his private life as well.'

'Not married then?'

'*Mmm...*' She hunched her shoulders under the effort of her answer. 'Some serial killers hold down perfectly normal relationships – wife, kids, the lot. Others are loners, or outcasts, even.' She approached the evidence board and trailed a finger over a few of the photographs pinned to it. 'Megan Lewis, if you're right, and Poppy Jones for sure, were killed in a way that was made to look like natural causes.'

'Meaning?'

'That their deaths were personal to him and not meant for a wider audience.'

'But that quickly changed,' Ginge reminded her. 'Look at what he did to Sandra Cole, and then Skye Dean. If that wasn't two fingers up at everyone.'

'He's lost focus,' Jenkins said. 'Would likely have started out with a clear-cut reason for what he's doing. Something that would have made sense to him, if not to most normal people. Then, as his mental health deteriorated further, he's become less able to control himself. Take Megan and Poppy, for example: they were paralysed. He could have done anything he wanted to those girls, but didn't. Maybe he was forced to act violently towards Sandra Cole and got a kick out of it. It was then only a matter of time before he combined control, violence, and sex, as a method of killing.'

Ginge was following along as best he could. 'But surely the killer's behaviour at work would change too. Wouldn't he be visible among the normal employees there?' He used the first two fingers of each hand to place inverted commas around the word, *normal*.

Jenkins half-nodded. 'Until now, his professional and private lives have likely been kept very much separate. I bet he was still functioning at a high level at work.'

'And now?' Reece asked. 'You think that might have changed?'

Jenkins thought long and hard. 'Starting to, probably. But let's hope no one points that out to him, because if those lines blur, then he won't think twice about dealing with it in the only way he knows.'

$\sim$

There was a dull knocking sound coming from the underside of the coffin lid. Knock, knock, knock, it went for all to hear. But none did, except Reece. He turned onto his other side – a dream not of Rome this time, but of a wet and grey graveyard somewhere – and cocked his ear to what he felt sure was a woman's voice. 'Can't you hear that?'

The girl's mother put a finger to her lips.

The dour-faced vicar shook his head.

Taking a few steps nearer the gaping hole in the ground, Reece asked, 'Are you all deaf?' but again got no response. 'It's *her*,' he said, and repeated himself in louder tones when still no one reacted. 'Your daughter is trying to get out.'

They all stared in silence. All gave him *that* look.

And then the vicar started up again.

Knock, knock, knock. 'There she is,' Reece said. 'Let her out, why don't you?' There were gasps and chatter from the onlookers, though none in support of the policeman who was marching towards them. 'If you won't, then *I* will.'

He saw ACC Harris pushing through the crowd, Brylcreemed combover stuck to his head like the shiniest of cowpats. 'What do you think you're playing at?' Harris demanded to know. 'That's it, you're done for this time.'

Reece looked to Chief Superintendent Cable. She was there too. 'You'll stick up for me again, won't you?'

'Go home,' she answered firmly. 'You're not needed here.'

There was laughter at the graveside; everyone mocking him in their own way.

'Fuck you!' he shouted, stood on the edge of the hole. 'Especially *you*,' he told the vicar. 'Idris and I never did like you, you pompous old sod.' Harris reached for him but slipped and fell to the floor, his combover breaking free to flop over a reddened face. Reece wondered how best to get down there. Into the hole. And how flimsy that coffin lid might be under his weight. He certainly didn't want to go crashing through it and injure the poor girl.

'Jump,' she called as though aware of what he was trying to accomplish. 'I've moved to one side now the drug has worn off.'

'I'm coming,' he said, taking a small landslide of earth and grit with him, and was careful to step only on the outer edges of the coffin when he got there. 'You're going to be safe.' Busy releasing the first of six thumbscrews holding down the lid, he felt something hit his back. At first, he thought it might have started raining again. Hail maybe? That's what it felt like. But no, this was something distinctly heavier. 'What the hell are you doing?' he asked, raising an arm against the shower of falling earth.

Harris peered into the hole. 'You were warned.'

Cable came alongside and shook her head. 'If only you'd listened.'

Next was the turn of the vicar. He made the sign of the cross and then walked away in silence.

Reece dropped to his knees and worked the last of the creaking thumbscrews loose. 'Look!' he shouted, and lifted the lid. 'Do you see what I was trying to tell you?'

'That's not my daughter,' said Mr Lewis.

The man's wife appeared a moment later. 'Not *her* at all.'

'What are you both talking about?' Reece turned his head away from them. Put a hand to his open mouth and froze. The girl wasn't alive. Neither was she Megan Lewis. He could see that too. Anwen stared at him – or would have done had the holes in her upper face contained eyeballs and not dirt 'n' worms. Her lips were retracted from yellowed teeth, held that way in something of a sinister grin. She was grabbing at his leg. Gripping hold of his trousers.

An engine started up on the wet ground above, the sound of a mini digger momentarily taking Reece's mind off the rotting corpse. 'I'm still down here,' he called to the driver of the digger. 'Get me out.' He pulled his leg free of his dead wife's hand and tried to climb the wall of the grave. But instead of the hole being the regulation three to four feet deep, it was twice that depth and sinking fast.

A bell tolled in the distance. Loud and slow.

Was it for him?

Did they think he was dead?

He opened an eye. Just one at first. Next, the other. Releasing his tight grip on the pillow, he grabbed for his phone from the nightstand – 4.30am – a new day. Throwing his legs over the side of the bed, he yawned deeply and let the rest of his body catch up in its own time before getting out onto his feet.

It would have to be a short run this morning.

In less than two hours he was due at the local cemetery. An appointment with the dead.

27

They were there to exhume Megan Lewis's body. It was just after 6am and semi-dark still. A thick frost had settled overnight. One that clung to the leading edges of the headstones like a sprinkling of silver glitter.

Angry with himself for not having worn a second pair of socks, Reece went in search of the man from the local authority. In his peripheral vision he saw a line of waiting cars, including a black Jag carrying Harris, Cable, and the girl's parents. Nodding as he went past them, he didn't stop to talk.

Reece could feel the parents' eyes boring into the back of his head with all manner of emotion, notwithstanding contempt. But this wasn't for *his* benefit. Not theirs either. This was for the girl. Their daughter. If Megan *had* been murdered – and he was as sure as he could be that she had – then she deserved justice like anyone else. Someone had to pay for prematurely ending her young life, and tearing apart what appeared to be a normal loving family. He couldn't understand why they still refused to accept that *this* was the only way to proceed, given the circumstances.

'I'm Detective Chief Inspector Reece,' he told the man from the council when he'd found him, and produced formal identification when asked.

'I'm Mr Squire,' the man said, stamping each foot in turn. 'Another ten minutes or so to kick-off.'

Reece leaned in close and spoke into the man's ear. 'You might want to show some respect, or you and me are going to fall out.'

Squire stiffened. 'I didn't mean anything by it. Turn of phrase, that's all.'

'How old are you?'

'What's that got to do with–'

Reece caught and pinched the man's elbow. 'It's a simple enough question.'

'Aargh. Fifty-five,' Squire replied, trying to break free.

'Wife and kids?'

'*No.*'

'Thought not,' Reece said, letting go.

Despite the early hour, there was already a heavy press presence on the peripheries. Not that the journalists and camera crews would have been able to see much, the grave being shrouded by a large white tent.

Stood just outside the flimsy structure were four men: two leaning on dirty shovels, the others sharing a smoke and bemoaning the state of the hard ground.

The man from the council checked his watch and said, 'It's time to begin.' He glanced at Reece as though seeking approval for his choice of words. When he got none, he produced a clipboard and set about checking details against those contained on the licence. 'And to which mortuary will she be taken?' he asked when most of the blank bits had been completed with dates, times, and signatures.

'The University Hospital in Cardiff,' Reece told him.

'Says here, you'll be re-interring the body later today.' The man looked up from his paperwork. 'That's very unusual.'

'Tox screens are all we need,' Reece said. 'I don't want this going on a second longer than it has to.'

'Fair enough.' Another date and signature were added to the pile. 'Today it is then.'

Once the vicar – Reece checked: not the one from the previous night's dream – was done with prayers, the two men with shovels entered the tent and broke the ground. Even from within the canopy, the sound of digging woke the resident crows, sending them into a frenzy of morning conversation.

It took almost twenty minutes for them to get down there. Until shovel struck wood. A large mound of earth set one side of the grave, a green carpet on the other, waiting for the coffin to be raised from its resting place.

Next to the flap of the tent was a larger casket that would protect the fragile cargo during its short journey across the city by private ambulance.

When Reece started back to his car, the black Jag and its occupants were already gone.

By the time Reece got over to the mortuary, the outer casket was already open, Megan Lewis's coffin resting on a wheeled trolley next to an empty extraction table. There was a hive of activity on the other side of the glass screen, most of it led by Dr Cara Frost. She was talking. Gesticulating. Quite clearly issuing instructions, though as yet, had not flicked the switch that would enable onlookers in the gallery to hear a word of what she said.

Stood next to Reece was Dr Twm Pryce. The man looked as

though the world was resting heavily on his shoulders. 'What a terrible thing,' he said, watching them lift Megan out of the coffin, positioning her for examination.

Some in the cutting room reacted to the noxious odour that came with her by turning their noses away. Not so Cara Frost, who took both control and the head end.

Pryce ran a handful of fingers through his neat silvered hair while they unwrapped Megan Lewis. 'I'm going to resign when this is over. Regardless of outcome.'

Reece turned. 'Why the hell would you do that?'

'Because I'm losing my touch, Brân.' Pryce pointed. 'Look at Cara. I was once like that: youthful, enthusiastic, and as keen as they come.'

'You couldn't have known about the paralysing drug. No one could.'

'Cara did.'

'But only because she had a hunch.'

'And that's my point. A little while ago, that would have been me.' Pryce stood and went closer to the glass. 'I've made my mind up, Brân. It's been coming a while.'

'What will you do?'

'Days off are for fishing. Same as they always were.'

'Not all day, every day.'

'I'll keep the evenings for drinking good whisky in Brecon.' The pathologist smiled. Or at least attempted to. 'That's if you're willing to spend time with a useless old codger?'

Reece put his hands in his pockets. 'You know you're welcome any time you want, Twm. But retirement...' He puffed his cheeks.

'When will *you* go?' Pryce asked without looking at him.

'Me? Ah, I don't know. The sharks are circling again. Cable really went for me yesterday. And Harris, well *he* thinks I'm–'

'A brilliant detective,' Pryce interrupted. 'Said so himself. Made me promise to keep schtum, though.' He tapped his nose. '"*The best he's ever known*," were his exact words.'

'Maybe it *is* time for you to go,' Reece said with half a laugh. 'You're barking mad.'

'True as I'm standing here before you,' Pryce insisted. 'He has no issue with your competence.'

Reece scoffed. 'He's got one hell of a way of showing it.'

For a moment, Pryce looked like he was struggling for the right words. Then ready or not, he said it anyway. 'Get yourself well, Brân.' He reached for Reece's arm. '*That's* their concern.'

'Did they put you up to this?' Reece pulled away, then increased the distance between them. 'You of all people.'

'I'm speaking as a friend.'

'I'm fine, Twm. The Italians nailing Anwen's killer has put me in a much better place these last few days.'

'But you *are* still going to counselling?'

'Yeah, for what it's worth.'

'Glad to hear it.'

Reece turned to the other man briefly. 'Will you give it a rest now, they're ready to start by the looks of things.'

There was an audible click from the public address system on the walls to their sides, as well as from a smaller set of speakers on the floor by the glass. It crackled and popped momentarily before Dr Cara Frost formally acknowledged them. 'We're ready if you are.'

All members of the cutting-room team wore full-length fluid-repellent gowns, gloves, and white helmets with visors that looked more suited to use by riot squads than they did anything like this.

Reece wasn't entirely sure he *was* ready, but waved a hand and nodded anyway. 'In your own time,' he told her.

It began with a walk-around and visual inspection of the naked corpse, Frost speaking clearly as she worked. He heard her say that early putrefaction was present. As was discolouration and bloating of the abdomen. The face was so swollen that the tongue and eyeballs protruded under the pressure of gas built up behind them. But the eyeballs *were* there nevertheless. There was fermentation on the thighs and forearms, evidenced by the presence of white slimy mould. They took photographs – lots of them – swabs from all body orifices, together with combings and cuttings of both pubic and head hair. 'I don't suppose you'll be able to find a needle track?' Reece said.

Frost shook her head. 'I'm not hopeful. We'll take some brain tissue and muscle biopsies. The bladder will be empty from the first post-mortem examination, but I'll take a good look when I get inside,' she said, reaching for a knife. 'Who knows, we might get lucky with a few tissue scrapings.'

Dr Richard Wellman was sat at home watching the early evening news. The feature headline was that the police now believed there to be four, not three victims of the stalker, though they neglected to disclose what had led them to that conclusion.

The newsreader told the public that the first girl's name was Megan Lewis: a twenty-something-year-old nurse – yada, yada – working at the University Hospital in Cardiff.

But *he* knew that already. Of course he did. Given that he'd been solely responsible for her untimely death.

He closed his eyes and recalled his favourite bit with the girl he referred to as his *prototype*...

. . .

He'd rolled off the bed and stood over Staff Nurse Lewis while she lay there dying. Stared into eyes he knew were pleading with him to share more air. '*Don't be frightened,*' he'd said. '*I'm here with you all the way.*'

She didn't gasp.

Nor did she struggle.

It was very peaceful, in fact.

Nurse Lewis simply went a darker shade of blue, then died.

The television images were of the exterior of a white tent set against grey headstones and distant hills. There were people stood nearby. One of them looked over his shoulder and stared into the camera. It was the policeman. The detective.

'You think you know,' Wellman said, tapping an empty wine glass against his teeth. He gave as good as he got, unwilling to blink until Reece looked away.

The reporter went on to explain to the morons at home what exhumation meant; why it had been applied for; and how the family must be feeling as they watched on.

A right fucking expert, if ever there was one.

But would they find traces of Sux this far down the line?

Of course they would. They knew what to look for now he'd given them enough practice to get good at it.

And there's plenty more to come. The pretty counsellor, for example. She knew way too much. Was starting to piece it all together. The medical director too, if he probed any deeper than he already was.

Wellman drummed his fingers on the armrest of the chair, a worrying thought suddenly crossing his mind. Were they all in this together? The medical director had sent him to the counsellor, who in turn was in cahoots with the detective. He knew that because he'd seen Reece going into the Cathedral Road offices. Even spoke with him outside.

Yes, they were in this together. It was a trap. Another trap.

He rose from the chair and made his way upstairs, the back of a hand pressed tight to his nose. Pulling the shirt-collar across the lower half of his face, he opened the bedroom door and gagged. 'Mother, it's time I got you buried.'

28

Mother peeked out of an eight-inch gap in the zipper of a hospital body bag. Just her face and a few well-fed maggots. The mattress she lay on took pride of place on the centre of the bedroom floor, safely contained within its original sealed sheet of clear plastic. Wellman had been careful to take the carpet up beforehand and store it in the spare room. The same was true of the bedroom furniture; only that had understandably required more effort on his part.

He knelt over the thick black bag, coughing and gagging with every stinking breath his body forced him to take. 'It needn't have ended like this,' he said, pulling the metal zipper closed to its end-point. 'All you had to do was love and bring me up as the son I am.' He tapped her cheek through the shiny material; a gesture he conducted heavy-handedly.

He got up to fetch a roll of packing-tape and long scissors from a drawer in the other room, a few wayward maggots crunching underfoot as he set off.

Sliding the black bag onto a separate sheet of clear plastic laid out on the boarded floor, he rolled *it* and its contents side-to-side. Five minutes later and Mother was all wrapped up like an insect cocooned at a spider-feast. Leaning back on his haunches, he let the tape and scissors fall to the floor, exhausted and out of breath.

It was done.

She was ready to go. And not a moment too soon.

He threw open the bedroom windows and gulped lungfuls of fresh air. Kept his head out there for as long as he dared before closing it again. Perhaps the time of year had something to do with it, but there were far fewer flies to get rid of than he'd expected. The cloying smell of death on the other hand – *that*, would remain with him for evermore.

Wellman didn't like being forced to move her. Knew that mistakes were more likely when actions were influenced by others. But the detective was already closer than he would have liked, and that worried him.

Grasping Mother by what might have been the ankles, he dragged her across the bedroom and out onto more sheeting that continued all the way up to the front door. He pondered how best to get her down the stairs with the minimum of fuss – put a foot against her head and pushed – sending her on her way like some ghoulish tobogganist.

He followed, careful not to slip on the plastic and do himself an unfortunate injury.

Back at the Midnight Club, Billy Creed was busy knocking seven shades of shit out of Kyle Cartwright. Jimmy Chin stood in front of the office door, blocking all possibility of escape. Cartwright ducked and dived, all the while spitting blood and pleading for his life.

'I told you to torch the fucking thing.' The veins in the

gangster's neck looked like lengths of metal cable bulging beneath his tattooed skin.

'We did, Billy. We took it up the water works and put a match to it, like you said.' That got Cartwright a hard palm-slap to the earlobe. '*Fuck. Aargh.* Shit, I've gone deaf.'

Creed pushed his face into the other man's. 'There's cameras all round there, you useless twat.'

'Nobody saw us,' Cartwright lied. 'Nobody at all.' The rolled-up newspaper caught him square on the bridge of the nose, showering Jimmy Chin with a fine spray of blood.

'Don't lie to me,' Creed said, swinging the thing about like a crazed swordsman. 'Security were there.'

Still playing for time, Cartwright whined, 'Security?'

Creed unrolled the newspaper and went straight to the page in question. The other pages, he tossed onto the floor in temper. 'See if you can't win first prize for guessing who this pair are.' The image was in familiar black and white: a large van with flames spewing out of the cabin, its centrepiece. A smaller van – one with *Security* written up the side in bold lettering – waited a safe distance away. 'You recognise them yet?' Creed asked, punching a hole in the paper where Albino Ron's head had just been. 'No fucker there, you say?' He grabbed Cartwright by the back of the neck and brought the man's head down against a raised table so hard that the wood made a splitting sound. He yanked the head up and down a second time before letting go. Reaching for his walking cane, he grimaced with the pain of it. 'You've got my knee playing up now, you little fuck!'

Cartwright said nothing about his head and pressed himself tight against the far wall of the office.

'Where's the machete?' Creed put the pointy end of the cane against the younger man's left eyeball and pressed.

'*Aargh.* It'll be burned, Billy. The whole thing went up like a bomb. Honest.'

The pressure relented by a small margin only. 'Let's hope for your sake you're right.'

Cartwright's hand hovered next to the cane, not daring to touch it.

Creed lowered his arm. 'I'm letting you off this time,' he said in a tone that bordered on being friendly. 'On account of you being Denny's brother.'

Cartwright exhaled. Made the error of relaxing just before the cane came up again, jabbing at him. His legs gave way, sending him crashing to the floor in fits of high-pitched wailing.

Creed turned to Jimmy Chin. 'Get him over to the hospital. He's got something stuck in his eye.'

Wellman's car turned full-circle almost, on a small roundabout on the outskirts of Llandaff. Past the BBC Wales studios he went, headed for Llantrisant Road and a rendezvous with a shallow grave and one hundred and fifty pounds of rotting flesh.

The houses were fewer in number the further he drove away from the city, pavements and street lamps swapped for thorny hedgerows and near-impenetrable darkness. It wasn't far off midnight, a thick cloud-base hanging low over Cardiff like some invading alien life form. It was picking to rain too, but nothing he'd call heavy, as yet.

There was very little traffic about thanks to the late hour. A few taxis, the odd car, and the last buses on their way back from town, mostly.

He was beginning to relax when he saw a police patrol car parked up at a junction just ahead. One of those BMW estate models. He scanned his dashboard: Lights on – check. Not speeding – check. Insurance and MOT – all good. He drove on, not daring to look at the driver as he went past. Using the rear-view mirror, he saw the police car pull out behind him; the occupants talking. The one in the passenger seat checking something on what looked to be an iPad-type device. Wellman drew a hand along the angle of his unshaven jawline. They were searching his details. Looking for reasons to pull him over. Just as well he hadn't used the Volvo. He banged the steering wheel with the palm of his hand and swore. *Calm yourself. They know nothing.*

The blue lights came on. No siren as yet.

Indicating left, he let his car roll to a full stop next to a raised banking; the vehicle leaning slightly towards its right-hand side. He was unlatching the seat belt when they pulled around him; the siren starting up and wailing like an injured cat as the patrol car accelerated towards the Danescourt roundabout and out of sight.

Five minutes further on and he arrived at the site of a housing *development* – if dozens of quick-build dwellings blighting an otherwise beautiful stretch of wild landscape could ever be referred to as such.

Opposite the site was a farm gate, and a sign tied to a leaning fencepost with **Private Keep Out** daubed in a hand-painted red scrawl. There were runs in the paint that made it look as though the lettering was bleeding. Wholly appropriate given the circumstances. He was in and out of the car for the shortest of hops, closing the gate behind him before driving off up the lane.

He'd previously walked this track as part of a ramblers' party many years earlier, and from what little he could see in the darkness, nothing looked to have changed much. Sure, the trees were taller, and the hedgerow fuller. But all in all, it wasn't too dissimilar given the passage of time.

He took the arcing bend slowly, lights off, eyes not yet fully accustomed to the darkness. The car rocked side to side on its squeaking suspension, deep potholes testing the mettle of the front shock absorbers. There was a turn further along on the left if memory served him correctly, leading to a dense circle of trees in a dip in the road. He wasn't wrong, and less than a minute later drove into the thick of it, two wheels coming close to slipping into a water-filled ditch.

Braking to a full stop first, he reversed into a space between two trees, got out and opened up the boot. Mother didn't smell anywhere near as bad now she was wrapped in thick plastic. But she *was* a tight fit for the small boot, and looked like a family pet curled up on a fireside rug.

An owl hooted somewhere nearby. The moon making a skittish appearance from behind its cover of cloud. With a torch and shovel, he went in search of a suitable burial site, leaving Mother on her own for now.

It wasn't long before he found one just the other side of the shorter of the two trees. The ground was softer there, water coming off the nearby fields keeping it that way. He guessed people would walk around it if they came in this direction, favouring a drier and less muddy area instead.

The spade hit a small rock, the noise travelling like a gunshot against a background of what would otherwise have been near-silence. He waited, listening for voices. Watching for movement.

When sure it was safe to do so, he started up again. More carefully this time.

Putting Mother in the narrow boot had been a much simpler task than getting her out. The plastic sheeting threatened to tear apart when he pulled at it. He stood shaking with rage before taking his fists to her, pummelling something that started off firm but soon went to soft mush under the unforgiving onslaught. He swung punches even when he was breathless. Kept going until his hands had gone somewhere beyond painful, through numb, and out the other side. Gripping the bumper of the car, he leaned his full weight on it until the lactic acid burn in his shoulders had passed. He was dripping with sweat and close to vomiting, such was the effort.

There was a dent in the sheeting where he'd thumped it. Enough of one for him to get a better grip and be able to pull Mother slightly more upright. With part of her out of the boot, it was then just a case of getting his hands round the back and pulling her towards him. She came up and over the high point of the loading bay in an arcing motion, falling to the floor at his feet with what sounded like something snapping, or coming apart.

The first couple of metres of ground were peppered with small stones, most of which tore slits in the plastic sheeting as he pulled Mother towards the grave. Once on the grass, she slid more readily. Easier still when he reached the muddier ground near the mound of earth and waiting hole. With a final exhausting shove, he got her in there, face down – though that mattered to no one, especially him.

29

R eece stared through the glass of the one-way window. 'What do you make of him?'

Dr Richard Wellman sat alone in the interview room of Cardiff Bay police station, his attention alternating between the hands on an expensive wristwatch and the battleship-grey walls of the almost-silent environment. He was alone; no legal representation required when one agrees to *pop in and answer a couple of quick questions.*

'Shifty,' Jenkins answered. 'Can't put my finger on it, but something about the man doesn't sit right with me.'

'I know what you mean.'

'And with him being an anaesthetist and all...' She arched an eyebrow.

'Another bit of good old-fashioned luck,' Reece said. 'Ginge knowing the guys who pulled him over last night.'

Jenkins nodded. 'Came across him twice. And well after midnight the second time.' She leafed through a handwritten report. 'Officially, there was nothing wrong with the car, except for there being a spade in the boot. Not that carrying a spade is a crime,' she quickly added. 'But the patrol crew got the same bad vibes we did.'

'Did they ask him about it?' Reece peered over Jenkins's shoulder and squinted, trying to get better sight of the handwritten entry.

'Told them he carried the thing during the winter months, in case it snowed.'

'You got a spade in your boot at the minute?'

Jenkins shook her head. 'Not sure I'd fit one in the back of my Fiat.'

'Me neither.'

'Maybe you should,' she told him. 'Snows a lot in Brecon, after all.'

Reece nodded as though considering it.

'This bit's interesting,' Jenkins said, working her way further through the report.

He sidestepped, still trying to get a proper look. 'What is?'

She put her finger to one of the entries and turned to look at him. 'There was fresh earth on it. On the blade and cutting edge. As well as a pair of muddy boots in a carrier bag. Our doctor's been digging – and at one o'clock in the morning.'

Reece took the report from her and read it again. 'Come on then, let's go see what he has to say for himself.'

'I'll be writing to the Police Commissioner,' Wellman said on first sight of them. 'This is beginning to feel like harassment.'

Reece settled into his seat and folded his arms. 'But you came of your own free will.'

'Even so, Detective Inspector.'

'That means you can get up and leave any time you want.'

Wellman turned his head towards the door and appeared to settle somewhat after that. 'What is it you wish to know?'

'You're happy to stay and help clarify a few queries?'

Another glance at the door. 'If you're quick about it.'

'Why did you tell my colleague you didn't know Harlan Miller?' Jenkins asked. She'd already drawn a large maze-shape on a notepad and was dragging the nib of her pen through it.

Wellman stood, his thighs banging against the table as he got up. 'I've already answered this.' He looked to Reece. 'I didn't agree to come here to go over old ground.'

Jenkins raised both hands in apology. 'Okay, let's stick to the events of last night,' she said, waiting for him to sit down. 'One in the morning is hellish late to be driving the empty streets, don't you think?'

'I'd been at the hospital.'

'We know you hadn't,' she said. 'Already checked before coming in here.'

Reece saw Wellman's eyes narrow. His shoulders tense.

'I was working in my office.'

'Working?'

'I have trouble sleeping.' Wellman leaned forward, just slightly, looking at Jenkins's ID badge. 'What did you say your name was again?'

She gave him rank and surname only. 'Why not work from home?'

'Because the files I needed were at the hospital.' He looked to the ceiling and exhaled loudly. 'We don't take them with us, you know. There are regulations governing such things.'

Jenkins leaned until the front legs of her chair lifted an inch or two off the floor. 'I'm told you've been expecting snow.'

Wellman frowned. 'What?'

'The spade kept in the boot of your car: you told the patrol officers that it's used for shifting snow?'

A nod. Nothing more.

'Why not a shovel?' she asked. 'People use shovels for

digging themselves out of snowdrifts. Spades are for digging, aren't they?'

'And your point *is?*'

'That it's covered in mud and soil – which means you've been digging, and not making snowmen.'

Wellman stared in silence, his jaw trembling as he bit down hard.

Jenkins rested her chin on steepled fingers. 'Why don't you quit with the bullshit, Doctor, and tell us what you were doing digging holes at one in the morning.'

Wellman got to his feet a second time, only the short stretch of table separating them. He towered over her, and for a moment looked like he might say something. Do something. Then, uttering nothing at all, made his way out of there.

'Yes?'

'Ginge said you wanted to see me, boss.' Morgan stood in the DCI's office doorway looking nervous.

Reece lowered his pen and shut the file he was working on. 'Come in and close the door.'

'Am I in trouble?'

'Have you done something wrong?' He pointed to a chair. 'Relax, it's just a chat I've been meaning to have with you.'

Morgan took a seat and patted down the trousers of a charcoal-grey suit. 'Okay.'

Reece waited until she was comfortable. 'You must have been under a lot of stress lately, what with *the...*' He nodded at her chest.

'The breast lump, you mean?'

'Yeah. Must have been a tough time for both you and...'

'Josh. The scariest days of my life,' she said, swallowing hard. 'Couldn't have done it without him. Or Jenks, for that matter.'

'But it's sorted now, right?'

'So they tell me.'

'You don't look convinced.'

Resting her hands in her lap, Morgan said, 'Something like this brings everything in life into perspective, doesn't it? Shows how easily loved ones can be snapped away from you.' Her head jerked up suddenly. 'Sorry, I didn't mean to–'

'It's okay, I'm learning to talk about it.' Even though he'd looked away, he knew she was still watching him.

'What was she like: your wife?'

Reece lifted a silver frame off the desk and stared at it. 'Beautiful, inside and out.' He turned it so Morgan could get a better look. '"*Practically perfect*" as Mary Poppins would say.'

'I'm sorry for your loss.' Morgan blushed a deep crimson. 'I've been wanting to tell you that for ages, but–'

Reece drew a sharp intake of air, interrupting her. 'But I'm a moody old bastard, aren't I?'

'You certainly have your moments.' She smiled and let out the shortest of giggles. 'But you've always got our backs – no matter how tits-up things get – and that's why all of us would willingly go down fighting with you.'

He nodded. Didn't know how else to respond. 'I just wanted you to know my door is always open.'

'Understood.'

'And if you need any time off at all...'

Morgan shook her head. 'Work was the only thing keeping me active enough to not be thinking about it all day long.'

He could relate to that.

'Was there anything else, boss?'

'Not unless you have something pressing on *your* mind.'

'There was one thing. It's about this stalker.' She checked the office door was closed, but kept her voice down even though it was. 'You're probably not going to like this, but I'll put it to you anyway.'

They were sat in the station canteen, Reece poking at a lemon cheesecake with a fork.

'Did you see Wellman's expression when you mentioned Molly Gantry's name?' Jenkins asked.

'It's still half-frozen,' he said, tapping like it was the shell of a hard-boiled egg. 'Three quid they charged me for that.'

'Take it back then.'

He pushed the plate away and rubbed his hands together. 'Wellman knew her all right. No doubt about that.'

'Still denied it, though.' Jenkins picked a bit of crust off the unwanted dessert and nibbled on it. 'Where do you think she is?'

'Honestly?' He sat back and watched Jenkins take a bit more. 'In that hole he dug last night.'

'Get out of here.' People on neighbouring tables stopped what they were doing to look at them. She'd been louder than intended.

Reece waited until most had gone back to their own conversations. 'No one's seen or heard from her in over a month. No banking activity either. Ginge already checked.'

'You think he had her body stored somewhere?' Jenkins pulled a face. 'What a thought.'

Reece shrugged. 'Or maybe he's only just killed her.'

'But you let him walk?'

'And I could have detained him on what grounds?' He waited for her answer.

'*Mmm.*' Jenkins took another bit of pie crust. 'You sure you don't want this?'

'Be my guest.' Reece watched her take a knife to it, laughing when the thing broke open and showered the table with bits of lemon curd and biscuit. 'Told you it was still frozen.'

'And you weren't wrong,' she said, scooping the crumbs up into a neat pile before dropping them onto the plate. 'Penny for them.'

'What?' Reece drew his eyes away from the far wall, and an advert for homemade apple pie and custard he'd already decided to try next time.

'You're miles away.'

He came to. Forgot about desserts. 'It's Ffion.'

Jenkins looked suddenly concerned. 'Everything all right with her?'

Nodding slowly, he said, 'She's offered to act as bait for the stalker.'

'And I hope you told her where she could take the offer?'

Reece shifted in his seat. 'Of course I did.'

'For a moment then...'

'But the more I think about it–'

'No way!' People were watching again, and Jenkins wasn't getting any quieter. 'She's only just had a health scare. You can't.'

'This guy will keep killing until we stop him.'

'But that's got nothing to do with Ffion. Put a tail on Wellman if you really think it's him.'

Reece leaned his elbows on the table. 'We could always do both.'

Jenkins sat up straight, arms gripped tightly across her chest. 'I can't believe you're seriously considering risking the life of a colleague?'

'We've got the means to guarantee her safety.'

'*Guarantee?*' Jenkins was on her feet, people around them

watching the performance as they might an episode of TV drama. 'Are you mad?'

So they tell me. Reece shot out of his seat and banged a hand against the side of his head. 'Barking, if you listen to that lot upstairs.'

The remark got the full attention of Chief Superintendent Cable, who, until then, had been stood at the far end of the canteen talking with DI Adams. She broke away from her conversation and headed towards them.

'I can't believe I'm hearing this. And from *you,* of all people,' Jenkins said.

Reece watched her walk away. 'Where are you going?'

'To talk some sense into Ffion.'

He saw Cable coming down one of the aisles so beat a quick retreat before she could catch up with him, zigzagging between tables and chairs on his way out. He searched *contacts* on his phone and pressed *call.* 'Maggie,' he said into the handset, 'about that conversation we had in my office the other day...'

When he got back upstairs, he found Jenkins stood in front of the evidence board, staring at photographs. There was one of Megan Lewis: the girl they now knew it had all started with. Poppy Jones was next, followed by Sandra Cole, and then Skye Dean. Harlan Miller was there too; but in a place of his own on the board.

Jenkins reached and moved Miller's photograph next to Poppy's. 'You're involved in this somehow. Collateral damage maybe?'

'What was that?' Reece came to a halt behind her.

She looked over her shoulder. Briefly. Then ahead again. 'If you're here to talk me round, then I meant what I said – Ffion's not up to doing this.'

'Thanks for that resounding vote of no confidence, Jenks.' Morgan entered with a trio of steaming mugs. She hunted for somewhere to put them, settling on her own desk being as good as any. 'And there's me thinking you and I were mates.'

'That's not what I meant and you know it.' Jenkins went and collected one of the mugs, leaving Reece's where it was. 'This killer's a clever bastard, and I'm not letting anyone put you in danger.' She turned to the DCI and rubbed her neck. 'I've been there okay, and it wasn't my idea of fun.'

'I've told her no already,' Reece said. 'Why are you still having a go at me?'

Morgan handed him his coffee. 'I'm a trained killer, remember?' She chopped the air with her free hand. 'Bruce Ffi, you called me if I remember correctly.'

'This isn't a game,' Jenkins snapped. 'You don't get up off your arse and press *play again*. If this guy gets close enough to stick you with that drug, then it's over. Kaput. Dead.'

Morgan looked ready to continue the discussion, when Chief Superintendent Cable entered the room.

'What was that about downstairs?' she asked Reece.

'Nothing. Misunderstanding.'

'That's not how it looked to me.'

'It's sorted now,' he said, sounding irritated.

Cable turned to Morgan. 'Are you involved in whatever's going on here?'

'Well, ma'am. It's a bit. It's a–'

'She wants to play honeytrap to the killer,' Reece said, scratching his head with both hands.

Jenkins hardly let him finish. 'And we've both said a big fat no to that.'

'I'd be all right,' Morgan insisted. 'There'd be plenty of backup. Besides, I do martial arts.'

'*Did*,' Jenkins said. 'Not anymore.'

'You don't forget when you've done it for as long as I did.'

'What did you have in mind?' Cable asked, moving the conversation on.

'You can't be serious?' Reece spun a half-circle. 'She's only just back from having her *thing* done.'

'They're breasts, for Christ's sake,' Morgan told him. '*Breasts.*'

He was about to respond when the phone rang in his pocket, and he went to the other side of the room to answer it. 'Maggie, what did you find out?' When he'd hung up, he was off to the office to collect his jacket.

'We're not finished here yet,' Cable called after him.

'Sort it between the pair of you,' he said, already out the door of the incident room. 'Jenkins – with me.'

30

Reece and Jenkins met with Simon Underdown – medical director – in the man's office and not the boardroom.

Underdown placed his hands flat on the tabletop, and in answer to the policeman's question said, 'I didn't act alone, I'll have you know. There were representatives from human resources, as well as the occupational health department involved in the decision-making.'

'But you must have been concerned Dr Wellman would pose a risk to vulnerable women in his care?' Reece countered. 'Especially after everything that happened in Brussels a few months back.'

'How could you possibly know anything about that?' The man looked aghast. 'The matter was dealt with in the strictest of confidence.'

Reece mentioned nothing about Maggie Kavanagh's help on that one. 'Dr Wellman popped into the station this morning to answer a few questions for himself.'

'And what an interesting chat it was too,' Jenkins said, fiddling with the zipper of her jacket.

'You can't seriously believe that Richard is in any way involved in this terrible affair?'

'The jolly in Brussels,' Reece said, ignoring the question. 'Tell me about that.'

The medical director blinked like he might be having an epileptic fit. 'It was no *jolly*, Chief Inspector. That was a highly regarded international conference.'

Jenkins clucked her tongue and shook her head. '*Mmm.*'

Reece spoke. 'But *matey-boy* went wandering, didn't he? Found his way into the bedroom of a young pharmaceutical rep. *She* woke up with him stood over her, and pretty much screamed the place down. *He* did a runner and got caught by hotel security.' Reece paused for effect. 'Some conference that must have been.'

'I don't like your attitude, Chief Inspector.'

Reece stretched his neck across the table, emphasising his point. 'And *I* don't like people withholding information relevant to a murder investigation. So, Doctor, unless you want my team crawling all over this place like flies on shit, you're going to tell me everything I need to know about Richard Wellman.'

The medical director went to a filing cabinet, returning a few moments later with a thin folder made from blue card. He dropped the folder onto his desk and sat down. 'We sent Richard for counselling as part of the Employee Wellbeing Scheme. Transpires, his psychological downturn was related to a recent bereavement in the family.'

'Who?' Reece asked impatiently. 'The *Mother?*'

'An aunt, I believe.' The medical director peered over the top of his spectacles. 'Richard wasn't the same after she died. Had a bit of a meltdown, but refused to take time off work. Wanted to keep himself busy.'

Reece pointed at the file. 'Can we get a copy of that?'

'Not without going through the proper channels, you can't.'

The medical director closed the cover and rested a hand on top of it. 'I've already said way more than I should have.'

'I'll drive,' Reece said, getting into the battered Peugeot.

'You going to bring Wellman in again?' Jenkins asked, slamming the passenger-side door three times before the lock would properly engage.

'Not yet. We still don't have enough evidence to pass the threshold test for the CPS.'

'You could give it a punt; you never know.'

Reece turned the key in the ignition and revved the engine hard until sure it wouldn't cut out on him. 'We need more. Something tangible to link him to those murders.'

Jenkins waited while Reece fiddled with the radio, the short screwdriver poking out the front of the car's dashboard like a spare gearstick. 'Wellman wouldn't be stupid enough to keep the drug and other bits and pieces at home, surely?'

'There's only one way to know.' Reece pulled away from the parking space to begin a slow circuit of the hospital.

'But how do we get the magistrate to agree?'

He watched her from the corner of an eye, suppressing a grin as best he could. 'You're a dab hand now.'

Jenkins slumped in her seat. '*Aw*, boss. If I get caught.'

'Tell them it was an order.' He gripped the steering wheel two-handed and shifted position. 'Actually, it *is* an order. I'm ordering you to make shit up in pursuit of a search warrant. There, happier now?'

'No. Not at all, in fact.'

'Tough.'

They passed Harlan Miller's place of death. The CSI tent was long gone; the bloodstains on the tarmac floor washed away by frequent deluges of rain. Short lengths of blue-and-white crime scene tape hung limply from the cemetery railings. A yellow square next to it displayed a date and time, calling for witnesses to the **Serious Incident.**

Jenkins nodded at the sign. 'Wellman up for that as well, do you think?'

Reece kept his eyes on the road. 'What if Miller was killed because of something he heard, or saw. At work, maybe?'

'Something that made him a threat to the girls' killer, you mean?'

'Why not?'

Jenkins thought about it before answering. 'It's as good as anything else we've got.'

'Put it all down on the paperwork for the magistrate,' Reece told her.

She turned side-on to him and stared. 'You mean I'm to include fact as well as bullshit?'

'Only if you think it'll help our cause.' They turned down City Road, stop-starting in a busier flow of traffic before pulling to a complete halt behind a parked patrol car.

'Why have we stopped?' Jenkins looked in all directions.

Reece nodded at the patrol car. 'Get that lot to take you back to the station.'

'And you?' she asked, undoing the seat belt.

'I'll be on Cathedral Road.'

Reece closed the office door behind him and went across the hardwood floor to *his* chair.

'Is this the way it's going to be with you from now on?' Dr Patricia Beven asked.

'I don't get you.'

'We had an appointment yesterday.'

'Did we?' He checked for diary entries in the calendar app on his phone. 'Nothing in here,' he said with a look of concern. 'Are you sure you're not mistaken?'

Beven lowered her head to the floor, arms folded. 'God, you're incorrigible.'

'I'm *what?*' He pulled a face and waited for her to explain what that meant.

'Incapable of being reformed.'

He broke into his best smile and kept it going for as long as he could. 'That's not what you've been telling the chief super lately. "Close to cured," wasn't it?'

'"Making progress," is what I actually said.'

'We're moving in the right direction, then?'

'Slowly – though it would help enormously if you were to give me a fighting chance, Chief Inspector.'

He sighed. 'When are you going to start calling me Reece, like everyone else does?'

'When *you* stop acting like a petulant adolescent.'

'Ouch.'

'Oh, I can dig the knife far deeper than that.'

'I bet you can. And twist it too, no doubt.'

'When I need to.' Beven took a seat opposite. 'This isn't a game, okay. I run a professional set-up here. *You're* sent to me with a problem. *I* get to the root of it. *Together*, we work on the solution. *Then*, at the end of the process, *I* tell your employer you no longer pose a danger to yourself or anyone else. That's how it works.'

'I'm not here to talk about me,' he said, fiddling with his tie. 'Not today.' He waited for the penny to drop.

Beven shook her head once she realised what he was asking of her. 'I've already told you there's nothing I can say on that subject. What you're asking could get me struck off the register in no time at all.'

Reece saw no point in holding back. 'And would it help any if I told you your life might well be in danger?'

Reece stopped before he got anywhere near his office. 'Don't tell me they didn't go for it?'

Jenkins looked defeated. 'A big fat *no*, is what they said.'

'Did you tell them about our chat with the medical director? And the stuff about Brussels?'

'Of course I did. But they were still having none of it. Not without solid evidence.'

'Like another dead nurse?' Reece went a few yards further and hung his suit jacket on a hook on the back of his office door.

Jenkins raised her hands above her head. 'Don't shoot the messenger.'

'We're going to try again,' he said, dragging an empty chair up next to her. She shifted a few inches, giving him more room at the desk. 'Patricia Beven emailed the medical director earlier today – not long after you and me left his office – advising him to pull Wellman from all clinical duties with immediate effect.'

'*No shit?*'

Reece told her what he knew of the wrist-grabbing incident. 'Beven was scared, you know. Said Wellman's whole demeanour changed in a split-second. And those FB entries in the diary that you and Ginge found at the Gantry house – I think they're a reference to a woman named Freda Beck.' He watched Jenkins try to work it out for herself, then put her out of her misery when she couldn't. 'He's unwittingly made his first mistake. Beck was the name of the aunt who brought him up. He told Beven as much during one of their sessions.'

Jenkins waved her hands to get him to slow down. 'Wait.

Wait. Why would Molly Gantry write this other woman's initials in her diary?'

'Because they were in regular contact with one another.' Reece had brought the diary with him and sat thumbing through its pages. 'Frequently too, if the number of entries in here is anything to go by.'

'You think Wellman killed them both when he found out?'

Reece shook his head. 'He wouldn't have mentioned the aunt's name if that was the case. No, I think he's still in the dark over the contact they had.'

'You going to tell him?'

'Not just yet. Get Ginge to find the most recent address for Freda Beck. As well as where she's buried.'

'Not another exhumation?'

Reece winked and double-clucked his tongue at the same time. 'More of a bargaining chip. What?' he asked when Jenkins kept staring at him.

'You got your way in the end,' she said. 'ACC Harris is putting Ffion out on the streets tonight.'

31

'I was about to go home.' Wellman stood on the threshold of his office doorway, a long coat buttoned to the collar, leather satchel hanging from a shoulder. He looked irritated by the late intrusion. 'It's been a long and frustrating day,' he said, noting the corridor was empty in both directions.

'Could we go back inside?' The tone used by the medical director was professional, if not overly friendly. 'It shouldn't take long, but we do need to talk.'

'Is there a problem?' Wellman re-entered the office and lobbed a bunch of keys that landed on his desk with a heavy clunk and rattle. When he offered the other man a chair, it was without turning to face him.

The medical director appeared to be playing for time now that he was sat down. Looked unsure of himself all of a sudden. 'Difficult case?'

Wellman shook his head. 'You're well aware my theatre list went down today. You'd have been notified at your morning business meeting.' He hovered near the other man's chair and bent at the waist. 'Better for both of us if you just get to the point, don't you think?'

The medical director cleared his throat. 'The police were here earlier today. Detective Chief Inspector Reece, specifically.'

'Is that so?'

'They know about Brussels. About you and that girl in the hotel room.'

Wellman balled his fists, though out of sight of the other man. *They're all in this together. Everyone conspiring against you.* 'And how might that have happened?'

'I really don't know. Someone must have told them.' Looking up quickly, the medical director added, 'Not me, obviously.'

Don't believe him. He's been talking to the police. 'Who, then?'

'Could they have spoken to the girl herself, do you think? The rep.'

'Wasn't there a silence clause attached to that settlement figure?' Wellman asked.

The medical director nodded. 'She'd risk having to repay the whole amount if she's been talking.'

It's not the pharmaceutical rep. It's the bitch on Cathedral Road. She's working with the police – with Reece – feeding him information. 'Surely, you could have told me this over the telephone?' Wellman hadn't shifted position since their conversation had begun, and remained uncomfortably close to the other man. 'I sense there's something else on your mind.'

The medical director ran a finger round the inside of his shirt collar. 'How long have we known each other, Richard?' He continued when he got no answer. 'I received an email earlier today – from Dr Patricia Beven. She's concerned about you.'

He's in it with them. After all these years of supposed friendship, he's fucked you over. 'And just what did *she* have to say?'

'Dr Beven thinks you require more specialist help than she has to offer.'

A psychiatrist, no doubt. They're trying to ruin your good name. 'And what's your view on this?'

The medical director took a deep breath before answering. 'I'm afraid I have no alternative but to remove you from all clinical duties with immediate effect.'

'You'd do that to me? To a good friend and colleague?'

The man seemed more confident now he had it out in the open. 'I'm going to speak with the Board first thing tomorrow morning and recommend we put you on an indefinite period of sick leave.' He stood and reached to rest a hand on Wellman's shoulder. Tapped it twice. 'It's in your best interests. You *do* understand, don't you?'

'You've told them already? The Board, I mean.'

A shake of the head. 'Dr Beven and I are the only ones who know at present. We've been very discreet, I can assure you. Oh, one last thing while I'm here. I've been meaning to ask since the recent meeting. That date of birth you gave the policeman: you didn't *mean* to mislead him, did you?'

You have to stop them. Put an end to it before it's too late. When the medical director leaned forward for his coat, Wellman brought the brass lamp stand down on the back of the other man's head. There was a dull thud and a cracking sound as the underlying skull gave way under the weight of the blow. He hit the floor in an untidy heap of sprawling limbs, cerebrospinal fluid trickling from his ears and nostrils. Wellman stepped over the fitting man, stooping to relieve him of the key to his office door while he Cheyne-Stoked his last few breaths.

In the annexe was a tall stack of cardboard boxes, filing cabinets, and green painted doors that hid pipework running from the bathroom and toilets on the next floor up. In one of the cabinet drawers were a couple of spare body bags, kept there for a job such as this. The spilled brain fluid smelled worse than a wet dog. The effort of getting the dead man wrapped and zipped up, beyond exhausting. He didn't have much time – nowhere near enough to rest – the cleaning staff would be in soon, and asking them to hoover around a leaking corpse was probably beyond the call of duty.

He pushed the boxes to one side and emptied a few of the cabinet drawers before pulling the complete units away from the wall. Taking the body bag by the foot end, he dragged the medical director from his resting place in front of the office desk, to the open green doors in the cluttered annexe. There was plenty of space between the pipes, and the black bag would ensure the stench of decomposition would be safely sealed away. In the unlikely event that anything did manage to escape; it could quite easily be blamed on the botched plumbing, as usual.

No one would be any the wiser for months. Years even. And by then, he'd have long since moved the medical director to another location.

The knock at the office door wasn't entirely unexpected, but nevertheless startled him. The rattle of keys had him move quickly. 'One moment,' he called.

'Sorry. I thought the room was empty.' The young man was dressed in a maroon-coloured uniform that came close to matching the birthmark beneath his right eye. His cleaning trolley was already wedged between the open door and its scratched frame.

'I told you to wait.' Wellman squatted to lift the lamp off the floor. 'I tripped and knocked it over,' he said, placing the brass stand on a semi-circular scratch that marked its place on the desk.

'Are you sure you're okay?' The cleaner raised a hand and pointed. 'There's blood on your shirt. Did you cut yourself?'

Jordan Patterson left Wellman to whatever he was doing and took his cleaning trolley up to the fourth floor. He put a mobile phone to his mouth and cupped the other hand over it. 'Zoe, come on, speak to me,' he said, when at first there was no response. '*Please.*'

'Piss off, Jordan. Do us all a favour and jump under a bus.' The line went dead on the other side.

He stamped his foot and pressed *dial* for a second time. 'Pick up, will you.'

'I'm warning you, Jordan.'

'Don't hang up.' He took a hand from his face and held it out in front of him as though trying to stop traffic. 'Don't,' he repeated, turning in circles. 'There's some weird shit going on at the hospital at the minute.'

'It's no bed of roses back home either.' Her tone was deeply sarcastic. 'What with two bedrooms sealed off and a couple of policemen stood on the front and back doorsteps.'

He heard her speak to someone else. 'You at home now?'

'Out having a drink. Not that I need your permission.'

'At the hospital social club?'

'That's for me to know.'

Patterson recognised several sounds familiar to him. Pool balls being racked. The jukebox in the corner of the room; its volume cycling up and down mid-song with no human command to do so. And the fire door banging against the brick wall as the smokers went outside for a sneaky cigarette. Yeah, he knew where she was all right. 'Wait,' he said when she told him she was finished talking. 'Just give me a few seconds more.' He could still hear the familiar background noise. She hadn't hung up. 'Lowri won't come anywhere near me; not since the police had us in for questioning the other day.'

'She's scared of you, Jordan.'

'I didn't kill them. Neither of them. I swear to God.'

'It's not me you need to convince.'

'Do you think they'd have let me out if they thought I had anything to do with this?'

'I don't know *what* to think anymore.'

He checked the corridor in both directions. Nobody coming. 'You and me both.'

'Look, is there any point to this conversation?' she asked. 'I'm trying to have a quiet drink and calm my nerves before going home.'

'That doctor – the weird one who used to freak Poppy out by staring at her...'

'What about him?'

'Was his name Wellman?' He'd read it off the name plaque on the office door. 'Big guy. Built like a brick shithouse?'

'Yeah. Why do you ask?'

'No reason.'

'Jordan, what are you up to?'

He was almost done. 'Don't tell anyone about this conversation.'

'If you think he's involved somehow, then go to the police and tell them what you know.'

'There's something I want to check first.'

'If you won't, then I will.'

'No, don't. You can't.'

'Says who?' She hung up again without warning.

He gripped the phone in his hand, raising it to the tall window. Stopped himself from striking it against the glass. What was he thinking, expecting Zoe to play ball and work with him on this? He tucked the handset safely away in the pocket of his tunic and kicked the wheel of the trolley. He'd somehow have to stop her shooting her mouth off.

~

Wellman let himself into the medical director's office with one of the keys taken from the dead man's coat pocket. There would be no one waiting at home, worrying as early evening wandered into the territory of late night. The medical director wasn't married. Lived all alone. Just as well.

Wellman sat and booted up a desktop computer that was as painfully slow as every other he'd used in the organisation. Thousands of employee hours wasted per annum by staff at their desks waiting for the spinning orb to morph into something more useful. He knew the login and password by heart, having inputted it on several occasions on the medical director's behalf. It hadn't changed. Good old Simon. Microsoft Outlook loaded – again, only after an age had passed – a mix of read and unread emails appearing under rapid fire and loud pings.

Dr Patricia Beven. There it was. Using the search facility, he gathered together all correspondence between the medical director and counsellor.

You two HAVE been busy. He read the content. Didn't like what he saw. Especially the bit where Beven advised that he be removed from all clinical duties pending full psychiatric review.

He deleted them all. Then emptied the *deleted* folder. Next, checked in the *sent* folder for evidence that any of this had been subsequently forwarded to the Chair of the Organisation. It hadn't. Not that he could see, at least.

Finally, he set an out of office alert, and left it at that.

32

'We should have dressed Harris up in a skirt 'n' heels, and put *him* out there,' Reece said. It was less than an hour to midnight and he was hating every minute of what they were about to do. The ACC had got wind from Chief Superintendent Cable that the team had earlier been discussing a sting. The same team that had then quickly dismissed it – though that counted for little by the looks of things. Under mounting pressure from the Police Commissioner, not to mention the Americans, under the guidance of Logan Johnson Jr III, Harris had ordered they get on with it that very night.

Reece had argued with his seniors. On the grounds of safety, mostly. Not to mention the fact the magistrate had kindly signed off his new application to search Dr Wellman's house. But with all available officers busy with the current charade, the warrant would have to be served the following morning – when most of the team would likely be knackered.

'I'll be all right, boss,' Morgan had said when they'd earlier left her in the hospital concourse awaiting the order to get started. They'd run through the plan one last time. Specifically: that the hired minibus – driven by DCI Reece – would go on ahead, dropping plain-clothes officers off at strategic waypoints to lie in wait as backup if required. Morgan would then walk the same route alone, attracting the attention of the stalker should he be out on the prowl. The only potential issue was a twenty-metre stretch of dipping pavement that sat in something of a blind spot. That concerned Reece, though they had no feasible alternative.

Jenkins was sat in the front passenger seat warming her hands on the vehicle's air blower. 'I've got a bad feeling about this.'

'You and me both,' Reece said. 'That's why we won't be letting her out of our sight for a minute.'

'Apart from when she goes through that blind spot you mean?'

Reece tapped his shoulder radio. 'She'll be using her microphone and earpiece to keep in contact with us when she goes through that bit.'

Jenkins looked unconvinced. 'Hope you're right.'

Reece turned to face two people sat together at the back of the minibus. They were from the medical team, and had kitbags forced into what little space there was between their feet. 'I'm banking on you pair getting a quiet night.' One of them nodded back at him.

With all drop-offs successfully made, Reece and Jenkins had then parked up in a side street, acting as a mobile command unit. 'Okay, Ffion,' he said into the shoulder radio. 'Let's get this done.'

Jordan Patterson couldn't let Zoe and her big mouth come between him and finding out what had happened to Poppy. There was something iffy going on with that doctor at the hospital. The blood on his shirt. The fact he was jumpy. The lamp on the floor, with the piss-poor excuse he'd tripped. There were no visible injuries to explain the blood spots. And the man had practically thrown him out of his office.

There was definitely some weird shit going on there.

Zoe wasn't picking up. Hadn't done since their telephone conversation nearly two hours earlier, and was obviously ignoring him again. Just as Lowri had decided to.

How could either of them believe he'd have had anything to do with what happened to Poppy and Harlan? Miller deserved a slap, true enough. He'd told the guy as much only the other night. But killing him – uh-uh, no way.

Left with little choice, Patterson had decided to go talk to Zoe face to face; to ask her to bear with him and not mention anything about the doctor to the police. Not yet, anyway. Not before he'd had time to do some proper snooping around.

When he got to the hospital social club, it was already closed, Zoe nowhere to be seen. He knew which route she'd use to get home, and needed to intercept her before she was within shouting distance of the police officer on doorstep guard duty.

There was a short burst of static, followed by, 'I'm about to turn off Allensbank Road.'

'Okay,' Reece said. 'The troops are out and about. If you need help, just ask.'

'There's someone coming on my side of the pavement,' Morgan replied almost immediately. 'Want me to cross, or keep going?'

'Your call.'

'Not big enough to be him. Hard to be sure though, because I'm still walking downhill.'

'Cross anyway,' Reece told her. 'Let's see what he does.'

'*Aargh!*'

'Morgan. Morgan, come in.'

'I'm okay, boss. Just some crap in the gutter. I'm good now.'

'And your man?'

'Crossing with me.' There was a tremor to the voice that wasn't there previously. 'He's reaching into his pocket.'

Jenkins moved in her seat, its ageing mechanism squeaking beneath her. She wore a look of deep concern; one hand resting on the pull-lever for the van door.

Reece spoke into the shoulder radio, 'Just say the word.'

'He's taking something from his pocket,' Morgan answered in what was little more than a whisper.

'Can you see what it is?'

'Careful, Ffion,' Jenkins said, even though the DCI's mic was closed at the time. 'Why isn't she answering?' she asked him.

Reece tried again. 'Ffion?'

Jenkins was staring at the side of Reece's head, her hand gripping the door handle now. 'Come on, boss, we have to move.'

'Ffion. This is DCI Reece.'

'I'm okay.' It was Morgan, back online. 'Sorry about that. He wanted a light for a cigarette. Harmless.'

'Is he gone?' Reece asked.

'Making his way up the hill.'

Jenkins released her grip on the door handle. 'Fucking hell.'

'You can't be too far from the blind spot now?' Reece reminded Morgan. 'I want you to maintain radio contact throughout.'

Her reply was next to impossible to decipher, the dip in the road combined with a thick treeline impeding voice as much as it did sight.

Jordan Patterson had broken into something of a slow jog once clear of the hospital boundary, and was making his way down Allensbank Road. It was picking to rain again. Or *spitting*, as the locals called it. Pulling the hood of his sweatshirt over his head, he saw her as soon as he took a right turn into the next street.

It was definitely her. Zoe wasn't exactly small, and walked with a distinctive side-to-side rocking motion that larger people often do. He didn't want to shout her name and risk giving her opportunity to call the police before he got there, and so he sped up, quickly closing the distance between them. Seemingly oblivious to the fact that racing towards her in the dark of night might cause more problems than it would solve.

Reece was sat with the radio in his hand. They'd not heard a word from Morgan for more than a minute.

'I don't like this,' Jenkins said. 'She has to be out the other side of it by now.'

'Does anyone see her?' Reece asked. No one did. 'Ffion. Ffion, come in.'

'We need to go.' Jenkins was reaching for the handle again.

'Not yet. *Ffion*, talk to me.'

There was a loud scream. Not from the radio, but from the adjacent street. 'Go, go, go,' Reece said, giving his team the command they'd been waiting for. He started the minibus' engine, didn't bother with the seat belt, and screeched off onto the other side of the road. 'Hold on,' he told Jenkins, and swung the vehicle hard right into the next street. Parked cars flashed by either side of them. Monochrome blurs in the darkness.

'There they are.' Jenkins pointed at a couple wrestling against the wall of a house.

'That's not Ffion,' Reece said, pulling on the handbrake. He pushed open the door and leapt out with the engine still running. 'Get off her, you bastard!' He took Patterson by his collar, swung him round and lifted a tightly clenched fist.

The girl screamed again, her assailant letting go of her in order to cover up ready for the oncoming punch.

The front door of the nearest house opened to reveal a burly man wearing little more than a bushy beard and a pair of *Bart Simpson* boxer shorts. He stepped onto the wet pavement in his bare feet and came their way. 'Fuck off,' he said, hitching a thumb at the struggling pair.

Reece had his fist cocked and ready to go if need be. 'We're police officers,' he said for the benefit of all those around them. The brief lapse in concentration was enough to allow Jordan Patterson to somehow pull free and scarper in the opposite direction to the way the minibus was pointing.

'You deal with her,' Reece said before sprinting along the pavement after Patterson.

'You've woken the kids,' the bearded man called after him. 'I'm gonna beat the shit out of both of you when you come back for that van.' He went over to the vehicle and removed the keys from the ignition. Waving them in the air, he shouted, 'I'll be waiting. Right here.'

Reece knew it was a one-horse race. Jordan Patterson might have had close to three decades on him in terms of age, but he wouldn't be getting away tonight. Pumping his arms, Reece brought his knees up high with every stride, the speed and endurance built from his daily runs paying off. He was catching Patterson. No doubt about that. 'Stop!'

Patterson went across the road without looking.

Reece followed. There were more calls for his assailant to

stop and give himself up. Shouts of *"Police,"* coming from a couple of uniforms loaned to him for the night. One of them was waving his arms up and down as though marshalling an aircraft onto its stand. Fat lot of good that was. Reece dived, tapped an ankle with a firm hand, and brought Patterson down against the wing of a parked car. Reece was slower to react than the younger man, but it was all over. The waving uniform had him. 'You're nicked,' Reece panted, staring up at a starry sky with the flat of his back resting in a pavement puddle.

Reece bathed a pair of scuffed knees in a bowl of warm water, and TCP solution he'd *borrowed* from the police surgeon's room downstairs.

Jenkins watched him. 'Not quite the result we were hoping for.'

'Bloody trousers are ruined,' Reece said, poking a finger through the gaping holes in them. Then he smiled. 'Top drawer tackle though, wasn't it?' He slapped a hand against the desk to demonstrate, spilling a small amount of water from the makeshift bowl. 'If the Wales selectors had seen me in action tonight...' He sat up straight and whistled.

'The wing mirror of that BMW is ruined,' Jenkins said, spoiling his moment of glory. 'No cheap fix there, I'd imagine.'

'I'll put a claim in for the car and my trousers at the same time,' he said, rolling them into a ball before throwing them across the room. They fell short of the intended bin. He sat for a while in his underpants and wet shirt, staring at the wall clock on the other side of the room. 'Jesus, there'll be no point in going home soon. We've got the search to do on Wellman's house in a few hours.'

'Never mind that,' Jenkins said. 'You need to go find something to wear before you get yourself arrested.'

Reece let his knees be, and got up with a stoop and groan.

'Where are you going now?' she asked when he headed for the door in wet shirt, underpants, and socks.

'Down to the custody suite to get a pair of those grey joggers they hand out to every waif and stray that wanders in here.'

'You can't. Not dressed like that.'

'Why not? There's never anyone about at this time of night.'

33

That wasn't exactly true. There were plenty of people about the station. Even at that ungodly hour. Cleaners for one. And most of them speaking in broken English as the DCI trudged on by, flashing half-moons of white arse-cheek at them as he went down the corridor.

'You should have seen the tackle,' was all they got in response to their giggles. He used the stairs, reckoning that as most people were downright lazy, he'd likely come across no one else. When he got through the door to the foyer on the ground floor, there was uproar going on at the front desk. He recognised one of two women immediately. It was *what's-her-name* – the wife of the missing CCTV engineer. She was drunk, and had already called the desk sergeant the c-word on at least two occasions he'd heard himself. Her embarrassed friend was doing her best to drag her away.

The woman turned, aware no doubt that someone was watching. She looked Reece up and down. 'And what the fuck have you been up to?' She came towards him; all teeth, spit, and sharp fingernails. 'Not looking for my Pete's killer, that's for sure.'

Reece raised an arm to fend her off. 'Hang on,' he said, under a deluge of flailing fists. 'Let me explain.'

A little over five minutes later and they were sat in an interview room: Reece, *Kath Hall* – he'd remembered her name – and her friend, who was looking no less embarrassed.

Hall was crying. Shaking as she spoke in fast bursts. 'I didn't mean to react like that. I'm sorry. It's just I can't sleep. And not knowing what they've done to Pete is driving me round the bend.'

Reece told her it was no big deal. That her assault on him would go no further. 'We're thin on the ground, is the truth. You must have seen the news lately?'

'Poor women.' Hall blew her nose in a paper hanky. 'Who'd do such a thing? And to nurses of all people.'

Reece had managed to get hold of a spare pair of jogging bottoms before taking the women to an empty interview room. They were at least one size too tight, probably two, and had him squirming in his seat trying to get comfortable. 'Pete's not come home then?'

Kath Hall was shaking. 'You still don't believe my husband's dead?'

'I didn't say that. It's just–'

'That gangster did for him.' She turned to the other woman. 'Didn't he?' The woman duly nodded.

'I need evidence.' Reece looked apologetic. *Something to keep Cable off my back.* 'I can't bring Creed in for questioning without it.'

Kath Hall reached into her coat pocket and passed him a folded sheet of paper. 'I've been looking through Pete's online diary.' She leaned forward and tapped the back of it. 'On the day he went missing he was supposed to meet BC at a snooker club.

That's what it says there in the five o'clock slot.' She'd stopped crying. Looked more hopeful all of a sudden. 'BC – Billy Creed – that good enough for you?'

Cable won't think so. 'I'll look into it,' Reece promised.

'When exactly?' She was angry again. Voice raised. 'Once I've waved enough money at a television camera?'

'That wasn't my idea.'

Hall patted both eyes in turn with another wad of hankies. 'If you won't do it for *me*, then do it for the kids.'

Reece recognised the signs of desperation. Had experienced most of them himself. 'Okay.' He paused, chewing on a thumbnail. 'I'll need something personal of Pete's. A toothbrush or comb we can get DNA off.'

Kath Hall let out a deep breath. 'You're going to take this seriously?'

Reece nodded. 'And I know just the officer who's going to help me.'

Reece was first to wake. He opened an eye and wondered where the hell he was until his brain caught up a few moments later. The office wall clock claimed it was just before five in the morning, and given the heavy blanket of darkness all around, he had no reason to doubt it. The others were asleep at their desks – a disciplinary offence ordinarily – a late finish to the Pete Hall discussion making it somewhat pointless for them to go home before the early start at Dr Wellman's place.

Morgan had mentioned nothing to Josh about her acting as stalker-bait; telling him instead that the team was busy working the night to prepare for an early-morning raid.

Jenkins had dropped into the chair at her desk with a noisy

yawn, bomber jacket drawn over her head, snoring noisily only minutes later.

Ginge had jumped at the chance of looking into the case of the disappearing CCTV man, and couldn't thank the DCI enough.

Reece gave the coffee pot a brief swill under the tap, returning after filling the machine with fresh coffee beans. Someone broke wind. Jenkins, the likely culprit, shifted position in her chair. Reece smirked. Stood there watching them sleep like a proud father checking on the kids before turning in for the night. They were becoming a great team. Even the wet-behind-the-ears newbie was showing huge promise. He was lucky to have them and knew it. Putting a couple of spoons in an empty glass, he walked the room shaking it like an improvised school bell.

'Jesus Christ,' Jenkins said, pulling the jacket tighter to her head. 'I've only just dropped off.'

'Morning, boss.' Ginge was up and off his chair like a sprinter out of the blocks.

Reece tossed twenty quid his way and said, 'Go see how many bacon rolls you can get for that.'

'Ginge!' Jenkins screamed when he switched the lights on to find a missing shoe. 'I'll staple your hands to the wall, if you do that again.'

'It wasn't me with the bell,' the newbie said apologetically. 'That was the boss.'

Jenkins reached across her desk and waved her stapler at him. 'Lights!'

'It can't be,' Morgan said, trying to lift her head off the desk. She wiped dried dribble from the corner of her mouth and sat there in a stupor.

Reece was busy clearing the surface of one of the unoccupied desks, getting it ready for when breakfast arrived.

. . .

'I managed to get eleven,' Ginge said, appearing in the doorway not ten minutes later. He waved a bulging carrier bag at them. 'They gave us an extra one free – said it was for you, boss. Something to do with a frozen cheesecake.'

'Juice.' Jenkins was staring at him. 'Where's the orange juice?'

Ginge peered into the bag, and then at Reece. 'You never said anything about juice.'

Jenkins pointed at the open door. Ginge was on his way again, this time accompanied by a round of loud laughter. 'Get back in here,' Jenkins said, stretching like a fireside cat. 'I was messing with you.' When at last they were all fed and watered, she was raring to go.

'I need to shower first,' Morgan said. She hadn't yet changed out of the clothing worn for the previous night's sting. 'I can't go out looking like this.'

'You're not on the pull,' Reece told her. 'Come on, it's time you lot were off.'

Patterson stopped playing with his hands and looked up when the door to the interview room opened. 'This is bullshit,' he said. 'Been here all night waiting for *him* to arrive.' He angled his head towards the duty solicitor sat on his left-hand side. 'I wasn't talking this time – not without a brief.'

Reece took a seat. 'You draw the short straw again, Giles?'

The man almost smiled, but opened a large notepad instead.

'You two know each other?' Patterson slumped in the chair and forced a hand down the front of his joggers. '*Great*. Fucking great.'

'Happy if I use your first name during the interview?' Reece pressed the red button on the DIR machine and waited for quiet. 'For the recording, could you confirm you've spoken to no one about the events of yesterday. Myself included.'

Patterson gawped like the detective had grown two heads. 'I was in a cell. Who else is there to talk to?'

'Just answer yes or no.'

'No.'

'What were you doing following Zoe home from work last night?'

'What did *she* tell you?'

'*I'm* asking the questions.' Reece waited patiently. Knew that most people, when nervous, couldn't resist the urge to fill awkward silences, often incriminating themselves.

Patterson was no different to the average man. 'I just wanted to talk, that's all.'

'What about?'

'*Things.*'

Reece glanced at the solicitor when he got no further explanation. 'You're up on a charge of physical assault on a woman, Jordan. Do you see how that looks under current circumstances?'

'Grabbing someone isn't assault.'

'I think Giles here will tell you it is.' The man nodded on cue. 'What was so important you had to pin a woman against the wall so she couldn't run off?'

'Nothing.'

'Come on, Jordan. Let's get this over and done with so we can all get home before *stupid o'clock.*'

Patterson lurched forward, making Reece flinch. He said nothing. Looked like he'd suddenly changed his mind – perhaps worried he'd give too much away if he continued. He ran a hand across his mouth, and said, 'There's a doctor at the hospital who used to stare and make Poppy nervous.' He shrugged. 'I just wanted to ask Zoe what she knew about him.'

'Hang on a minute.' Reece got up. 'DCI Reece is leaving the interview room,' he told the DIR machine before putting it on pause. He was short of breath and perspiring when he got back. 'Him?' he asked, holding up a black-and-white photograph he'd taken off the evidence board in the incident room. It was one Ginge had downloaded off the internet, and showed Richard Wellman at some sort of awards ceremony.

'You got your eye on him too?'

'Stay out of this, Jordan,' Reece said.

'You *do*, don't you? You think it's him. You think the doctor is the murderer.'

34

Jenkins slapped the search warrant into Wellman's open palm and waited for him to step aside. 'I think you'll find everything is in order, Doctor.'

'What the hell are you playing at?' he said, refusing to get out of her way.

'No games on our part. We're here to search these premises for evidence linking you to a Mrs Molly Gantry.' Reece had told his team his intention was to first establish a connection between Wellman and the woman thought to be his mother, and in so doing, the Volvo. Next, place the car at the scene of at least one murder, and then see how things progressed from there.

'This is preposterous.'

'Stand back, please.'

'You can't come–'

'In you go,' Jenkins told a line of waiting uniforms. No need for the *Big Red Key* on this occasion. They pushed past the man in the tartan dressing gown and filed down the hallway before splitting into smaller teams. Some went through to the living room. Others climbed the carpeted stairs. Each team calling out when the rooms they were responsible for had been systematically *cleared.* The CSI contingent stayed where they were for the time being, waiting for the nod telling them the place was safe enough to enter.

'I don't understand,' Wellman said, turning to follow the last of the uniforms inside. 'I've already told you: I don't know the Gantry woman. Never heard the name before your chief inspector started asking questions about her.'

'You can't go in there.' Jenkins put a hand on his arm to stop him going any further. 'If there's anything you need from the house, then someone will get it for you once we're finished here.' He stared at her hand. Then deep into her eyes with a level of contempt that made her physically shudder. 'Move away from me, sir.' She repeated the command. Louder, making sure she got his full attention.

Wellman blinked. 'I need my things,' he said politely. 'I'm working at the hospital this morning.'

Jenkins shook her head. 'Afraid not, sir. I'm going to have to ask you to accompany us to the station.'

His eyes narrowed. 'On what grounds?'

Reece had phoned only minutes earlier, instructing her to bring the doctor in – kicking and screaming if necessary. 'New developments in the Poppy Jones case.'

'And what's that got to do with me?'

She was almost ready to go. 'That's what we intend to find out.'

Wellman took a step closer, invading Jenkins's personal space. His smile was thin-lipped and cold. 'You're going to regret this.'

Ginge was on a roll, quickly linking fingerprints found on the inside of the partly burned-out van, to one Kyle Cartwright.

Another five minutes spent digging around in various police databases told him that not only was Cartwright a violent offender, but surprise, surprise, also a known associate of Billy Creed.

'Boss.'

Reece was tidying his desk. Killing time before going downstairs to meet Jenkins when she arrived with their suspect in tow. Jordan Patterson could go free. He'd been warned in no uncertain terms not to interfere with the investigation. To leave Zoe and the other members of the household well alone. 'What?' Reece shouted through the open office door.

'You'll want to see this.'

'Can you bring it in here?'

Ginge took the laptop with him and put it down on a pile of files on the crowded desk. 'Look,' he said before the screen blinked and went blank. He started tapping at the keys. 'It shouldn't be doing that, sorry.'

Reece screwed his eyes shut and counted five back to one. 'Just tell me what you've found.'

'There was a van torched near the Welsh Water plant the other night. Made the local paper.' Ginge got the laptop booted up again and scrolled to the online version of the story. 'Kyle Cartwright,' he said, pointing at the screen. 'And Ronnie Boyce.'

Reece nodded. 'Albino Ron. What's your point?'

'Well, boss – there was a machete and what looked like bloodstained rags in the back of the van.' He showed the DCI an image of a blade set alongside a scale of measurement. The metal was tarnished with colours ranging from black through to light blue and yellow. The wooden handle was completely destroyed, leaving only a short shank of metal that would have slotted into it. The blade itself had a pronounced back-bow, bent that way by the intense heat of the blaze. 'Forensics found evidence of what might be organic tissue along the cutting edge,'

Ginge said. 'It's burned up pretty bad, and they're not hopeful of extracting any useful DNA from it.'

Reece scratched his head. 'How does that help us?'

Ginge grinned. 'There was another set of prints pulled off that van, and they don't belong to Cartwright or Boyce.'

'Creed?'

'Already checked.' Ginge shook his head. 'But I think I might know who.'

So did Reece. He slapped the newbie on the back. 'You get that toothbrush and comb from the wife yet?'

'In the lab, boss. Sioned Williams is taking DNA off them as we speak.'

The troops were filing in as Reece arrived at the custody suite, Jenkins issuing orders as she led the way. 'We're not charging him as yet,' she told the desk sergeant. 'Just holding him for questioning while we conduct a search at this address.' She handed the sergeant the necessary paperwork and waited for the man to read through it.

'How did he take it?' Reece asked when he got her to one side.

'Well pissed off. And lots of threats to report us to anyone he could think of.'

'Rattled then?'

'First time I've seen him flustered.' She looked over Reece's shoulder and nodded. 'You letting that one go already?'

He turned to see Jordan Patterson being led out of his cell by one of the custody officers. Saw Wellman double-take when he clocked him. The change in the doctor's body language spoke volumes. 'Give me a second, will you?' Reece walked off. Stepped in front of Patterson when he looked like he might say something. 'You remember what I told you earlier. Leave it to us.'

'I knew it.' Patterson glared at Wellman. Got agitated and pointed a finger in warning. 'You *were* up to no good when I saw you yesterday.'

Reece pulled him to one side. Pushed him against the corridor wall. 'What do you mean by that?'

'Nothing.'

'Jordan, I'll nick you again if I have to.'

Patterson pulled himself free and marched towards the exit. 'Leave me alone!' he shouted when Reece went after him. 'All of you. Just leave me the fuck alone.'

When Reece got back to the custody desk, they'd finished booking Wellman in.

'You want coffee before we start?' Jenkins asked.

A nod. 'Coffee sounds good.'

'Can I meet you there?' She waved her phone at him. 'I've almost managed to get Charlie somewhere to stay.'

Reece frowned. '*Charlie?*'

'The homeless guy with Harlan Miller's phone.' She was already walking away. Dialling while she spoke. 'One more call to Veteran's Welfare should do it.'

'Don't be long,' Reece told her. 'We've a busy day ahead of us.'

When at last they sat down with Wellman, he was no happier. 'You know how it goes,' Reece said, prior to reeling off the preliminaries. 'So,' he continued, 'here we are again, Doctor.'

Wellman's solicitor was an insipid-looking man. Downtrodden and down at the mouth. Reece imagined he wore cardigans and slippers at home, answering to an overpowering woman named Doris. Or something like that. He'd instinctively known he wouldn't like him even before the man uttered his first words.

'My client has a right to know why his home was ransacked this morning, and why he's been brought here for questioning.'

Reece turned to Jenkins and addressed her with a deep frown and scolding eye. 'You been out ransacking again?'

She raised both hands in denial. 'Not me, boss. I don't think we're allowed to do that sort of thing these days.'

'More's the shame,' Reece said with a shake of the head. 'Not her,' he told the brief. 'Not the type.'

The man went bright red – like a teenager caught with his hands on more than just a mucky magazine. 'I'll be reporting your flippant behaviour to the Police and Crime Commissioner.'

'It might be a long queue,' Reece told him.

One shade closer to puce, the solicitor repeated his earlier comment about his client's legal entitlements.

'Jordan Patterson,' Reece said, ignoring him.

'Is that a question, Chief Inspector?' The solicitor again. And no less florid.

'I couldn't help but notice your response to seeing Patterson downstairs earlier.' Reece sat back. 'Sooner you tell me what's going on there, the sooner you're going home.'

Wellman stared straight ahead. At Jenkins mostly, even though it was Reece asking the bulk of the questions. 'Never heard of him.'

'Now I know that's not true,' Reece said, wagging a finger. 'And it got me wondering how you'd know the ex-boyfriend of Poppy Jones.'

Wellman leaned closer and whispered something in Insipid's ear. He got a nod in return, and only then answered. 'I've seen him at the hospital. Wasn't aware of his name.'

'Where've we heard that one before?' Jenkins asked the DCI.

When she faced forward again, Wellman was giving her the same icy stare he had during the search of his home. 'Patterson definitely knew you,' she continued, unperturbed. 'What was it he caught you doing yesterday?'

'He's a *cleaner*,' Wellman said through gritted teeth. 'He didn't *catch* me doing anything.'

Reece joined in again. 'The boy cleans – has to make a living somehow – why does that make him any less of a person in your eyes?'

Silence. The same stare.

'The upstairs of your house smells like Molly Gantry's.' Jenkins sat back and folded her arms. 'Both of you use unnecessary amounts of bleach. That a family thing?'

This time it was Insipid's turn to lean in close. After which Wellman replied with, 'No comment.'

'Did you tell him to say that?' Reece shook his head. 'Now you've definitely got me thinking he's hiding something.'

The brief had quite obviously had enough. He got to his feet, prompting Wellman to do likewise. 'Chief Inspector – let's end this pointless charade. Do you have anything with which to hold or charge my client?' The man waited. 'Yes, or no?'

35

Jordan Patterson had already joined most of the dots and didn't like what he was seeing. He'd chosen to mention nothing to the police about the doctor's bloodstained shirt. Had almost blurted it out in a moment of anger; managing to rein things in again before it was too late. He wanted no one poking around that office – not even DCI Reece – not until he'd had a good look at the place himself.

'I didn't know you were in work today,' the woman said, and leaned on the handle of her cleaning trolley. It lurched to one side, dirty water swishing about in a half-filled bucket, some spilling onto the floor. She took a mop and dabbed half-heartedly at the puddle.

'I'm on an extra shift,' Patterson told her. 'Came up here to give you a quick coffee break.'

'Bullshit, Jords, you're up to something. And no good too by the looks of it,' she said, flicking a wrist full of fingers in his face.

'Look, there's no one else free for another hour at least. Take it or leave it.'

'*Ah*, fuck it. You here long enough for me to sneak round the back for a cheeky fag?'

'Take your time, I'm done after this.'

She handed him a bunch of keys. 'If you're on the rob, then I want a pack of twenty for keeping my mouth shut, okay.' With that she was gone, waddling down the corridor towards the lifts, the heels of both shoes worn on the insides, like doorstop wedges.

Patterson waited until the woman was fully out of sight before moving on with the trolley. There were so many doors and corridors in a hospital of this size that he couldn't be sure which one he needed until he came across the nameplate. *Dr Richard Wellman*. This was it. Patterson checked his watch. Had no idea how long DCI Reece would be keeping the doctor at the police station. Turning the key in the lock, Patterson let himself in and shut the door behind him.

Wellman was already on his way back to the hospital, struggling with the city traffic as much as he was with thoughts of what that policewoman had said. She'd got so far under his skin that he'd almost lost all control and reached across the table in the interview room and throttled the bitch in front of DCI Reece. Fortunately for her, they'd not been alone together. But there was time.

There was always time.

DS Jenkins – she hadn't given him any more than that – had spoken about Aunt Freda, and how she and the woman he knew as Mother had been in regular contact. He didn't believe a word of it. Wouldn't believe it. Not until they'd presented him with the diary, complete with dates and times. And even then, he'd sat there repeating 'no comment,' like some fucking imbecile.

Aunt Freda had deceived him. Even on her deathbed she'd said nothing, doing her utmost to take her secret to the grave. He banged a clenched fist hard against the steering wheel and swore loudly. It wasn't supposed to be like this. Should have been easy. Women succumbing to death by natural causes. Instead, he had bodies coming out of his ears. Old. Young. One hidden in a cupboard at work. Even his own mother rotting in the woods off Llantrisant Road. The wheel got another hammering.

Just as well the hospital was only another five to ten minutes away.

~

Patterson wandered the empty office, not knowing what it was he'd come to find. It had seemed like a good idea when he left the police station. Now, not so much. He turned in a full circle, hoping something might catch his eye.

But what?

It looked like any other office he'd ever been in. Had the usual desk, computer, lamp, and mail trays. Smelled a bit odd. Unpleasant. He ran a hand along the upright stem of the lamp. It had a slight bend in the metal. He stopped when his finger encountered something raised and crusty on the underside. He picked at it. Rubbed the brown crust between finger and thumb. Old blood, pure and simple.

The doctor would have him believe it was his own. Impossible. He could never have tripped and injured himself on that part of the desk ornament. Someone else's then? Patterson didn't know. Wasn't trained in such things.

He found filing cabinets in a small annexe room, each of them competing for space with a forest of cardboard boxes. Lifting the lid off one such box, he peered inside and found it full of old papers and files. It smelled musty in there; as though it hadn't been opened in years. Checking two others, he noted the same. He closed the lids, then tried the nearest filing cabinet. More paperwork. Some dates on the files were from ten, even twenty years earlier.

And a few were older than that.

Drawers opened and closed easily, and in quick succession. All except one. He pulled at it, this time with so much force the entire cabinet rocked on its front end, shifting a few inches forward with a hollow sounding bang. He froze, breath held, waiting for the occupants of the neighbouring office to come and knock on the door. Nobody did. Carefully, he slid the cabinet back into place. These things were easy to get into and didn't usually require the correct key – just something similar in size and shape.

He'd left the pile of master keys on the trolley in the other room. Checking through them, he found one that might do. On the first attempt, it refused to turn in the slot. He removed it, put it in his mouth and wet it with saliva. He tried again. Bingo – he was in.

The drawer was empty, except for a laptop kept inside a canvas shoulder bag. He had no time to fire the thing up. He'd have no clue how to, either. But he knew a man who'd be only too willing to help for as little as a couple of free games of snooker. With the drawer locked again, he dropped the laptop into a net bin that hung from the handles of his trolley, and covered it with paper towels and a dirty mop head.

He'd just unlocked the office door when the tall, dark outline of someone he recognised appeared on the other side of the frosted glass.

Reece pushed a clear evidence bag across the table. 'Recognise that?' Even with two good eyes, Kyle Cartwright might have struggled. As it was, he had an oval-shaped cup of plastic stuck over the left one, making it all the more difficult. 'Pick it up if you need to, it's yours after all.'

'Says who?'

'Says these. That's you and Ronnie Boyce,' Reece said, tapping each photograph in turn. 'No doubt about it. You did everything short of stopping to wave, you stupid sods.' He paused to laugh. 'Billy's none too pleased then.'

Cartwright was fiddling with a piece of tape that had broken free of his cheek. 'No comment.'

Reece tossed more photographs at him. One by one. 'There's you turning up in the van. You putting a match to it. That's you running away. And then there's these.' He showed Cartwright pictures of the machete and bloodstained rags. 'Damning, wouldn't you say?' What Reece wasn't telling him – mostly because Cartwright hadn't yet asked – was they had no DNA evidence linking him to either of the exhibits. Temperatures inside the van had likely got up to around three hundred and fifty degrees centigrade to warp the metal blade. And with DNA denaturing at somewhere near half that, the only prints they had were from some of the outside surfaces. Still, no harm in giving it a punt. Reece put one last photograph on the tabletop. 'And all because of this man.'

'Never seen him before.'

'That's Pete Hall. The man Billy blamed for his knee, not to mention your brother Denny's early departure from this world.'

Cartwright stared straight ahead.

'Billy had you kill him, didn't he? Told you to torch the van, and blinded you in that eye when you screwed up.'

'No comment.'

'Did he get to Ronnie Boyce first?' Reece asked. 'Only, we can't find him anywhere we've looked.'

Cartwright shifted. Despite him lacking his elder brother's imposing bulk, there was still an air of menace to the man. 'No *fucking* comment.'

Ginge hadn't said a word as yet. Didn't need to. Was sat listening to the boss at work.

'Billy believes just about anything that leaks out of this station,' Reece said. 'He's so paranoid that if I plant a seed in his head, then it won't be long before he's kicking yours about the city like a football.'

When Ginge looked like he might at last say something, a loud knock at the door interrupted him before he got it out.

It was Morgan. 'Boss, I need a word outside.'

'*Now?*'

She nodded. 'It's Rome. They said it's important.'

Reece paused the DIR without further explanation, leaving the room in a hurry. When he'd finished the long and difficult phone call with Colonel Gianfranco Totti, he'd been numb and unsure of what to do next. Anwen's killer had hanged himself while in custody. Had taken the coward's way out, unwilling to face up to the consequences of his actions.

These things happened. In justice systems all over the world. Even in one station he himself had worked in.

But that made it no less painful.

His beautiful wife deserved better.

He'd wandered the landings at the station after that; Chief Superintendent Cable finding him in bits on her way out of the building. She'd tried to take him to a quiet office for tea and sympathy.

He didn't want her pity. Or anyone else's for that matter. It was over. Hopeless. And nothing could make things any better.

There was only one thing left to do. Without returning to the interview room to pick up his jacket, he marched through the foyer, oblivious to the desk sergeant's repeated attempts to get his attention. Out into the cold and dark night he went, headed for the barrage and the swollen sea.

36

'Can you open it?' Jordan Patterson was sat alongside his favourite table in the snooker hall. It was late evening. Not far off closing time. The regulars finishing their last frames before making a break for home via the local chippy. It was dark but for a half-dozen rectangular islands of light-green baize cloth. He'd not known the days when men from the local docks and coal yards had snuck in for a frame or three before going home to their families. The days when curtains of fag smoke had made it almost impossible to get a clear sight of the other end of the table, let alone the far side of the room. He wasn't old enough. 'Look,' he said, 'if you can't, then I'll find someone who can.'

'Like who?' his friend, Gittings asked. 'There's no one else round these parts with my level of skills.' He cracked his knuckles theatrically. Then drummed his fingers against the laptop's keys.

'Open it then.' Patterson sounded exasperated and looked up to see if anyone had heard him. Nobody was watching; not even the tattoo-faced owner prowling near the till. The man was a gangster, or so he'd heard, and had got his kneecap shot off in a hit gone wrong. *What goes around...* as they say.

'What's on here, anyway?' Gittings looked suddenly worried. 'Tell me it's not kiddie porn.'

Patterson was on his feet, leaning over the other man. 'Fuck sort of question is that?'

Gittings raised a hand in apology. 'I'm just saying I'm not into paedo stuff.'

'Will you stop it.' Patterson spoke through clenched teeth, one eye fixed on the gangster who was busy throttling a man with dirty white dreadlocks. 'You'll get us both killed talking like that round here.'

'What's on it then?'

Patterson shook his head. 'I'll know if I see it.'

'What sort of answer is that?'

'You're starting to do my head in, mate. Concentrate on opening the thing.'

'Already have.' Gittings handed over the laptop. 'Security on these things is shocking,' he said with a loud snort. 'I'd consider making a complaint to the manufacturer if it wasn't for the fact I make a damn good living as a hacker.'

'Shit, you're right, you've done it.'

There were raised voices coming from the opposite end of the room, and when Patterson looked, the gangster was busy pinning Dreads to the table with a snooker cue pressed hard against the man's throat. He could hear the gangster asking as to the whereabouts of Kyle Cartwright. Patterson knew that name – had been in school with Kyle – but had never been stupid enough to go anywhere near the psycho. Not then. And not now, if he could help it.

'You two.' The voice was deep and menacing.

Patterson kept his head down. Didn't dare make eye contact.

'Oi.' Louder this time. More threatening. 'You two!'

Now Patterson raised his head. But only fleetingly. Long enough to let the gangster-man know he was listening.

'You've got to the count of ten to make yourselves scarce.' The snooker cue had been handed to a man with an enormous jaw. Dreads was on his back, his wrists bag-tied to the pockets at the near end of the table, the gangster loading snooker balls into something that might have been a football sock.

Wellman had found the laptop missing within minutes of getting back to the office. No prizes for guessing who the culprit was. He cursed himself for not having stopped the man when he had the opportunity. But he'd been preoccupied. Wasn't thinking straight – and let him leave without comment or challenge.

DCI Reece had the cleaner doing his dirty work. Wellman had seen them conspiring together at the station only a couple of hours ago. Pretending to argue. The cleaner doing a splendid job of racing off and out of the building in a contrived strop.

Just about everything Wellman had done in the planning stages was on that device. Facebook searches, and background checks on Molly Gantry, included. He'd deleted the search history, obviously. Had emptied all temporary folders and stored caches. But the police would use forensic software to trawl the hard drive in search of incriminating evidence. Not to mention, issue his Internet Service Provider with warrants for information relating to his browsing habits.

The thought festered like an open sore. He punched the empty cabinet in a fit of rage, leaving a fist-sized dent in one of the drawers' front.

Someone knocked on his office door a few moments later.

'Richard, are you okay in there?' The owner of the voice sounded concerned. Do-gooders always did.

Wellman answered without moving from where he was. 'One of the cabinet drawers got stuck. Had to give the thing a bit of a kick to get it open.'

'I'm next door for another five or ten minutes, if you need me.'

You offering to hold the thieving bastard down while I gut him? 'Thank you. That won't be necessary.'

'I'll be here all the same.'

Aren't I the lucky one? Wellman paced the room. His head felt like it would explode; heart racing in his chest. Getting that laptop back had suddenly become a priority.

Using freeware downloaded from the internet, Gittings had managed to retrieve much of the device's deleted history. It had cost Patterson a burger, fries, and Coca-Cola to do so. Mostly on account of them needing somewhere with an active wifi connection to get it done.

They'd found references to Poppy's Facebook account on there; visited by the doctor a dozen times or more. There were accounts belonging to other girls too, a Megan Lewis featuring prominently. *The* Megan Lewis that Patterson had seen on the news the other day – the one taken from her grave for more tests at the hospital.

There was already sufficient evidence to hand over to the police and be done with it. But Gittings had found something else on that laptop; information that intrigued Patterson enough to have him come down to Cardiff's docklands to take a look for himself.

.   .   .

It was beyond cold on the quayside. March hadn't fully shaken off winter as yet, and all Patterson had on was his cleaners' tunic and trousers. Those and a thin black hoodie. He'd seen homeless people further along the dock, crawling in and out from under container units. They were warming themselves on basket fires, their grubby faces lit up in tones of yellow and orange.

He blew on his hands and set to work on the lock. It wasn't of the type he'd found on the filing cabinet back at Dr Wellman's office, unfortunately. This one was a padlock that ordinarily required a round key. But it was also a cheap inferior Chinese copy of the real deal. And that meant it was next to useless.

Using a technique borrowed from countless hours of watching YouTube videos on his phone, he made short work of the lock, the thing popping open in his hands. The door was of the up-and-over kind, and squeaked noisily when he set it in motion. Stopping to check no one was coming, he left the door in the open position when he went inside.

It was even darker in there. And cramped too. The bulk of the available space taken up by what looked to be a vehicle covered by a grey tarpaulin anchored to its wheels with claw-straps.

Squatting, he loosened a strap on one of the front wheels, a Volvo trademark coming into view on the kerbed hubcap. He switched position and did the same on the passenger side of the vehicle. Lifting the tarp over the wheel arch and front wing, he saw the bodywork was painted silver; pockmarked with rust spots that were bubbled and flaking in several places.

He stiffened, a noise outside the cause of his increased state of anxiety. It sounded like shoes scuffing across hardened concrete. Going to the open door, he stuck his head out there, into the alley, his breath condensing on the cold and salty air.

Apart for the noisy gulls, he was as sure as he could be that he was still alone.

He squeezed round the back of the vehicle while talking into his phone. 'I want to speak to someone working on the Poppy Jones murder.' It was a tight squeeze, and he breathed in to give himself more room. 'DCI Reece: isn't that his name? Looks like Al Pacino.' He waited while the woman on the other end explained that there was no one from the team in until the morning. He'd stopped moving. Was half-stuck. Wedged between wall and bumper. 'Can you take a message, then?' he asked, trying to rotate his leg free. 'I can't speak any louder. Are you sure you've written it all down?' he said when finished.

There it was again. The same noise he'd heard a few minutes earlier. He pushed up on tiptoe, figuring that might help get his knee unstuck.

'Where is it?' The figure stood in the open doorway – tall and wide – holding something in both hands.

'You killed Poppy.' That's all Patterson could think to say.

Wellman poured fluid from a bottle into what looked like a mask lined with wadding of some sort.

'I've told the police,' Patterson said, trying to escape as the doctor edged round the side of the car. 'They're on their way.'

Wellman laughed, and reached a long arm. He couldn't get much closer than he already was, though that didn't matter. 'You're lying,' he said, pressing the mask against Patterson's thrashing face; pinning his head against the block wall. 'Breathe. Make it easy for yourself.'

Patterson swung punches but couldn't reach the taller man's head and face. Banged his fists against forearms that refused to relent. He was getting sleepy. Every thirsty gulp of air propelling him ever closer towards certain death. And then he was gone. Asleep. Enveloped in total darkness.

. . .

When Patterson woke, he was lying face-up on the car's bonnet, spread-eagled and unable to move. He tried to breathe but couldn't manage that either. The doctor was stood over him, fingers pressed gently to the side of his neck.

'Three minutes and thirty-seven seconds. That's how long it took your Poppy to die.'

The world was fast caving in on all sides. There was no white light. No robed figure beckoning him with a kindly smile. He was fucked and knew it.

The doctor spoke one last time. 'Looks like Poppy will have outdone you by a good ten to fifteen seconds.'

37

There was no shortage of empty parking spaces outside the Norwegian Church at such a late hour. Not that Reece needed one. He'd travelled the short distance from the police station on foot. Along James Street, turning right at the Millennium Centre for the quayside.

There must have been a concert on; the pavements awash as they were with people hailing taxis. Some used mobile phones to check their rides home were on the way. That they hadn't been forgotten and left out in the cold. He could hear their excited conversations as he pushed through the throng.

He'd seen flyers for Elvis Costello and The Imposters over the previous weeks: on lamp posts, billboards, even the table in the station foyer. *Oliver's Army* had been a decent enough song in its day, he'd give Costello his due on that. But try as he did, Reece couldn't remember much else he liked of theirs.

The whitewashed church dated back to the days of the Industrial Revolution. A place of worship for Norwegian sailors at a time when Cardiff's Docks had been the world's greatest exporter of coal. It had become his thinking place since Anwen's death. Somewhere he went when he needed to talk things through with her. In life, he'd never have shared such details of the day job – for no other reason than to shield her from the evil people do. But things had changed. She knew first-hand what they did, and there was sod all he could do about that.

Opposite, and well beyond the protection of the tidal barrage system, was a storm leaving Weston-super-Mare, its course set for the shores of south-east Wales. It would race inland, gathering speed before running out of puff somewhere in the mountains.

It wasn't raining yet. But it wouldn't be long before it was.

Walking alongside the man-made lake, navigating by the lights of the barrage ahead and those of the city behind, he could think of nothing but the dead man in Rome. The murderer. The coward. The bastard. Could almost see him swinging from what would likely have been a belt gone unnoticed by some incompetent custody officer.

Reece squatted to pick up a couple of flat stones. Did so by feel alone. They were smooth and icy cold. Like Anwen's skin when he'd kissed her for the last time at the mortuary. He threw the first of them, listening, counting the splashes as it skimmed the water in the darkness. 'A tripler,' he said proudly.

'*Throw one for me*,' he heard her say.

And so he did. Positioning himself just right, he swung an arm and counted, 'One... Two... Three... Four. A quadrupler, if there's such a word.' He looked skywards. 'You've been practising up there.'

He went further on. Towards the open sea. Stopped to stand above one of five sluice gates – each capable of allowing over a quarter of a million litres of water per second to flow through. He stood listening to the thunderous roar, mesmerised by the awesome draw of it.

The wind was picking up. The storm announcing itself to the people of Wales with the loudest of war cries.

Raising himself onto one of the higher railings, he felt surprisingly calm for what he was about to do. He gripped an upright of cold steel and hung over the bubbling torrent. 'I can't do this anymore,' he said, readying himself to fall.

Amid the crashing noise of sluice-gate water was a sudden clap of thunder. This one bringing with it a crackling lightning show high above the pointed spire of the Norwegian Church.

It caught him unawares.

Had him stop what he was doing and refocus.

Anwen was sending him back. Telling him that it wasn't yet his time.

The sudden explosion of thunder overhead made Wellman jump; the lightning so close that it looked like a 5th of November firework display in nearby Bute Park. And the rain – that was of a kind he'd rarely seen the likes of in this country – buckets of water falling horizontally from the heavens, forming puddles and fast-flowing streams within minutes. It got in through the flat roof of the lock-up, wetting the walls, dripping on the grey lifeless face of Jordan Patterson.

But now wasn't the time to stand around like an open-mouthed tourist. Wellman had the laptop back in his possession, giving him the upper hand again over the police.

There was nothing linking him to any of the crimes. Not that he knew of, anyway. They wouldn't have let him walk free of the station if there had been.

DCI Reece and his cronies knew about Aunt Freda. Could even pick up a few stray fingerprints if they dusted the old house he'd recently sold to a couple of young newlyweds. But that didn't make him a murderer. And they'd find no matching prints at any of the crime scenes.

Thoughts of Aunt Freda angered him. Why had both women been in regular contact all this time? If she'd known where Mother was, then why keep it to herself.

Because they were in it together, you fool. Been playing you ever since you were a kid. He swung a muddy boot at the bumper of the Volvo. 'Bitches!'

It took over ten minutes to drag the thieving cleaner off the bonnet of the car, and stuff him in the driver's seat. There was more room on that side of the lock-up; the door able to open fully wide. Wellman was exhausted with the effort. Was no longer a young man. Leaning on the wing with gloved hands, he took a few minutes to catch his breath before slamming the driver's side door shut and pulling the dusty tarpaulin back into place.

On his journey out of the city's docklands, he saw a lone figure making its way along the lakeside path, flashes of lightning illuminating the man only momentarily. He was hunched at the shoulders and soaked by the heavy rainfall. Just another down-and-out, Wellman supposed. Not his problem. All was well again.

Or was it? He chewed on a gloved knuckle, suddenly deep in thought.

Dr Patricia Beven could still stir things up. She was, after all, leaking what should have been confidential information to the detective. Wellman knew he could ruin her career for doing that. Have her struck off and out of work. But that wouldn't help his cause any.

She knew too much.

Had to be dealt with.

Silenced indefinitely.

∽

Reece whimpered in his sleep, thrashing about as though he were emerging from a drunken stupor. The dream was different tonight. Anwen was there of course. And in danger, as was always the case. But on this occasion, Rome wasn't the venue. The scooter riders nowhere to be seen.

It played out widescreen, and in monochrome, Reece watching himself as though he'd become a fly on the wall.

He was at work. Had phoned home earlier in the evening to let Anwen know he'd be late. They were about to close one of the biggest cases of his career. Catch the stalker and put him away for several life sentences.

Although Reece knew the killer's identity, the CPS wanted more. Demanded evidence that would hold up to legal challenge in the highest courts of the land. How much did they need? Couldn't they understand the longer the man was left free to roam the city streets, the higher the likely body count?

'We've got the green light,' Jenkins said, bursting into the room. 'CPS are on board with us throwing the book at him. Let's go, go, go.'

Reece was on his feet. Could actually see himself taking the stairs to the ground floor two at a time. When he got to the foyer, Jenkins and the rest of the team were nowhere to be seen. 'Where are they, George?' he asked the desk sergeant.

'You're late, Brân. They left hours ago.'

How could that be? Reece shifted in his sleep. Rolled onto his other side and immediately back again. Outside the station was a field and snow-covered mountains. Nonsense, he knew. There should have been streets, flats, and houses.

He saw a man walking towards a white-washed cottage, his fists clenched, carrying what might have been a needle and syringe. 'You leave her alone, you bastard.'

George told him to watch his language. 'There's people about,' the desk sergeant said, brushing snow off his shoulders.

Reece didn't apologise. Had no time to wonder where the police station had gone, and studied the wintry landscape instead. 'Brecon, not Cardiff!' he shouted into his phone. 'Our man's in Brecon. Jenkins, you're going to the wrong place.'

When he searched his jacket pockets for car keys, they were gone. The phone too. He'd had it only a moment ago – what the hell was going on?

No phone, no car, he'd run. It was fifty-something miles door to door, but Anwen's life was at stake here. He raced along the pavement, soon finding himself quayside in the bay. 'Which way to Brecon?' he asked a man selling boat trips from a deckchair in a kiosk. 'This is a police emergency.'

'It'll be far quicker if I take you,' the man said, starting an outboard motor with a single pull of a short cord. The speedboat weaved in and out of the busy road traffic, banking sharply side to side as it went.

Reece watched road signs go by on the edge of the dual carriageway. 'Oi.' He pointed the opposite way. 'We should have turned off there.'

The bald speedboat driver laughed and blew cigar smoke at him, the scent of patchouli oil strong in the air.

Reece froze. 'You! Creed.'

'Don't look so worried, Copper. I'm sure the good doctor will make sure she's okay.'

38

'Jenks, this came for the squad during the night.' George stuck an arm through the window at the front desk, waving a folded bit of paper like he was fighting to get an autograph. 'Haven't seen Brân yet, so you best have it.'

She stopped and took it from him. 'What is it?'

George shrugged. 'Just another crank caller, I bet. Switchboard's been inundated with them since that American flashed his money on camera.'

She wasn't listening, and read the note to herself. 'Did anyone respond to this?'

'Were we supposed to?' he asked, sticking his head through the hatch when she made off towards the stairwell. If the desk sergeant said any more after that, she couldn't hear him. She burst into the incident room, breathless and able to speak in part-sentences only. 'Where's the boss?'

Cable stepped out of Reece's office. 'Did you hear from him at all last night?'

Jenkins was slowly recovering from her sprint up the stairs. 'No. Why?' She looked from Cable, to Morgan, to Ginge, and then the empty office. 'What's the matter? What aren't you telling me?'

Ginge explained how Reece had left mid-interview the previous evening, giving him little alternative other than to bed Kyle Cartwright down in a cell until morning.

'All started after he got a call from Rome,' Morgan said. 'Wasn't right after that.'

'Do you know where he might be?' Cable asked. 'His jacket is still here. Car's gone, though. We've checked.'

Jenkins tried Reece's number, giving up when he didn't answer after several attempts. She handed the chief super the note George had given her downstairs. 'I'd like to follow up on this, ma'am, if that's all right with you?'

Cable handed it back. 'Take a uniform, just in case.'

Reece had little to no idea what made him take a spur-of-the-moment detour to Cathedral Road that morning. The dream, perhaps? Something about it was still nagging at him, chirping away inside his head like a small and annoying bird. Even his morning run had failed to get rid of it. He should have been going straight to the station. First off, to apologise to Ginge, and then get Kyle Cartwright to spill the beans on Billy Creed.

Cable and Harris could go take a running jump. If the gangster *was* responsible for the death of Pete Hall – and Reece had no reason to believe he wasn't – then their repeated threats of a desk job would fall on the deafest of ears.

Reece had parked his car a few streets away from the Cathedral Road address of Dr Patricia Beven. Could find nothing closer on either side of the busy road. Lo and behold, it had started raining again. Big fat spots making wide splatter marks on the cracked paving slabs. He looked to the sky, wondering how anything could be left up there after the previous night's deluge, and for the time being, put all thoughts of his encounter with the barrage out of mind.

When he got nearer the counsellor's place, he saw a familiar figure, the man's back to him as he pulled the front door closed. 'Doctor.'

Wellman turned, the door inching open again unnoticed. 'Chief Inspector, what are you doing here?' He looked nervous. Flighty, even.

'I could ask you the same thing,' Reece said, blocking his way.

'I need to be at the hospital.' Wellman moved onto the shingle border in a second attempt to get round him. 'There's an emergency on its way in.'

Reece let him get as far as the pavement. 'Just a minute,' he said, starting down the path. 'I said, *wait*.'

Wellman stopped momentarily to glance at a window on the upper floor of the building. 'You're wanted upstairs.' He rested a gloved hand on the metalwork of the gate. 'I had no time to stay and watch, more's the pity,' he said with what might have been a smile. 'You'd better be quick, Chief Inspector, the lady needs you.'

Reece ran to the front door and pushed it against the wall inside with a clatter of its heavy brass fittings. 'I'll exhume her once I'm finished here.' He wasn't sure Wellman could hear him. Didn't know if he'd take the bait, even if he had. 'Your Aunt Freda's next to be dug up.'

Jenkins had tried ringing Reece countless times without luck. She was travelling the short distance to the docklands with a wet-behind-the-ears uniform in tow. Morgan and Ginge had been left at the station, their mission to locate the missing DCI.

The patrol car slipped and skidded in mud as it crawled down the narrow lane, the young driver coming close to scraping its doors against the walls of passing lock-ups. 'It's just here,' he said, pulling up alongside the one of interest to them. 'Number thirteen.'

'Unlucky for some.' Jenkins got out and pulled at a broken padlock looped through a ring-and-flap latch. 'Give us a hand with this, will you.' The lock-up door squealed open, sending a large flock of seagulls on their way. She went straight in, mud squelching over the fabric of her new Nike Downshifters. Gripping handfuls of rough tarpaulin, she pulled it away from the bonnet and windscreen to reveal a silver-coloured Volvo, with Jordan Patterson sat in the driver's seat.

'He's dead, sarge,' the uniform said, stating the obvious.

Jenkins donned a pair of blue examination gloves and opened the car door. There was no need to check for a pulse – Patterson was displaying the classic Q sign – mouth open, tongue lolling to one side. She went round to the passenger door of the vehicle, glad for once to be slight in stature. The door knocked against the block wall when she leaned in to open the glovebox.

Rummaging inside, she found a faded owners' manual and old-style tax disk. And hidden beneath those, she struck gold. Rolling the knife in the palm of her hand, she noted it had all the characteristics documented in Harlan Miller's post-mortem report. 'Get this round to the station,' she said, dropping the weapon into a clear plastic tube she fetched from the boot of the patrol car. 'Tell them to get a full crime scene team out here.'

'What about you?' the officer asked before doing as told.

Jenkins looked across the dock, towards rows of blue container units rusting in the salty air. Charlie had been over the moon when she'd given him the news about the self-contained flat. Couldn't thank her enough. Would be moving in, in just under a week's time. 'Someone's got to play scene guard until reinforcements arrive,' she said, looking for somewhere to sit. 'Might as well be me.'

The patrol car had only been gone a few minutes when her phone rang in her jacket pocket.

～

Reece raced up the stairs towards Dr Beven's office, phone wedged tight under his chin. 'Listen,' he said firmly when Jenkins tried to speak first. 'Wellman's got to Patricia.'

'Is she dead?'

'I don't know. I only just caught him leaving.' Reece hammered on the locked door with his free hand. 'Get an ambulance over here.'

'Will do. Where's Wellman now?'

'You got a key for this?' Reece asked the bemused accountant when he appeared from the office next door. Speaking into the phone again, he said, 'He'll be on his way to the Thornhill Crematorium if I'm right. Get over to Freda Beck's plot and arrest him when he gets there.' The accountant reappeared moments later with the spare, Reece hanging up without warning.

They were in. The man in the beige tank-top following close behind. Beven was on the furthest couch, fully clothed but worryingly blue.

'Patricia!' Reece grabbed under both armpits and pulled her onto the hardwood floor, no time spent on niceties. They were up against the clock. He felt for a pulse in her neck. Slow and weak. She was alive, but only just.

'She's not breathing,' the accountant said.

Reece leaned over the cyanosed face, not knowing if he could keep Beven alive another five to ten minutes until more specialist help got there. He tilted her head and lifted her jaw. No respiratory effort. He leaned over and put his lips to hers, watching her chest rise and fall. Maybe he could. He certainly wasn't going to give up without trying.

Again, and again he did it, settling into a rhythm that was in sync with his own rapid breathing pattern. He stopped for a moment. 'Go outside and make sure the ambulance knows where we are when it gets here.' He lowered his face to her. 'Come on, Patricia, don't do this to me.'

Jenkins had done as told. Phoned it in and sent fast response vehicles speeding out to the city crematorium. They'd taken Morgan and Ginge with them. The ambulance well on its way.

Jenkins would be next to make a move over there, just as soon as the lock-up was secure, all evidence inside gathered or guarded. Her back was to the open door when she realised she was no longer alone.

39

Reece couldn't be sure that Wellman had taken the bait and was headed over to the crematorium. But it was very likely he was. The earlier threat of exhuming Aunt Freda had been an out-and-out lie on the detective's part, there being no obvious reason to suspect she'd succumbed to the same illegal end as the other women. It was Reece's hope that the festering thought alone would be enough to overwhelm the doctor and make his reaction to the statement predictable.

It was all over, in any case. Wellman had been caught this time, and there was no going back. If Reece was right, then he'd want to pay his last respects to his dead aunt while he still had the opportunity.

Time had almost stood still during the umpteen cycles of mouth-to-mouth resuscitation. The paralysing agent wearing off eventually, Patricia Beven emerging from her ordeal groggy, but with her higher functions seemingly intact. Once she was safely on board the ambulance, Reece was on his way to the crematorium.

He turned left on the junction at the bottom of Cathedral Road – not waiting for the lights to turn green – across the bridge spanning the swollen River Taff and round the front of the castle. When the little Peugeot hit the speed bumps in the road, the DCI's body shook almost as violently as the car did. It felt like someone had connected the steering wheel to a pneumatic drill. Rattling and squeaking loudly, the 205 didn't dare fail him.

Reece was soon hammering up Manor Way – a long straight stretch of road only a mile or two from his destination point. He braked for the changing traffic lights on the busy crossroads adjacent to the golf course, accelerating away again once sure it was safe to do so.

Three. Four minutes at the very most.

'*You.*' The front bumper of the Volvo pressed uncomfortably against Jenkins's legs when she took a step away from the lock-up door. She reached a hand behind her to steady herself.

Wellman's reaction to finding the intruder was characteristically matter of fact. 'You didn't think I'd fall for that exhumation nonsense, did you? DCI Reece must take me for a complete fool.'

Jenkins forced herself to appear confident – was anything but – stood up straight and spoke loudly in the hope that someone in a neighbouring lock-up might hear them and come to investigate. 'He's got your number,' she said. 'You're finished.'

'Not quite.' Wellman took a small brown bottle from his pocket and held it to the weak morning light. 'Enough for one more, I'd say.'

Jenkins looked round the doctor, searching for any sign of blue lights coming down the lane, listening for the loud sirens of patrol cars. But apart from countless bits of litter somersaulting like tumbleweed in the wind, and the screeching of gulls overhead, there was little else out there. 'Is that how you did it? How you incapacitated them.'

'Sevoflurane,' he said, reading its name off the label. 'A wonderful inhalation agent. The more you struggle and hyperventilate, the quicker its rate of onset.'

'Why? What had any of them done to you?'

Wellman took a mask and wadding from the other pocket. 'Nice try.' He looked behind him. 'We're pushed for time as it is. Let's begin.'

Reece swung the Peugeot through the double gates of Thornhill Crematorium. Accelerating along the winding driveway, he passed armies of miniature wooden crosses, and wreaths of artificial poppies lying where grass met tarmac. People dressed mostly in black turned as he sped by. Some shaking their heads. Others, a weak arm in protest. A man in navy-blue overalls stepped behind the bulk of his mowing machine. Another jumped away from the road, a well-used sweeping brush and shovel still gripped in hand.

Pulling into the busy car park with a final squeal of the car's ageing suspension, Reece left the vehicle unlocked and went in search of the vicar.

The man in question was short and plump, had a rosy complexion and a purple nose that was much too broad for its owner's pockmarked face. Reece didn't recognise him from any of the dreams he'd had lately, and that had to be a plus he decided.

'You asked to see me,' the vicar said, looking mildly irritated having been disturbed between back-to-back funeral services.

Reece stood beneath a wide concrete overhang, shielding from a new downpour. 'I need to find a plot somewhere out there,' he said, turning to survey a couple of hills that were full of them.

'And would it be for yourself, or a family member?'

'No, no. I mean the plot's already out there.'

The vicar frowned. 'And might I ask why the interest?'

'It's in connection with a murder investigation,' Reece said, trying not to look too irritated by the delay. He was shifting from one foot to the other, aware that Wellman would be off again soon enough. 'I need to find the plot belonging to a Mrs Freda Beck.' The vicar headed inside without explanation. 'Where are we going?' Reece asked with a last fleeting look towards the hills.

'I don't store the details in my head.' The vicar shuffled along ahead of him. 'We have a records department for such things.' They went beneath a sign marked, *Bereavement Office* – to an area of the building that wouldn't have looked out of place in a modern-day business block – and towards a woman whose name badge read, *Natalie*. The woman looked up from what she was doing at the photocopying machine and flashed a well-practised smile. 'Natalie will assist with your request.' The vicar checked a pocket watch. 'Now, if you'll please excuse me, Chief Inspector, I'm already running several minutes late for my next appointment.'

'That's the boss's. There in the car park,' Morgan told the driver of the high-performance BMW. Parked out on the road and getting in the way of the arriving hearse, were three more vehicles, each of similar spec – their lights flashing in blinding neon-blue. 'Pull up next to the Peugeot.'

'I can't see Jenks yet,' Ginge said from his seat in the back. 'Must be stuck in the bay, still.'

Once on foot, they made way for a large group of mourners

coming down the steps. Again, for a separate group who'd stopped to read cards attached to rows of floral tributes. Morgan pulled at the collar of her coat, holding it overhead like a makeshift umbrella.

'I can see him,' Ginge said, pointing into the distance. 'Next to the taller monument over there.'

Morgan shielded her eyes from the rain and squinted. 'I think you're right. Come on.'

'No sign of Wellman, though.' Ginge finger-combed a handful of soaked hair from his forehead. 'I hope the boss is right about this.'

Reece trudged through wet grass and soft earth, mud squishing over his leather shoes, their smooth soles slipping and sliding like he was walking in thick snow. Ahead of him was a marble cross, but no Dr Wellman. Reece put a hand to his mouth and scratched his wet beard – turned full circle – checking the other plots around him. It was the right grave for sure. Freda Beck's name was on it, confirming it was. 'What the hell?'

There were two familiar figures making their way through the quagmire, grabbing at one-another's coat sleeves in repeated attempts to stay upright, a couple of uniforms in hi-vis jackets following close behind.

But still no Wellman.

'Where is he?' Morgan asked once she was close enough.

'He should have been here,' Reece said. 'Fuck!' He punched the space in front of him with a clenched fist. 'I was sure he'd come.'

'What now?' Ginge asked.

Morgan lowered her head to the worst of the weather. 'Worth checking with the hospital, do you think?'

Reece didn't. 'Where else could he have gone?'

Ginge waved his phone at them. 'Shall I stop Jenks coming over here?'

Lifting his head, Reece shook drips from it. 'Where is she?'

Morgan told him about the phone call during the night. The note from George. And Jenkins's request of the chief super to let her go follow it up herself.

Reece felt his knees buckle. 'Shit!'

Wellman hadn't expected to find Jenkins at the lock-up, and was surprised when he did. With the police certain to make an arrest within the hour, and his career in ruins, he'd decided to finish things, as his father had done all those years ago. And in what better place to commit the act, than Mother's car?

Jenkins was asleep and positioned on the bonnet of the Volvo. He had two remaining vials of Suxamethonium Chloride in his coat pocket. Both originally intended for him. There was one syringe and a single needle; sharing not an issue under current circumstances.

He'd decided the detective had to die on first sight of her – she'd been disrespectful after all – a suitable finale to what was a *calling* cut short.

He flicked one of the vials with a fingernail, fully separating air and solution. His hands were trembling as he drew the drug into the syringe, and put it down to thoughts of his own impending death. 'Time to die,' he said, getting to his feet, the needle hovering close to Jenkins's right thigh.

'Itchy's not going to let you do that.'

The voice came from somewhere over his right shoulder. Turning, he saw a dishevelled looking man stood in the doorway of the lock-up. 'This is no business of yours. Go away and I'll let you be.'

'Not until you put that thing down,' Itchy said, pointing towards the loaded syringe.

There were sirens to be heard in the distance. Not yet louder than the gulls calling overhead. Wellman came towards him, jabbing the air repeatedly with his makeshift weapon.

Itchy's ripped coat was on the floor outside, getting wet in a muddy puddle. He folded his shirtsleeves back to his elbows. 'You're going to regret this,' he said, raising both fists in a southpaw boxer's stance. He pulled twice on an imaginary bell cord hanging above him. 'Ding. Ding.' The first left hook caught Wellman over the liver, almost rendering him unconscious from the outset. As he tottered unsteadily on his heels, a right uppercut shifted his jaw sideways, violently shaking his head, adding to the insult. The second left hook was probably unnecessary, given that the doctor was already falling backwards and towards the Volvo.

Jenkins shifted sluggishly, disturbed by Wellman landing on her, and the sirens of the police cars pulling up outside.

Reece was in one of them, but only until it slid to a full stop. 'Elan. Elan, are you all right?'

She fell into his arms, shaking herself awake. 'I thought...'

'It's done,' he told her. 'Over and finished with.' Wellman mumbled something on the floor. Reece kicked the syringe to one side and dangled his cuffs out in front of him. 'You up to doing the honours?'

Jenkins dropped to the floor, straddling the man. 'Doctor Richard Wellman, consider yourself well and truly nicked.'

40

THE FOLLOWING DAY

Jenkins was stood cleaning the evidence board with a handful of alcohol wipes, the best part of a month's work reduced to wide swirls of black and red ink with the swish of a hand. She was humming a tune. Justifiably content with the outcome. 'Charlie's due an award for saving my life, you know.'

Morgan was next to her, busy taking photographs down, piling them on the edge of the nearest desk. 'You've started making a habit of this. Getting to be a right little attention seeker.'

'Bollocks I am.'

'It was a joke.'

Jenkins let it go. 'An excellent result, all things considered. The girls, Miller, *and* Patterson all cleared up neatly.' It was true. Even the Americans had gone home with an answer to accompany the body of their dead son. The family had spoken to ACC Harris by telephone from the airport, asking him to pass on their sincere thanks to DCI Reece and the Cardiff Murder Squad. Even Logan Johnson Jr III had been suitably impressed. Jenkins looked across to the DCI's office. He was in there, but with the door closed.

'What about Molly Gantry?' Morgan asked, searching for a box big enough to put the crime scene photographs in.

Jenkins cleaned ink off her hands with a couple of paper tissues and some old-fashioned spit. 'Forensics say the soil on that spade is common to lots of places around here.' She shook her head. 'Might be the last we hear of her.'

Morgan went back to what she was doing. 'Perhaps they'll find her next time they bulldoze another wood to make room for a housing estate?'

'Maybe,' Jenkins said, lobbing the tissues into the box before her colleague could move it out of range.

'Oi.' The photographs were packed and labelled for storage. Morgan put the box to one side. 'Kyle Cartwright's willing to cop full blame for Pete Hall's murder. Revenge for what happened to his brother is what he said.'

'No surprise there. Wouldn't have survived two minutes if he'd turned Queen's evidence.'

'Suppose not.'

Jenkins went back to her desk and took a seat. 'Boss,' she said in greeting when Reece emerged from his office.

'I heard what you said about Molly Gantry. I'm not giving up that easily.'

'Where do you even start?' she asked.

Reece went over to the simmering coffee pot and helped himself to a half-cup. 'We know the patrol car stopped Wellman somewhere along Llantrisant Road.' He stirred two sugars into the dark beverage. 'We'll get a couple of dog teams to search along the route.'

Jenkins pulled a face, obviously unconvinced.

'I've just come off the phone to the hospital,' Reece said, changing the subject to something less contentious. 'They're letting Patricia home later today.'

Jenkins smiled broadly. 'That's great news.'

Morgan and Ginge agreed. 'You saved her life,' Ginge said with all the excitement of a proud son. 'There's no doubt about that.'

'When did he stop calling her Dr Beven?' Morgan whispered.

Jenkins winked. 'Watch this space.'

Reece reached for his suit jacket and stuck an arm in it. 'You two can stay here and finish clearing this lot away.'

Ginge looked disappointed. 'What about me, boss?'

'You ever driven a Peugeot 205?'

'It's a bit small to be honest. Not sure I'd fit.'

Reece took a short screwdriver from his jacket pocket and tossed it to the newbie. 'We'll push your seat back as far as it goes and listen to some Deep Purple on the way.'

The look of disappointment quickly turned to one of concern. 'On the way where?'

'The hospital.' Reece was already out on the landing, Ginge following with a lolloping trot. 'Rumour has it, they've misplaced the medical director.'

THE END

ACKNOWLEDGEMENTS

Although writing a novel is a mostly solitary affair, it is next to impossible to achieve without the help and support of others. With that in mind, I'd like to thank my ARC group, who did a magnificent job finding plot holes and typos in the manuscript. Without you, the book would not be what it is today. My editor, for teaching me so much about the art of writing. Everyone at Bloodhound Books. You've been magnificent. And most of all: my readers, for taking a chance on me. I will forever be in your debt.

Lightning Source UK Ltd.
Milton Keynes UK
UKHW010725020221
378105UK00003B/162